Adventures Off the Beaten Path

A Novel
Inspired by True Events

Terry J. Kotas

with Artwork by Travis Johnston

Black Rose Writing | Texas

ISBN: 978-1-68433-750-7
PUBLISHED BY BLACK ROSE WRITING
www.blackrosewriting.com

Printed in the United States of America
Suggested Retail Price (SRP) $18.95

Adventures Off the Beaten Path is printed in Chaparral Pro

*As a planet-friendly publisher, Black Rose Writing does its best to eliminate unnecessary waste to reduce paper usage and energy costs, while never compromising the reading experience. As a result, the final word count vs. page count may not meet common expectations.

Dedicated to:
Manny and Free Spirit Dave
Two great guys, gone too soon.

Sail on, sail on sailor

Route of S/V Casablanca

Adventures
Off
the
Beaten Path

Off the Beaten Path
Lyrics by George Gray

We chase the moon's path through the stars
Hear the wind's song through the stays
We smell the islands as they near
And dream of warmer days

We make our way through coral heads
And see the reefs below
The palms blow gently on the shore
The white sands are aglow

We've traveled days to get here
We've left the storms at sea
Our friend, our boat, has kept us safe
The Gods have let us be

The dolphins led us to this place
Through dreams and hope and fear
The savage sea has calmed again
The stormy skies are clear

And as the journey nears its end
We will sit with friends and laugh
We'll plan our next adventure
Off the beaten path

Prologue
Calamity on the Beach

Playa La Ropa beach, located nearly 1 mile from old town Zihuatanejo, is your typical Mexican Riviera tourist destination. A wide white sand beach separates the steep cliffs from the beautiful bay. Perched upon those cliffs there is a mix of grand hotels and condominiums, all with winding stairways that serve as access to the beach. The temperature varies slightly throughout the year, mostly in the mid-80s. Here you can frolic in the waves, sunbathe or for the adventurous types there are Hobie Cats, jet skis and speed weenies to rent. For a small fee, you can strap yourself to a surplus parachute and a speed boat will pull you up to several hundred feet for a majestic view of the harbor. Keep in mind there aren't many personal injury lawsuits in Mexico, so fly at your own risk. This half mile of beach is crammed with restaurants, or more precisely open air palapas, nearly all sporting thatched roofs and offering cuisine which varies from tacos to lobsters, Italian to French. However, the restaurants all have one thing in common: Margaritas!

Folklore seems to suggest that this national concoction was invented at a fancy hotel in Ensenada in the 1950s and was named for a patron at the bar whose name was, yes, that's right: Margaret. Restaurants all over Mexico use this popular drink to lure customers to their establishments, and La Ropa was no exception. Two for one, free with dinner and dollar margs all day were advertised. Of course, the key ingredient is Tequila or as some call it "Ta Kill Ya". Now bear in mind not all Tequila is created equal, some are aged over a period of years in wooden casks and kept in cool dark rooms which is reflected by how smooth it is and the price you pay. However, on the other end of the spectrum you have brands that are aged in plastic bottles in the tropical sun. This grade of Tequila can usually be found on sport fishing boats where it is used to subdue large game fish that have just been landed. So, I guess the moral of the story is one should be very careful when it comes to 'almost free' Margaritas.

· · · · ·

It was on this beach that two men stood over a prone body, that of another male, lying face down in the sand. The sun was nearly touching the horizon as beach goers walked along Playa La Ropa, hoping to see the infamous green flash at sunset. No one seemed the least bit interested in the seemingly lifeless body, like it was a common everyday occurrence.

"I think he's dead," the taller of the two men mumbled.

"He'd better not be or we're in deep shit," replied the other.

Then a low, eerie moan emanated from the dead guy's sand encrusted lips.

"Let's get him turned over," one of them slurred, and with that the two men unceremoniously flipped the six-foot body onto his back.

The shorter of the two men let out a mild gasp when he caught sight of the dried blood and the one-inch gash that was its source.

"That cut on his forehead looks nasty," the man stated agast.

"Naw, head cuts always look worse than they are," this coming from Sparky, who has exactly zero background in the medical field.

"Let's get him sitting, then we can try to clean him up a little."

"Ok buddy, now sit up, that's a good boy..."

Then, suddenly, Jim started to giggle. Trying to stifle the low laugh made it worse, and before long both men were laughing heartily.

"How'd he lose the sleeve from his shirt?" Sparky questioned then let out a large uncontrolled belch, then added, "Come on, we need to get him to one of those beach showers."

As he bent down to help him up, Jim said, "Come on buddy, we're taking a little walk."

Struggling, Jim and Sparky finally managed to pull their nearly unconscious friend to his feet. Then staggering, the ungainly trio headed for the nearest shower to rinse him off. Luckily, these showers dot the beach and are provided by the various hotels so their guests can wash the sand and saltwater off before going up to their rooms.

Once the cold water washed over the inebriated individual, the real world came crashing back, along with a severe headache, an urge to pee and a trace of nausea thrown in for good measure. After a solid 5 minutes in the rinse cycle, complete with all of his clothes on, but minus the shirt sleeve, the intrepid party goer begged for an end to the water torture.

"Stop already! What the hell? Enough of the water boarding!" he pleaded.

"Well, who says the dead can't come back to life?" Sparky said with a bit of a smirk.

"I can't believe how much my head hurts," murmured the newly brought back to life man. Then, looking at the one called Jim, he asked, "What are you staring at?"

"You've got a nasty looking cut on your head," Jim replied, and with that, the drunken laughter started anew.

Now, even with the majority of a pitcher of Margarita flowing through his blood stream, the third guy was now well on his way to sobriety.

"Guys, it's not that funny," then after a moment, "What happened? Remember we were supposed to watch each other's back?"

"Well, after the server, Carlos, brought the last round.... that was his name, right?"

"No, it wasn't Carlos, it was Francisco."

"No, I'm pretty sure it was......"

"Guys! Focus! Please!"

"Boy, are you in a foul mood. You must need a drink," and with that peals of laughter once again broke out between Jim and Sparky.

"I'm glad to see you two think this is so damn funny. I've got sand between my teeth, in my pants, I'm soaking wet and my shirt is ripped up!"

Before anyone had a chance to comment, a hotel security guard approached the three and inquired, "Are you men guests at this hotel?"

"No," Jim said with just a trace of guilt.

"Then you cannot be here doing.... whatever it is you're doing," he said with an air of conspiracy and a wink, "This is a family hotel."

"We were just using your shower to rinse off," offered Sparky.

Then Jim and Sparky helped their charge to stand up and the motley trio staggered down the dark empty beach. After a short silent walk Jim asked, "Did he wink at us?"

"What exactly happened back there?" the banged-up guy wanted to know.

"Well, I think the guard thought...."

"No, not that.... I mean at Elvira's," he clarified his question.

"After that guitar player came over and played *La Bomba*, you got up and said you were going to dance your way to the baño. Sure enough, you danced right out of the palapa with people clapping for your performance. About 45 minutes later, when we realized you hadn't come back, we got worried and ordered another round. An hour later you still hadn't come back, so Jim and I paid the bill thinking your disappearance was just a ploy to keep from paying your share," Sparky informed him.

"It's an old Canadian trick, eh," This from Jim who is Canadian.

"Yeah, anyhow, when we got to the beach, there you were laying peacefully, face down in the sand right next to a beached panga boat. You must have tripped on the mooring line stretched out in front of the boat. That's when you conked your melon, ripped your shirt and went beddy bye."

Now reality was setting in for the ones called Sparky and Jim. Turning to the sand laden, cut up, one sleeve guy in the bright tropical shirt, Sparky said, "You're going to catch Hell."

"I think we all will," added Jim solemnly.

Sparky was right. Maybe he even understated it a bit, but the one thing that was for sure, the poor SOB was in deep trouble.

Oh, by the way, that messed up, sand covered, completely soaked guy with the brand-new tropical shirt.... the one missing a sleeve and covered with blood. That guy is ME. My name is Rick, and I just missed my birthday dinner with my wife. The shirt had been her gift to me.

Chapter 1
Making Plans

"A goal without a plan is just a wish."
~ Antoine de Saint-Exupery

A year before that incident which Sheryl dubbed 'The Calamity on the Beach', we had been finishing up the final preparations that would allow us to depart my hometown of Gig Harbor, which is located in the perpetually wet State of Washington. We had been living there aboard *Casablanca*, our Fantasia 35 cutter rigged sailboat, since our arrival from the Hawaiian Islands.

Before returning to Gig Harbor, we had been in Oahu while I was recuperating from a particularly nasty arm injury which I had suffered riding out a storm at sea. So, instead of having Sheryl sign my cast (with something on the order of 'tough break' ha-ha) I convinced her to marry me (joke's on you S).

We had known each other for a handful of years, beginning with our first meeting in Emery Cove Marina in San Francisco Bay, where we became good friends. I had sailed into the Bay aboard my first cruising boat, *Rick's Place*, on my way to Hawaii. It was a brief stopover, but in a short amount of time it was obvious she had fallen hard for me.... at least that's what I told myself.

When I left the dock heading for Hawaii on *Rick's Place*, I discovered her toilet trained tabby cat named Jack had snuck aboard my boat. Weather considerations and the distance I'd already traveled prevented us from turning back. That's how Jack ended up sailing thousands of ocean miles with me on that small boat. Here I would like to dispel Sheryl's contention that I took the cat as a lame way of making sure she and I would meet up again. Simply unprovable. But it worked!

Unfortunately, I ended up losing *Rick's Place* in a storm. Fortunately I did save Sheryl's cat, which led to us reuniting and eventually cruising together on my new boat.

Several years later we were married in Oahu and on our 28-day ocean passage back to Washington, Sheryl became pregnant. I'm still not quite sure how that happened. Don't get me wrong, I really do understand how nature works. However, as anyone who has made a long off shore passage can tell you, doing shifts of 3 hours on 3 hours off 24 hours a day for the better part of a month tends to make one sleep deprived, cranky and a little grungy so there's usually not a lot of room left for romance.

But what Nature gives, Nature can also take away. An addition to our family was not in the cards, at least not at that time. To help ward off the disappointment, Sheryl focused on her job at the local garden shop in Gig Harbor; I continued in earnest, getting *Casablanca* ready for our next cruise. After three months of installing upgrades to the electronics, painting the topsides and purchasing a new Genoa, *Casablanca* was ready to go. But we still had not really pinned down any specific destinations.

This is where I should add that I was lucky to have married into money. My wife had recently sold her flower shop down in the Bay Area. Although not really rich by any stretch of the imagination, we then had enough money to go long-distance sailing if we supplemented the cruising kitty doing odd jobs along the way.

"I've made a life decision," I announced, grabbing Sheryl's hand as she walked down the dock towards our boat, our home. 'Life decisions' was the term Sheryl and I would jokingly say, giving some plans more importance than they really deserved.

"Come on, we're going to the club house," I proclaimed.

The clubhouse at our marina was a two-story wooden building that was so well maintained it never seemed to age. It had showers and laundry facilities on the ground floor, and the second floor had a kitchen and large open area that could be used for meetings or parties or simply a TV room.

"Rick, I'm starved. Can we do this later?" She pleaded. I could tell she'd had a long day.

"No, no.... just give me a minute," I said, fiddling with the DVD player that sat on top of the 32" 1990s era TV set. "Here.... sit... you have to see this. Someone left this disc here.... now watch."

I knew that what I was about to show Sheryl would pull her out of the funk she'd been in. A "resume" icon appeared in the upper right-hand corner and then the screen was filled with an image of two grunting giant tortoises, obviously in the midst of some reptilian love making.

Exasperated, my wife said, "This is what you wanted me to see?"

"Trust me, just give it a sec," I encouraged her.

The scene changed. Suddenly small penguins were racing just below the water, darting after little fish. Then the video panned to a dozen or so marine iguanas, piled on dark volcanic rock looking like something out of the black lagoon. We both sat mesmerized for the next half hour, seeing sights that looked so foreign and magical at the same time. But the most dramatic scene came near the end of the video, as the camera panned back revealing a snug aqua blue bay with several sailboats bobbing peacefully at anchor. I was sold! And I hoped Sheryl was too.

While the credits rolled at the end of the documentary, Sheryl asked the obvious question, "Where was that filmed, Rick?"

"That's where we're going to sail to next!" I said with a hint of manic enthusiasm, "The Galapagos!"

With our cruising plans coming into focus, Sheryl and I attacked the remaining boat projects with renewed vigor, but as the days ticked down, we had both side-stepped around the elephant in the room, or rather the cat in the cockpit.

Jack, the seafaring cat, had more sea miles than most cruisers I know, but, like the rest of us, he was aging. Being at the dock for a year had the same effect on him as it had on us. We'd all lost some of our balance, a bit of muscle tone and probably some stamina as well.

"Do you even think they would let Jack into the Galapagos?" Sheryl asked while petting the sleeping feline.

"Yeah, I checked the rules.... got them off the internet. As long as he has a health certificate, he would be good to go. The real problem comes if and when we travel to Hawaii on the way back to the mainland. To avoid a month long quarantine there he would need to get something called the FAVN titter test for rabies."

"Are you making this up?" Sheryl asked skeptically.

"No, but thanks for asking. Anyway, we would need to take Jack to our veterinarian where they would draw some blood from the Big Blob, spin it down to plasma and then send it to the University of Kansas for processing."

By now Sheryl's mouth was hanging open in disbelief. I knew what was coming next.

"You are such a big liar," she said, looking for something to throw at me.

"No, its fact. We're just lucky I stumbled upon this nugget of info when I was researching for the Galapagos or Jack would have been confined to the gray cage motel for a month when we reached Hawaii."

"Rick, seriously, do you think Jack would do OK coming along this time?"

Knowing how much Jack meant to Sheryl and after the disappointments of that past year, I knew I had to do the right thing.... so, I lied.

"Sure.... he'll do fine."

A week later we found ourselves at *Pets R People Too*, the veterinarian's office that we use for Jack's health needs. Sheryl and I were in the waiting room when they brought the big lump back after the procedure. Two things garnered my attention right off the bat. First Jack had a one-inch shaved spot on his front leg (or arm, as my wife would say). The vet, a short and thin young lady with dark hair and tan skin, noticed my stare and informed me that was where they inserted the needle to get the blood. The second thing I noticed was the vet had very long and somewhat deep scratches on her arm.

Again, noticing my stare, she informed me with a tight smile, "And this is where your cat drew blood from me."

"Yep, that's Jack's claw marks alright. Believe me, I know from experience," I said, smiling sheepishly. Her expression went unchanged.

She then explained, "The lab in Kansas will send the results directly to Hawaii so you should be able to bypass quarantine all-together. You will just need to contact the Department of Agriculture at the airport when you get there."

As she left, we heard her mumble to her assistant something about 'that damn cat'.

"How could she say that about sweet Jackie?" Sheryl said, somewhat taken aback.

• • • • •

Several days before the good ship *Casablanca* was to set off for points south, Sheryl and I went to visit my mom. First, a bit of background about Muriel. She grew up in the wilds of Canada, a somewhat nomadic life. Her father was a forest ranger, so the large family rarely lived in one area for more than a couple of years. Being the oldest of the six kids, she not only helped around the cabin, but she would also accompany my grandfather out bush-whacking trails and even helped with some surveying. She grew up in a time and place where a two-seat outhouse was the latest in modern conveniences. She eventually met my father when she was in her early twenties, and they married, then migrated to the United States where they became citizens. They spent their first years of matrimony traveling the States on a motorcycle. About the time my mom found out that she was with child, my father passed away. Mom raised me as a single parent, often working two jobs to support us. Looking back, I feel fortunate that Mom didn't put up with any nonsense from me while growing up. She was quick with a paddle, but at the same time caring and understanding.

"Rick, have you noticed your mom is acting a little different lately?" Sheryl asked me.

"That's what I've been trying to tell you these last couple of months," I said with just a bit of exasperation then continued, "You know what's going on Sheryl, it's that guy she met at the retirement community."

"You mean Walter?" she said, looking at me with a playful smile.

"He thinks he is the second coming of Fred Astaire, with all that dancing he does at the community center, and what's with that goofy bow tie he always wears?" I asked rhetorically, somewhat under my breath.

"Rick, I think it's cute, and I think maybe you are just a little jealous of your mom paying attention to another man. Who knows, if things work out, you might get yourself a new dad."

By then, she was grinning ear to ear.

As we pulled into the *Common Gardens* parking lot, I tried to explain in a thoughtful manner what I thought of her analysis and blurted out, "You're full of BS!"

The Commons was a retirement facility laid out much like a one-story condo complex. There were 50 one-bedroom units with all the amenities, including washers and dryers. Each place had a private patio with access to a large garden area and courtyard. One building housed the recreation hall where the weekly Bingo game is held, as well as dances for the senior citizens.

We found Mom working outside on her patio, tending to some tomato plants that she had growing in small pots.

"Ricky! Sheryl! It's so good to see you," as we both received the customary bear hugs from Mom. "So, I spec you guys are ready to go, eh?"

"The weather looks good for the next couple of days," Sheryl said. "But we will let you know for sure when we decide to go. Plus, we will stay in touch on the cell no matter where we are."

The three of us sat and chatted, or I should say that my mom and Sheryl chatted. And here, I should point out that I suspect that my mother likes my wife more than me. She probably really wanted a girl, but ended up raising a mischievous, crazy boy. Anyway, as I tuned back into their conversation, I heard my mom say, "and he really wasn't the brightest bulb in the drawer growing up."

"Hey, I'm sitting right here," I reminded them. Mom continued, "I just don't know how much longer I will be here."

I immediately piped up, "Mom, what are you saying? You're still healthy and active and you'll probably out live us all!"

"See, Sheryl, this is what I mean…. sometimes he just isn't all there."

My wife's response, between giggling, was something to the effect that I wasn't the greatest listener. "Rick, what your mom was saying is Walter has asked her to marry him, then move into his place."

With that, my wife jumped up and the hug fest started with tears flowing like a Seattle rainstorm. I, on the other hand, couldn't get control of my slack jaw and continued to just stare at the two of them.

A knock on the door had Mom and Sheryl wiping their eyes and me just trying to land back on this planet. To say it came as a surprise would be an all time under statement. Don't get me wrong, after all those years of being alone I couldn't be happier for her. But Walter? Really?

Sheryl answered the door and in waltzed Mom's next husband. And I mean he actually waltzed in, pretending that he was dancing with a partner! Then he proceeded to make several shuffling loops around the small living room before he stopped next to Muriel where he planted a big kiss on her cheek. Brother give me a break. Of course, Sheryl zoomed over, gave Walt a big hug and kiss, then the tears started up again. Walter, really?

It was decided that a celebratory dinner was called for, so off we went to a nearby restaurant. Throughout dinner, good old Walter, who had positioned himself strategically between Sheryl and Mom, kept up a running conversation, often flirting with my wife, then turning his full attention to his bride to be. Both of them were eating it up. I could see that Muriel was about as happy as I had seen her in a long time.

Walter insisted on paying for dinner, after which the four of us strolled back to *The Commons*. As I summoned the courage to talk about their upcoming nuptials, Walter, as if reading my mind, told me that a simple ceremony down at the courthouse was how they would tie the knot.

As we neared the main entrance, Mom took my hand, and we lingered back as my wife and Walter went ahead.

"Ricky, I know marrying Walter comes as a bit of a shock, but he is a good caring man, and, you know, he reminds me of your father, which is what I love about him. You know what else? He reminds me of you, so how could I go wrong, having the spirit of your dad and my favorite son around me, protecting me and making me happy?"

I reached out and wiped the tear that was running down her cheek, and she did the same for me. Walter? Really?

Chapter 2
Coasting

"In the end we only regret the chances we did not take."
~ Lewis Carrol

With the help of a few friends from the marina, our dock lines were cast off and with that Sheryl, Jack and I were on our way to the Galapagos!

Well, actually there would be numerous stops along the way. We would be traveling about 4000 sea miles, and there would be several countries to explore before we could expect to see our first boobies (the blue footed bird).

Our first stop would be Neah Bay, at the western most tip of Washington State. When we motored out of Gig Harbor, an air horn was blaring from the overlook, a place where people often stop to watch the marine traffic comings and goings. Looking up, we saw Mom and Walter waving enthusiastically as *Casablanca* slowly slipped by. We had said our goodbyes the night before, so we were delighted to see them bidding us farewell.

"I'm surprised to see Muriel and Walter at the overlook. I thought they might come down to the dock this morning," Sheryl said as she looked through the binoculars.

"You know Mom, she didn't want to make a big emotional scene," I said, and Sheryl's response was classic, "I think she was afraid of YOU making a big emotional scene." Yeah, right, I thought.

My first experience with Neah Bay was on my maiden voyage to Hawaii. I stopped there as most boats do when leaving Washington. It's strategically placed making it a good harbor to wait for favorable weather as well as get fuel or last-minute provisions before making that big left turn into the Pacific.

Having said that, it's also a place you can't leave soon enough. Many derelict boats crowd the bay, so anchoring can be a challenge. We tied up at the only marina in town while we waited out what was forecast to be a short-lived blow along the coast.

As Sheryl stepped off the boat with the dock lines in hand, she promptly slipped on the guano covered finger pier and landed on her ass. Man was she mad... at me ...for laughing.

"Dammit, Rick! It's not funny!"

"I'm sorry, are you hurt?"

"No, but that's no excuse to laugh," she said, a slight smile forming on her red face.

I jumped off the boat and took the lines. As she picked herself up, I could hear her cursing under her breath about how gross the place was. Luckily, she had her foul weather overalls on, so it was just a matter of hosing off the offensive goo.

Neah Bay is at the watery intersection of the relatively calm Strait of Juan de Fuca and the often-tumultuous Pacific Ocean. Its location allows boaters to venture into the nearby Pacific in search of salmon, halibut and other game fish, yet still have the safety of a nearby harbor to return to. That's why it draws thousands of sport and commercial fishermen each year.

The popularity of fishing was none more evident than when I went to take a shower at the marina restroom, where much to my chagrin two fishermen were using a shower stall to clean and gut their mornings catch.

As I passed by with my shower bag, the men looked up and exclaimed, "Some catch, huh?" All I could get out of my mouth was, "This is the shower, right?"

"Oh, don't worry, we do this all the time," came their response.

I quickly showered in an empty stall, leaving my tennis shoes on, and then broke for the door once I had finished.

Meeting Sheryl outside, I casually asked how her shower was. "Smelled fishy," was her only response.

"Well, we are leaving in the morning, I don't care what the sea condition is," I announced. I couldn't wait to leave this filthy place in our wake.

On my first trip to Hawaii, I had chosen to stay one hundred miles offshore as I traveled down the Pacific Coast. My reasoning was that there would be less danger of coming in contact with fishing nets, crab pots or the land. However, if you are that far out and some terrible weather comes your way, there is no place to hide.

With this in mind, we decided to risk the possible encounters with unknown objects and follow the coastline, staying generally five to ten miles offshore.

•　　•　　•　　•　　•

Leaving Neah Bay (as quickly as possible, I might add) we set a course south, our goal being Newport, Oregon, which would be a two-night jaunt.

The morning we left we had a nice westerly wind blowing 15 knots on the beam, seas that were a gentle 5 to 6 feet coming from the north, as well as clear skies. Not a bad way to get our sea-legs back.

While we were provisioning back in Gig Harbor, we brought many of our supplies down to the boat in cardboard boxes. Jack the cat decided he really liked one in particular. It was about 8" by 10" in dimension, and Jack could barely squeeze his rather generous body into its confines. But none the less, he would sit in it, lay in it and sleep in it and Sheryl dubbed it 'Jacks waiting room'. So, when it came time to leave, we kept it on board so he would have a comfy place to retreat to if the going got rough. This was Jack's safe spot.

It was quite a sight on that first day in the open ocean to see Jack, snug in his waiting room, sliding from one side of the floor to the other, in cadence with the swell that would gently rock *Casablanca* from side to side. And the entire time Jack slept soundly.

During the summer months along the coast, fog can be extremely dense and can settle in quickly with little warning. Such was the case as we approached Newport on the morning of the third day. The previous night the sky had been clear, with the stars seeming close enough to touch.

That morning *Casablanca* approached the Newport entrance buoy, which was about one mile offshore, when suddenly, as if a curtain had been lowered, a fog bank engulfed our little boat, briefly disorienting her crew. We had the sails down and we were motoring slowly toward the entrance channel, all the while hoping the fog would lift just enough to see the shore.

We switched on the radar and could make out the approach, but never having been there we were just guessing where we should be positioned in the channel. While Sheryl drove and monitored the radar display, I stood on the bow and tried to see through the dense blanket, hoping to pick out a channel marker.

"Rick, I can see the buoy on radar, and it looks like it should pass to your right any minute now."

I could hear the gong that was built into the buoy and it sounded very close, but fog is funny that way you can never be sure what direction the sound is coming from. We passed the marker and through the gloom I could just make out the brightly painted 12-foot-high floating structure, not more than a boat length away. That was close.

Then, just as I was starting to relax, thinking about a nice hot shower, minus the fish filets, Sheryl's panicked voice brought me back to reality.

"Rick, come here quick!" she called. Hustling to the cockpit, I saw Sheryl pointing to the radar display where I clearly saw the next channel marker on the small screen, and it was roughly a quarter mile ahead. But what had gotten her immediate attention were 15 to 25 small dots spread from one side of the channel to the other. They appeared to be flying at us like a mad swarm of bees. And very fast.

"What are they?" My wife's voice had just gone up a pitch.

Trying to keep the panic under control, I instructed, "Let's just take the boat out of gear and float until they go by."

"Why are so many boats going that fast in this fog?" She questioned.

"I've got no idea; I just hope the hell they see us."

Then the lead group came roaring toward us. The fog was dissipating, but there was still only about 50 feet of visibility so we could hear them before we could actually see them. Then we began to see flashes through the mist as the contingent flew by, headed to open water. Several of the runabouts swerved at the last instant to avoid slamming into *Casablanca*. It was, as they say, pandemonium. It scared the crap out of both of us. Ten minutes after we first spotted the herd on radar, they were gone with just a few stragglers passing by. Whew.

We once again put the boat in gear and proceeded on our course. The sun continued to burn off the fog and after a few minutes the public dock was in sight. Once tied up to the pier, it became clear why all the small boats seemed as if they were on a Kamikaze mission. A sign posted at the head of the dock proclaimed this day to be opening day of halibut fishing, starting apparently at sunrise (or whenever a boat is trying to enter the channel....in the fog). They obviously take their fishing seriously in Newport, I just hoped they don't use the restrooms for gutting and cleaning.

The next two days were spent completing several small repairs that inevitably seem to follow an off shore passage. We also found time to visit a fabulous aquarium and the West Coast's NOAA weather information and forecast center.

After learning we were traveling by small boat, Sheryl and I were escorted through the forecast center and introduced to a nice, very young-looking forecaster whose name was Jill and she was sporting a large baby bump.

On her desk were three large computer screens, each showing a satellite image of a different location on earth. Jill explained to us, "Raw data is dumped from the satellites to a computer that is located in the basement. The computer, which we call AL, whirls and whistles and throws off a little smoke, then spits out its interpretation, which we promptly ignore."

Seeing confusion on our faces, she stifled a giggle and went on, "Just kidding. AL is usually pretty close, but we take a look at his output and tweak it when we need to."

After fielding several questions, I hit little miss giggles with the one question every sailor asks: "Why is it that sometimes the predictions are not even close?"

Jill responded, "Have you ever heard of the butterfly effect?"

"Of course. It's the premise that a butterfly flapping its wings in one part of the globe affects weather in a distant part of the world," I replied.

Another restrained giggle then she added, "You're basically right, but here's the problem, instead of just one butterfly, or cause, we have hundreds of variables all over the globe affecting the weather."

With a twinkle in her green eyes she said, "Let me ask you a question. For the most part, are the forecasts that you use fairly accurate?"

"Yeah, for the most part, I guess," I replied.

"So, not a bad record for having hundreds of butterflies influencing the forecast," she stated proudly and then went on to say, "If you have a cell phone, I will give you my direct line and you can give me a call as you go down the coast. I will give you the best weather info I have at the time.... or make something up." That last part she said with such a straight face that it took me a second to catch on to her joke until she broke into a big grin.

We said our goodbyes to our new friend and, on our walk back to the boat, Sheryl pointed out that we had just acquired our very own weather person for the remainder of the coastal trip. Score.

When we left Newport, we made the decision that if the weather remained decent, we would just sail straight to the Bay Area about three days south.

Going under the Golden Gate Bridge in my own boat always sets off a variety of emotions. So, when Sheryl asked if those were tears around my eyes, I tried to say that it was the wind irritating them.

"But there is no wind right now," she said, smiling, while putting her arm around me.

That was my second time entering the bay and passing under San Francisco's iconic structure, but it still brought forth a flood of emotions.

Growing up in the Northwest and reading about people from our area sailing to far-off lands, their first major accomplishment was reaching San Francisco. So, just making it under the Gate, you receive an "Atta-boy" for achieving that milestone.

After the relative quiet of offshore travel, the amount of activity that is going on once you pass under the bridge is staggering.

Float planes, fast ferries, tour boats.... they all seemed to be conspiring to make sure we had to take the longest possible route to Emery Cove

Marina. Once the marina was finally in sight, a mere two miles away, both Sheryl and I were able to relax, with all the marine traffic behind us.

"When we get to the dock and get squared away, we are hitting that pizza joint near the dock master's office," I said, my mouth watering as I remembered the place from my previous visit. "I hope it's still .... SHIT!!!"

Sheryl yelled up from below, "Rick, it wasn't that bad.... maybe a little doughy but...."

"Dammit, you won't believe this," I shouted. "You better help me up here... Hurry!"

Within minutes we are surrounded by no less than a 100 high performance sail boats (Sheryl thinks maybe 20 but lets' call it 30 to 100) in some sort of regatta. There was yelling from the different captains as they passed our bobbing sea home. Some were nice warm welcomes, some others were even nicer welcomes that included a middle finger, I guess for emphasis. Come to find out it was a major race event, and we were right at one of the turning buoys.

Ten days had passed since we had thrown off the dock lines in Gig Harbor and tied up to the dock at Emery Cove. When there is a new arrival at a marina, they usually send someone down to take your lines, but it's not usually the Harbormaster. But this was special and Diane, who had capably run this marina for nearly twenty years, was there waiting for us.

Sheryl and Diane were good friends, going back to the days when my wife lived aboard her own sailboat in that marina. And it is also the marina, I am sure it was the very slip, that I pulled into some years ago, where I dropped off my sailing buddy after an arduous trip from Washington. It was then that I met up with Jack the Wanderer and his owner the lovely Ms. Sheryl. And, as they say, the rest is history. For the record, Sheryl had pursued me vigorously for a month before I left for Hawaii. However, when asked about that, she will probably deny the entire story.

We had planned on staying at the marina for about a month as Sheryl had a mother living nearby in a town named Pacifica, as well as a married sister with twin boys that lived close to the marina. My wife was also excited to show me the 'real San Francisco' — the one that she had grown up in, went to school in, and became a successful small business owner in.

That night, I sat in the cockpit with Jack, who was doing some needy nuzzling, and listened to Sheryl on her cell phone catching up with her friends, her mom and who knows who else. I then realized that a very busy month lay ahead.

Chapter 3
Reunion

"Arriving in San Francisco is an experience in living."
~ William Saroyan

One month later:

"Oh my God, I am soooo excited that we are finally on our way!" Sheryl proclaimed with enthusiasm, as we crossed beneath the Golden Gate on our way south.

The wind was a pleasant 15 knots and *Casablanca* was on a comfortable beam reach as the three of us happily watched the City by the Bay receding in the distance. Well, I am not sure Jack really had any feelings on the matter, but he appeared very content. I set the autopilot, sat back and tried to make sense of the whirlwind of experiences our month in San Francisco Bay had provided.

Everything had started out with the usual pattern of long showers, utilizing good laundry facilities, going out to dinner and, of course, boat repairs. Then came the family visits, the close friend visits as well as what I call the "fringe friends" visits. Oh, and did I mention the police visits?

For the record, Sheryl is what I call a beach roamer hunter/gatherer. She collects shells, beach glass, bones, various kinds of sands.... just about anything that has washed up with the tide. I had concluded early in our relationship that my wife is a collector like none other. However, when we arrived at her mom's beachfront home in Pacifica, my jaw nearly hit the floor. Outside, surrounding the porch, were glass balls, net floats in various states of condition and, of course, shells.

Wind chimes made from driftwood and shells adorned the short roof over the porch of the early 1950s vintage, one story, cabin. It was clad in weathered gray cedar siding and had probably been a vacation get-away for folks from the city years ago.

Sheryl's mom met us at our rental car and as the two hugged and cried and laughed, I stood back, just taking in the unspoken love that was passing between the two of them.

"Rick, get over here and give me a hug and a kiss," commanded Betty, or Bets, as she prefers to be called. She wrapped me in a bear hug that was surprisingly strong for someone her age. In her early 70s, she was very much her daughter's mom. Tall with a medium build, she still had long blonde hair, though beginning to turn naturally gray. And just like her daughter, she had a sharp wit.

"Remember what I said in Hawaii at your wedding?" she asked me.

Recalling that day on the beach, I answered, "Yeh, you said you would kill me in my sleep if I didn't make her happy."

"No, not that, but it still holds true. No, I mean that you two needed to get your butts down here for more than just a pass-through visit."

Looking over my shoulder, Bets was making sure Sheryl was out of ear shot, before she asked, "How is she doing? Is she still holding up ok after the loss?" A mother's tears were just beginning to show in Bets' eyes.

"Don't worry, she is a strong girl and with all the support that came from you and Joni, it made all the difference in the world." By that time, I was close to tears too. Dammit.

Released from my interrogation/bear hug, we caught up to Sheryl on the front porch. Then, stepping inside the cabin, I was astonished at the number of shells and other beach bric-à-brac adorning every shelf or ledge. I have had the opportunity to see some exotic shells in my travels, but nothing compared to what I was seeing in my mother-in-law's house. Bets could tell you where each and every one had come from, right down to the name of the beach where she had found them.

She and her late husband had traveled the world "shelling" as she called it.

"Back in the old days we didn't worry too much about whether there was a critter in them, but as times change and we became more responsible, it became quite the scavenger hunt, you know, trying to find shells with nobody home," Bets explained.

Sheryl chimed in with, "Remember that time when you and dad got home from... I don't remember which beach you went to, but when you opened your suitcase the smell was absolutely hideous?"

Then Bets continued the story saying, "I will never forget that smell as long as I live. It was straight out of hell. Sometimes, I would sneak a shell or two into our luggage and not tell your father because he would get so nervous, worried that some officials were going to tear through our bags. Anyway, I had stashed two small shells, not knowing one was occupied, and when we opened the suitcase after we got home....... Well, let's just say we threw out some of our favorite family fun wear that day. Boy, was your dad mad."

"Family fun wear?" I queried.

"I was just kidding about that, but..." she trailed off as she walked over to an antique roll-top desk and plucked a paper out of a stack of many and handed it to Sheryl. "These are my last wishes."

Reluctantly my wife took the paper, but soon the solemn look on her face was replaced with a surprised grin. "These are shells," Sheryl said with a puzzled tone.

"Yeah, so?" answered Bets.

"Well, I thought.... never mind," Sheryl said with a sigh of relief.

"You two need to be on the lookout for these babies for me — they would make your fathers and my collection nearly complete. I'll get some pictures of them for you before you leave."

We stayed for several hours, had a delicious dinner of clam chowder (what else would you expect from a shell collector?), made plans for several more visits and a commitment to take the entire family out for a day sail on the bay.

"That shell collection was insane," I said as I started up the rental car.

"Yeah, I was always the hit of the parade during Show & Tell. In fact, mom even donated a bunch of shells to the school district for use in some classes." Answering an unspoken question, she went on, "There are hundreds of shells crammed in and around that house."

The next day it was more family fun time, this time it was with Sheryl's sister, Joni.

Joni, who is the complete opposite of her sister, lived with her husband Kenny not far from the marina where *Casablanca* was moored.

Sheryl is tallish, somewhat reserved and introspective, and always has a sense of purpose, while Joni, on the other hand, was like a pinball gone mad. The mother of three-year-old twins, she is non-stop motion. Constantly on the move cleaning, wiping, feeding, scrubbing, picking-up and putting down. The twins, whom I call Rick and Jack (even though their names are Leo and Isaac) are seemingly always one kitchen catastrophe shy of great destruction. They have the energy of their mother times two.

The sisters talked like sisters who hadn't seen each other in a while. Non-Stop. This included when one or the other had to use the bathroom. Shouts of laughter, claims, and counter claims resonated through the modest condo.

As I walked out of Jack and Rick's (that would be Leo and Isaac's) toy infested room, the low volume conversation between the girls suddenly stopped. Both sisters wore a look of guilt.

"So, is Kenny away at some kind of conference?" I asked. Kenny works for Pixar, the film makers, whose offices are just a short walk from their condo.

"Yeah, all this week," Joni replied, clearly distracted as she answered. "It's too quiet in the twin's room. Rick, what are they up to?"

My quick reply was, "I gave them a pack of Camels and a lighter."

Sheryl took this opportunity to step in and politely asked me to go back and check on the boys, her words being, "Rick don't be an ass, go to the boy's room and make sure they're ok and do not come out until I tell you to. Think of it as a time-out for giving them cigars."

"Cigarettes."

"Just go!"

After the visit, the short walk back to *Casablanca* held little in the way of conversation. Sheryl seemed in deep thought. Thinking back to the muted conversation I had interrupted at the condo; I knew something was going on.

"Well?" I prodded.

"Well, what?" she answered looking at me out of the corner of her eye.

Right then, I knew I had her. Sheryl and her sister's secret would soon be mine.... or not. I would just have to bide my time on this one.

Our time in the Bay Area had flown by, but there were still a couple of 'must do' things on Sheryl's list. Upper most would be to show me the flower shop she had owned when we first met. It had often been stressful with long hours, but she had loved that store.

Eventually she sold the shop, married me and with that financed our lives. So, one day we hopped the subway, jumped on a bus, took an Uber, then walked through the business district and stopped in front of a newly constructed low-rise condominium complex. Looking at Sheryl I could see a small tear making its way south down her cheek.

"It's gone," she whispered through quivering lips. Those assholes tore down my shop! I wanted to see it again and to show you, Rick. Dammit!" Her voice raising with every word.

Knowing my wife as I do, she doesn't just throw out cuss words without good reason. Plus, I could see that she was hurt that her prior life's work had been bulldozed into oblivion. I sought to comfort her in her time of need and consoled her with, "Hey, but ya got good money from those assholes." I really need to work on my comforting skills.

Leave Eve. It's the day before we point *Casablanca's* bow south to Mexico and hopefully beyond. Sheryl and I were doing last minute shopping at an upscale mall near the marina. It was mid day, so there was a mix of shoppers, people taking early lunches and even a few mall walkers. As we approached the exit door a women's scream echoed through the concourse, "HELP ME!

HELP ME!" and at once all heads turned toward the direction of the screams. Sheryl and I looked at each other and laughed.

"Rick, that was Lucy yelling," she said as the mall cop pushed past us.

"HELP ME....... HELP ME!"

"That's Lucy, alright," I concurred. I couldn't keep from laughing.

We had met Lucy about a week before when a beautiful 60ft motor yacht came into Emery Cove and tied up to the end of our dock.

We didn't see the occupants until the next morning when the family consisting of mom, dad and 12 yr. old Jimmy (although that might not be his name) headed for the City by the Bay for a day of wonderful tourist activities.

Jack and I were on the bow of *Casablanca* while Brian, the assistant dock master, was checking nearby dock boxes. All of a sudden, a women's blood-curdling scream resonated down the dock.

"HELP ME..... HELP ME!"

The plea was coming from the newly arrived yacht, just five boat slips down from us.

"Let's take a look," I said, jumping onto the dock at the same time Brian was on his hand-held radio calling the marina office saying we were on the way to check out the commotion.

"AHHHH! LEAVE ME ALONE!" came the voice which was definitely in distress.

The office had told Brian that someone across the street had heard the screams and called the police. It was strongly suggested that we not do anything until the authorities arrived.

"GOD DAMMIT! LEAVE ME ALONE!"

Emeryville is a small suburban patch of land that boarders Oakland on one side, San Francisco Bay on another, with Berkeley and the I-80 freeway completing the rectangle. None the less, they have their own police department, which turned out to be about 5 minutes away from the marina by car or 3 minutes walking.

As the police car braked hard in the marina parking lot, Sheryl, accompanied by Jack the cat, strolled up to where I was standing and asked, "What's going on Rick?"

"A woman is screaming to be left alone, sounds domestic," I said at a whisper.

Brian tried the knob on the main entry door of the big motor yacht. Had it not been locked, it obviously would have been an easy in. He then did a quick search which revealed every door, hatch and a large window were, of course, locked.

About that time the Emeryville police officer could be seen hurrying down the dock in our direction. Two things caught my eye, one: he had the look of a war veteran with his muscles, close shaved hair and a very serious look, and two: he had a very serious look.

I was astonished by how many items were on his belt. Handcuffs, Taser, radio, extra bullets, night stick and what looked like the biggest handgun I had ever been close to. If something bad went down, he would be the one to hide behind.

Brian gave officer tough guy what we knew, and that we hadn't heard anything for several minutes.

As Brian finished his status report, a weak voice could be heard to say, "Help me Larry."

Then two things happened almost at once.

Sheryl elbowed me and said, "No one is in there you know." She turned and walked back to *Casablanca*, with Jack right at her heals. She was being rather smug.

About that time Officer No Nonsense took out his night stick and with one very well-placed strike, knocked the handle right off of the door, allowing him to kick it in rather easily.

Then I yelled to my wife, "But somebody is in there…. you heard it."

She replied over her shoulder, "It's not the family."

Alright, she was really acting smug.

"Oh shit!" was the response from officer Fife.

And as good luck would have it the family that owned the boat with the now broken back door, could be seen trudging down the dock like the worn-out tourists that they were.

However, their pace picked up when they realized the police were at their boat. I chose that time to casually start side stepping back to *Casablanca*. As Mom and Dad and Little Jimmy (turns out his name is Larry) passed by me, the father in a controlled, but strained voice announced, "That damn parrot better not be causing a problem again or she is gone, I swear."

After a third of the Emeryville police force had gone, a real heated domestic discussion took place for most of the marina to hear. We found out that in Larry's spare time he would give language lessons to his Macaw parrot, named Lucy.

The next day, Lucy the parrot, was exiled to a local pet store.

Chapter 4
Cape Fear

"If you're going through hell, don't slow down."
~ Winston Churchill

With the Golden Gate Bridge rapidly fading from view *Casablanca* and her crew were once again at sea. Although we were not on a hard and fast schedule, we definitely felt the need to get our sea-legs back and to continue moving.

All three of us were laying in the cockpit, Jack had perched himself on Sheryl's stomach as she laid prone on the port side of the cockpit. I was propped against the back-seat rest watching for ship traffic, all the while the wind vane tirelessly steered *Casablanca* south towards Mexico.

There was a gentle 6-foot swell coming out of the north and the wind was coming from the northwest keeping us moving right along with a full Genoa and reefed main.

"So?" I finally asked Sheryl.

"So what?" She questioned back.

"I think you know...."

"I swear Rick have you been drinking? What the heck are you yacking about?"

"All that whispering at your sisters house, that's what."

"Rick, that was a month ago...... why have you waited this long to ask?"

"Well, it's been bugging me for a while," I replied, even though it was really because I had forgotten about it.... and had just remembered.

"Joni just thought she might be pregnant again, and she was waiting for the right time to tell Kenny."

"Why couldn't I know about it?"

"Because you are a big blabber mouth."

"Are you saying I can't keep a secret?"

"Pretty much, yah."

"Not true."

"True."

"Nonsense," I stated, "I guess we will just have to agree to disagree."

"Let's agree that you're an idiot and leave it at that," she said with a smirk on her face.

Guess I won that round.

As we approached the divide between Northern and Southern California, we received a troubling weather prognostication from my new friend at NOAA. Seemed a big change was coming: the winds and seas were going to build considerably. We would need to get around Point Conception before the weather worsened.

As a bit of background, Pt. Conception is a large bulge on the North American coastline where, at times, the wind and current will work in unison to provide some really hairy conditions. This has resulted in the area being referred to as 'The Cape Horn of North America'.

The prudent mariner has to plan his or her rounding of this infamous Cape very carefully. But the reward on the other side is the warmer climes of Southern California and maybe shedding the long johns and fleece. To aid in this timing the *Casablanca* crew would stop in San Luis Obispo, the last safe anchorage north of the point. Our stop would allow a lingering front to move down the coast and give the wind and the seas time to calm before we needed to proceed. Timing is everything; we really didn't want to get caught in bad weather rounding The Cape.

"It's going to be a race to the point," I said staring out the window after we had dropped the anchor in San Luis Obispo, "and the calmest winds are going to be around midnight."

Sheryl asked, "When is the next front supposed to hit?"

"If the predictions hold the winds will start to pick up around daybreak bringing big seas and gale force winds. So, if we can make the thirty miles in six hours, we should be good," I said with confidence, while thinking of a plethora of things that could go wrong but trying to sound upbeat.

For the next eight hours we comfortably rode the anchor in the bay's protection. We could still see the ocean swell and hear the wind, so the tension of having to wait made sleeping or any sort of rest impossible for me. I had hoped to raise the anchor around midnight, then gradually sail a southwest course that would take us away from land to about 5 miles off shore. There we would turn south, round the point and then actually head on an eastward track following the coast of California.

Unfortunately, that day of all days, my 'IN' at NOAA had chosen to take the day off, something about having a baby. So instead, we listened to the VHF radio for the automated weather report.

"Rick, you have been checking the weather constantly; you need to get some rest," Sheryl prodded. She was right. I would turn on the weather forecast every hour and listen for any changes in the storm's progress. That robotic voice from the weather station was driving the three of us insane.

"If we don't get around Conception tonight, it looks like this thing could last for a week," I cautioned and went on, "then we would be stuck here for a while."

Then adding, almost to myself, "It's going to be close but once we round the point, we're set, we will be out of the junk. The Cape should block all the weather nonsense as we travel eastward."

Around 10 pm I went up on deck to check the conditions and I was relieved to no longer hear the surf. With just two hours to go I was on pins and needles. I had a hard time staying still for more than the length of the weather report. On the other side of anxiety, I could hear Sheryl softly snoring in the aft cabin. I was tempted to leave early, but if experience was any indication, the longer we gave the seas to flatten, the happier Jack would be, and by extension Sheryl. But happiest would be, yours truly.

The night was dark. The moon was half full (or maybe the other way around), the clouds would occasionally block out its light and the decks were wet from dew. Let me emphasize again, it was DARK. Sheryl and I both double checked our safety harnesses as there would be a slim chance of recovery if one of us went over the side, given the conditions.

"Let's do this." I tried to sound more enthusiastic than I really felt.

Five minutes to twelve we started the engine, and I began pulling up the anchor. Sheryl turned the bow toward the open ocean and upon leaving the bay, we were quickly surrounded by a thick fog.

"Not exactly what I wanted to see," Sheryl said as she stared at the gray wall in front of *Casablanca*. Within minutes the dodger windows were completely covered in moisture. The visibility had dropped from 100 yards to about the length of the boat before I could say, "oh shit!"

"Rick, it's not doing any good trying to see ahead of us, I'm just going to concentrate on the radar screen." There was real tension in her voice.

"Sounds good, I'm gonna hand steer, so if you see anything just tell me which direction you want me to go."

We were confident that anything bigger than a row boat we would pick up on radar. The potential problem would be the small buoys holding crab pots or fish nets that would be too small for the radar to identify, but just the right size to get caught in the propeller.

On the plus side, the seas were around six feet spaced about fourteen seconds apart, and we could live comfortably with that. The wind was northwest, blowing between 12 to 16 knots.

After traveling quite a while, I broke Sheryl's concentration with, "Well that first hour slipped by pretty quick."

"You nut, it's been exactly 20 minutes.... you should have rested when you had the chance."

"I'm just kidding," I uttered, totally beat. Then, changing the subject, I pointed skyward, "That's a weird effect." Looking straight up we could see clear skies and stars with an occasional moon beam thrown in.

"Wish that clearing was down here," Sheryl lamented turning back to the radar.

That gray wall of fog had a way of giving a person vertigo. That person being me. To combat it, I was constantly moving my eyes and changing positions while the cold wet night crept into our bones.

We were no longer listening to the radio weather forecast for updates because at this juncture we were committed. But we had a potential problem; we weren't making the speed we had anticipated.

"I would sure feel better if we could speed up a little, there must be a current or something slowing us down," I murmured while doing the mental math to figure out if we would be around the point before the gale kicked in. Sheryl and I knew it was going to be close when we started out but as it was, we would be about an hour behind our planned schedule.

As we were approaching our turning point, the ocean swell began to take on a different feel. Since the impending storm had started somewhere off the Washington coast and its waves were traveling faster than the wind, we had begun to feel a change in the sea conditions and knew it wouldn't be long before the wind caught up.

When we left the harbor, I had put a double reef in the main and had the Genoa full out. The wind had been slowly creeping up and before we knew it had reached 20 knots, so *Casablanca* was finally picking up speed. I then reduced the Genoa down to about 90%.

The increased speed was a double-edged sword. We needed the speed to stay ahead of the gale, but not so much speed that we could accidentally jibe or lose control or miss seeing a buoy, so our concentration was heightened. At that point we had to focus on the radar while straining to see what was ahead of us as well as worrying about the weird creaking noises coming from the rigging.

With about half an hour to go before our waypoint turn, Sheryl checked and rechecked our current position as well as the intended route to make sure she had not overlooked any danger.

I had expected that when the wind picked up it would help dissipate the fog, but no sir. In fact, I swear it made it worse. The wind was a solid 25 knots, and we had just passed close to a fish net buoy, luckily without getting tangled. My nerves were about shot.

"Hey Hon, you should take a quick peak down below to check on Jack and make sure everything is still stowed okay," I suggested explaining, "When we make the turn the wind will be on our beam so I suspect we will be on our ear for a little while."

"You got everything up here under control?" Sheryl asked nervously.

"Yeah, just hurry."

With just two miles to go before the turn a howl came out of the fog and the resulting wind slapped the boat like a giant hand. With 35 knots on the stern the bow dug in and threw sheets of water over the entire length of the boat. Sheryl struggled up the companion way and got the drop door in place before the next big gust.

Yelling to be heard I said, "I AM GOING TO START TURNING EAST A LITTLE EARLY."

"WE SHOULD BE OK! BUT MAKE IT A GENTLE TURN AT FIRST," Sheryl yelled back.

I began slowly turning the steering wheel just a couple of degrees at a time, my reasoning was we could keep the wind on our stern quarter while we angle into the turn, as opposed to taking it full on the beam. The dangerous part of that maneuver was that we would be inching closer to land. I rolled in the Genoa leaving just a small triangle. With only the double reefed main driving *Casablanca* we still had the rail buried in the water.

Suddenly there was a crash from below; it sounded like the pan cabinet made a deposit on the galley floor. The sounds of two pots and a pan sliding and crashing together made me cringe. Sheryl made no move to go below. We were both holding on for dear life, me on the wheel and Sheryl with a death grip on the dodger frame. The spray in the air was slowly taking the place of the fog.

"ONE MORE MILE AND WE WILL BE BEHIND THE POINT!"

"RICK, LOOK," Sheryl called out. Looking to where she was pointing, I could see the beginning of the sunrise below the cloud deck. One final gust of only 30 knots had us guessing that the end was near, figuratively speaking. And sure enough, within 20 minutes, not only had the wind dropped to the low teens, but the seas had laid down as well. We had made it around the infamous Cape.

"Gees what was that? Those last two miles were nuts.... then it was like somebody threw a switch," I said with relief filling my voice.

Within three hours the wind had completely died, and the motor was chugging away. The fog had lifted and even though it was just before 10 in the morning it was warm, so much so that when Sheryl returned to the cockpit after cleaning up the mess below, she was wearing shorts and a long sleeve t-shirt.

"Welcome to Southern California! Hey that's about the first time that I have seen your bare legs since we left Washington." After leaning over and planting a big kiss on her lips I told her, "Those are probably the worst winds we're going to see for a long time."

Will I never learn?

Chapter 5
The Dodge

"Life is like a dance, sometimes you lead, sometimes you follow."
~ John Michael Montgomery

By midafternoon we had tied up to a dock at the Oxnard Yacht Club. We were members of the local yacht club back in Gig Harbor which has a reciprocal agreement with clubs up and down the coast. This meant we were entitled to stay for free and that included the use of the showers, laundry as well as other perks. But all we were looking forward to right then was getting cleaned up and enjoying a peaceful evening with no night or anchor watches.

Waking the next morning, refreshed after a great sleep, we pushed on to San Diego. This would be another overnight passage. The weather was fair, having left the nasty stuff up north, so we anticipated a pleasant trip under a nearly full moon. However, we would have to cross one of the busiest, most congested waterways in the world: the entrance to Los Angeles Harbor.

As we approached the greater LA area, the shipping traffic kept both of us on our toes. Personally, nothing worries me more out at sea than ships, you always wonder and worry if they are actually seeing you. Thankfully, before we set out from Washington, I had purchased an AIS receiver that works in conjunction with our VHF radio.

AIS stands for Automatic Identification System. By international agreement, all large ships in transit are required to have an AIS transponder on board. That device sends a signal out from the ship so that other vessels know the ship's position. *Casablanca* can receive signals from the properly equipped ships that are as far as 15 miles away. The signal then displays on our chart plotter, giving us the approaching vessels name, speed, and most importantly, how close it will pass to us, given our present course.

This has taken about 80% of the worry out of ship sightings for me. The remaining 20% of worry is taken up by ships that don't show up either because their radio is off or disabled for any number of reasons.

But there is one other culprit that doesn't show up on AIS: The US Navy. Sheryl and I had discovered this on that overnight passage to San Diego. It puzzled us that we were seeing the lights of 2 large ships and had even spotted them on radar but the AIS display remained blank. But when a Navy ship called us on the radio inquiring as to our course and destination, we realized it was the Navy keeping their transponders off.

After responding with the requested information, we were told that we had stumbled into one of their maneuvers and they requested that we maintain our present heading for at least 45 more minutes. For the rest of that night we were the most guarded sailboat anywhere in the world as the two big warships circled *Casablanca*, keeping us in the center of a 10-mile circumference all the while moving south.

By daybreak, after leaving the protection of the warships, we had the San Diego entrance buoy in sight. Unfortunately, so did two enormous cruise ships. Throw a departing aircraft carrier into the mix and it made the waterway seem extremely narrow and very busy. We chose to stay just outside the channel markers, figuring it to be our safest place to navigate.

We had originally planned to make this port of call a touch and go, meaning we would get some essentials then shove off for another overnighter down to Ensenada, Mexico. But the good luck we had been having to this point took a hit.

This bit of bad luck had actually planted its roots at our Bon Voyage party back in Gig Harbor. A dear friend had made a couple of flowers out of palm fronds as a parting gift. Each flower was about the size of a silver dollar with a short stem hanging down. They were supposed to be for good luck but come to find out no such luck.

Now fast forward to rounding Pt. Conception where these two small innocent looking 'good luck' charms ended up on the cabin sole due to the rough weather.

Fast forward one last time (this is the last, I promise) to 5 miles off of San Diego at five in the morning.

"Rick, I smell smoke."

Those words got my attention, and I charged down the companion way yelling, "Turn off the macerator!"

After Sheryl turned off the breaker, we both converged into the head at the same time, getting in each other's way. I quickly opened the cabinet door to gain access to the pump that discharges waste from our holding tank. Although the smoke was light, the acidic smell was overwhelming.

"Well that's not good," I mumbled jerking my hand away from the still hot, now dead, electric motor.

"I will need to take a look at this once we get to the dock," I told Sheryl, then added, "On the bright side at least we weren't already in Mexico where it would be much harder to get parts."

The next day as I was sitting on the finger pier in the marina with the offending pump and its casing in pieces all around me, my wife came back from the store just in time to see my discovery.

"What's that?" She said pointing to the stringy mess in front of me.

"Let me ask you a question first. Have you seen those two palm flowers that Rod made for us at our party?"

"I think so, but I can go look," she replied sounding puzzled.

"No need. This mess," I said pointing to the gunk, "is what's left of them."

"But how?" She asked breaking into a somewhat contained laughter.

"Not funny, not funny," I said trying to sound firm but failing miserably.

"They were hanging way out of the way but probably fell as we rounded the point in that rough weather, and we didn't notice," Sheryl surmised while trying to contain a left-over giggle.

Jack the cat had a bad rap for eating things he shouldn't, and those palm fronds went to the top of that list.

Shaking my head, I mumbled, "I thought those flowers were supposed to bring good luck."

"Oh, but they brought good luck," Sheryl replied.

"So how is this mess that's in front of me in any way good luck?" I inquired.

Climbing on to *Casablanca* she rubbed Jack's sleeping head as she passed him and said over her shoulder, "They're not still in his stomach and I would call that lucky."

Point taken.

Chapter 6
Hola!

"Sometimes the road less traveled is less traveled for a reason."
~Jerry Seinfeld

In order to reach Ensenada during daylight hours we would need to depart San Diego around midnight. Let me just say again for the record: I am not a big fan of night departures and I don't care what time of night it is. Dark is dark. We were greeted by fog as soon as we cleared the harbor just as we had been when we rounded Point Conception. Thankfully, the curtain lifted an hour before sighting the Ensenada entrance buoy. By midmorning, and with the help of the marina dock crew, *Casablanca* was securely tied to a finger pier.

Sheryl and I had sailed to Mexico a few years back, so we knew the drill for checking into the country. The Mexican government in Ensenada has done a wonderful job of combining all the offices that concern customs and immigration into one building. The route to those offices from the marina passes right by the passenger disembarkation point for the cruise ships in port. This can make the short walk to the port captain's office seem like running a gauntlet as there are always a dozen or more street merchants lined up selling everything imaginable to the visitors coming off the cruise ships. The whole scene can be a little overwhelming and intimidating if it's your first time going through there. We were in luck; there were no ships in port that day, so most of the venders were absent with just a few making half-hearted attempts to sell their wares.

Once we completed our paperwork and after paying a small donation to the country by way of entry fees, the last step was to play 'red light-green light'. This is supposedly a random process to determine if further inspection of an incoming vessel is needed.

To play the game a boat captain or their representative steps up to a button on the wall which in turn is wired to what looks like a miniature traffic light. A press of the button and if the green light shows up, you're on your way no worries. However, a red light and you are likely to have an official visit to your boat at dockside. Sheryl hit the button and.... a RED LIGHT flashed, a bell rang for what seemed like five minutes but best of all everyone in the office turned to see who was unfortunate enough to win the prize and take the walk of shame.

They then informed us that an official from the port would come down and inspect *Casablanca* at the marina. This was standard procedure and when port captains have come aboard in the past, we have always enjoyed talking with them and offering them refreshments.

Miguel, an inspector from the customs office arrived at the dock later that day. He was about thirty-five years old, slight of build and he had a big toothy smile. Luckily for us he spoke very good English. While we chatted, he talked about his family and growing up in Ensenada. But during the conversation I could tell that something was distracting Miguel.

"Señor, I believe your cat es dead," he uttered pointing at the fifteen-pound ball of fur named Jack.

"No, no he is fine," Sheryl reassured him as she walked over and picked up the seemingly comatose feline. "See," she added as she held Jack up to show the concerned official. The lazy cat couldn't even be bothered to open his eyes. I don't think Miguel was convinced.

While we were in Ensenada, I got a call from my mom letting us know she and Walter would be in La Paz in a couple of weeks and asked if we would be close by.

"Sure, we should be there by then," I assured her.

And then Mom asked to speak to Sheryl. Handing the phone to my wife, I wandered down the dock while they talked. When she finished the call and caught up to me, I asked her what Mom had to say.

"Not much, really, just making sure everything was good," then continued, "Your mom is still so protective of you."

"What does that mean?"

"Oh, nothing, I guess it's just hard for her to break the old habit of worrying about you. Were you always in trouble growing up?" she questioned.

"I was an angel," I said dead pan.

With that Sheryl started choking on the water she had been drinking.

Having made that commitment to my mother I had broken one of the hard and fast rules that cruisers live by. That rule states "You can pick the time to meet someone or you can pick the place to meet someone, but you cannot pick both". Bad things can happen as a result of trying to keep to a time schedule. We would be putting that old adage to the test.

After Jack's comatose display for Miguel, we decided to stay in Ensenada for a couple extra days to allow all three of us to recharge our energy levels. Although for Jack, I think that ship had sailed.

From previous experience sailing the Mexican west coast, we knew that there would be several overnighters in our future. A crew has to be super vigilant because the chances of running over an unlit small boat, fish net, lobster pot or even a bale of pot increases significantly once a boat crosses the border.

After spending a very relaxing three days at the dock, we untied our lines to resume our trek south. The sun was bright and there was a gentle swell out of the north that morning as we motored out of the harbor.

"Rick! Look at all the dolphins heading our way!" Sheryl exclaimed as she climbed out of the cockpit and raced forward to the bow with camera and enthusiasm in hand.

To my eye there was something different about the way this massive pod of dolphins was acting. We were used to seeing the loping, tail slapping, having a good time, goofballs of the sea playing around the boat, but these guys were going full tilt and looking like they were trying to stay out of the water. I engaged the autopilot and joined my wife on the bow for a better look.

"Wow! Look at all of them!" She was snapping pictures, whistling, calling them and just plain having a great time. They were in a nearly straight line about 200 ft. across and the group gave the impression of one long wave coming at us.

As the pod drew near, they began to split up half going on the port side and the other half on the starboard side of *Casablanca*.

Then I realized what was going on.

Three very large fins were racing behind the pod. Orca! Before I could fully appreciate what was happening one of the huge mammals grabbed its intended target, thrashed around, and disappeared leaving a trail of blood.

The stunned look on Sheryl's face when she turned to look at me broke my heart. I'm sure she had never seen anything like the display we had just witnessed, and I coaxed her back to the cockpit. I held her and dried her tears knowing the best thing for me to say at the time was.... nothing.

For the next several hours Sheryl was understandably quiet, and I wasn't having much luck cheering her up. I even resorted to dragging Jack up to the cockpit as a backup, but a sleeping cat wasn't going to make her feel any better. Then Mother Nature stepped in to make things right. Sheryl was down resting up for her night shift. Evening was fast approaching when I heard the distinct sound of a whale blow. As I searched the smooth sea for the source, I again heard the mighty mammal's signature sound only this time it seemed on the opposite side of the boat.

"Hey, Sheryl! Whales!" I yelled.

Still groggy she quickly joined me in the cockpit, asking, "Where? I don't...," and before she could finish her sentence two large gray whales appeared simultaneously on either side of *Casablanca*. One was so close that the distinctive stench of sea food breath permeated the air. That promptly brought Jack bounding up the stairs, moving faster than I thought he was capable. But the real showstopper was sighting a calf that was not at first apparent. The young mammal blended right in as it held its position next to mom. For the next hour the 'family' escorted *Casablanca* and crew down the Mexican coast. They would ease close enough for us to see barnacles on their bodies, then slowly move away. Sheryl had positioned herself on the bow with her harness hooked to a lifeline where she had the best spot for viewing and photo ops. I chose to stay at the wheel in case we needed a sudden course change. With the night descending on our small boat it seemed, at least for that moment, our little slice of the universe was back in harmony.

Night passages always have a drama all their own. Maybe it's the mysterious noises that begin coming from inside the cabin during a night watch or perhaps the eerie 'voices' that whisper out when the wind freshens. I swear I have heard *Stairway to Heaven* playing in the rigging many a night. It's always something.

On our third night out at sea I heard, "Rick, honey wake up," Sheryl was whispering and gently nudging me. When I didn't respond, she shook me a little harder. She then placed her lips near my ear and said, "I know you're awake I heard you get up and use the head."

"What's up?" I asked trying to stifle a yawn.

"Come take a look."

Grabbing a hoodie, I followed my wife up the stairs to the cockpit and saw that *Casablanca* was easily motoring through smooth, lazy rollers.

"There's a mast light dead ahead, and it's showing its red port side light." She handed me the binoculars.

"Hard to see through this haze," I observed.

"Yeah, sorry to get you up, but I even adjusted the autopilot to take us further offshore."

"Still nothing on radar? I'll try to call on the radio," I offered.

After repeated attempts at contacting the approaching vessel through VHF, my concern was peaking.

Finally, as the lacy haze began to lift, with it came clarity in more ways than one.

"That's MARS!" laughed Sheryl, and she again handed me the binoculars.

"Huh," I muttered, then halfway back to my bunk I turned, trudged back to the cockpit adding, "This stays between us."

Yeah right.

Further down the coast while recouping at anchor from one of the long night passages, we were boarded by the Mexican Navy. Never having been boarded before we were not sure what to expect. A large Mexican Navy ship had pulled into the bay and immediately dispatched an inflatable. This crew boat was about 25 ft. in length with two very large outboard motors and was manned by four people in full military garb. Luckily for us there was another sailboat nearby, and that was the Navy's first stop. This gave Sheryl time to dig out our visas, boat documents, the veterinary certificate for Jack and anything else she could think of.

"They're heading this way," I said keeping Sheryl appraised while she scrambled around making sure the docs were in order.

"I had this file stashed thinking we wouldn't need them until La Paz." She sounded flustered.

The approaching craft presented a menacing sight with fully armed and uniformed individuals complete with helmets and dark goggles. The rifles were an attention getter but not as much as the bandannas that partially obscured their faces. Why the masks?

When the inflatable was just a few feet away, an officer outfitted in more relaxed attire (and minus the rifle) called over in near perfect English, "Buenos Dias I am Lieutenant Vasquez with the Mexican Navy. We are requested to board your vessel."

"Yes, please come aboard," I replied nervously.

The helmsman expertly brought the craft next to *Casablanca*, and as he did so a sailor at the bow grabbed our lifeline and steadied the maneuver.

The Lieutenant then stepped aboard closely followed by his two biggest, most heavily armed escorts.

Shaking my hand, he informed us that this was just a routine boarding, kind of a 'Welcome to Mexico' if you will.

Casablanca is a small sailboat even when it's just my wife, the cat and me, so having three more individuals, two of whom were decked out for war, made for a very awkward, crowded space. In addition, the added weight as the guys climbed aboard caused *Casablanca* to rock to that side. That, in itself, was no big deal, except it caused the barrels of the M-16s they were carrying to wave around wildly as they tried to regain their balance. I was really hoping they had the safeties on.

We offered cold drinks to our guests, but the lieutenant declined, and his men just stood stoically, unsmiling and cradling their cannons.

After we explained to him where we were coming from and our intended destination he asked if he or the Mexican Navy could help us in any way.

We assured our visitors that there had been no problems thus far. I was hoping to wrap up the little get together quickly because the wind was coming up and the two boats were starting to bang into each other.

The lieutenant rejected my invitation to have a look below saying it wasn't necessary. He spoke a few words in Spanish to his men then stood up to leave and unfortunately Jack chose that moment to clamber into the cockpit. As a bit of background Jack is an overly large male tabby that doesn't get the exercise he needs, hence the hugeness. Before the lieutenant could leave the cockpit, Jack started doing a figure-eight between Mr. Vasquez's legs, rubbing and paying particular attention to the Lieutenant's spit shined boots.

When the Lieutenant looked down and saw Jack, the expression on his face was a mixture of disbelief and a little fear. Sheryl rushed to grab Jack, not knowing if Vasquez was a 'cat guy'.

"Gato Gordo!" exclaimed the startled officer as he sat back down.

Then a flurry of Spanish, that included the words Gato Gordo more than once, took place between the Lieutenant and his crew. Before we could stop him, Jack was on the officer's lap! The Navy guys, finally looking more relaxed, took turns coming into the cramped cockpit to see, what I guessed, was the largest 'gato gordo' they had ever seen. Jack sucked it all in even as the waves were starting to show whitecaps and the two boats began a crazy out of step dance.

When the navy tender was finally out of ear shot Sheryl inquired,

"Did you catch that fish smell?"

"Look on the deck where they stepped aboard," I said pointing to a pile of mush that at one time had been a flying fish.

"Ugh, that's gross. The guys must have stepped on it releasing the lovely fish market smell that got Jack going."

With a bucket of sea water and a brush I scrubbed the remaining blood and guts off the deck, all the while pushing the cat away, who was convinced there was a meal to be had.

"He is addicted to flying fish," Sheryl stated.

"No," I said, "he's addicted to eating."

Our last night in the Pacific gave way to our first sunrise in the Sea of Cortez. We had made good time coming down the coast since we had continued overnight five times, instead of stopping to anchor every night. The weather had been kind, but that was all about to change.

Once we rounded Cabo San Lucas at the tip of Baja, a completely unique weather pattern kicked in. A brief explanation for that change goes something like this: When the summer hurricane season ends on the 30th of November, high-pressure cells can develop over what's called 'the four corners' in the United States. That's where the borders of Nevada, Utah, Colorado and New Mexico all meet. Then if a low-pressure cell develops to the south, a river of air flows from the high in the US to the low, often lasting days at a time and sometimes with gale force winds. That's called a Norther.

One other consideration with these north winds is the Sea of Cortez is notorious for what they call 'square waves' that some mariners nickname refrigerators. These nasty waves are a result of the short period between the wave-tops that occur during a Norther, which is about three seconds, as compared to the Pacific where they are spaced about twelve seconds apart, even on a bad day. The pounding a small boat and its crew takes going north in a Norther is enough to rattle your fillings.

A few years earlier on our first cruise to the Sea, our inexperience showed when we chose to set out in a 'light' Norther. About a mile out of the anchorage the five-foot waves would bring *Casablanca* to a complete stop. The resulting spray would almost envelope the entire boat. The engine would struggle to overcome the smashing seas and just as we would start to get some momentum another wave cluster would again stop us in our tracks. Needless to say, we turned and headed back to the protected anchorage.

"We have five days before meeting your mom and Walter," Sheryl reminded me.

"It's about a hundred and fifty miles to La Paz, so if we can avoid a north wind, we've got it made," I stated realizing I was probably being too optimistic. That's why you never commit to meeting someone at a set time and place.

"We have four days before the next Norther according to the weather report on the net, so we should really push to get there," Sheryl said seeming anxious to get to the city.

"It will be interesting to see Perry's resort. I heard it got hit by Hurricane Newton," I ruminated.

Joseph Perry was an old family friend that had stepped into my life when I was a youngster, giving me my first job and kind of helped my mom keep me on the straight and narrow. For some reason my mother didn't think that the *Three Stooges* were the best male role models, so she appreciated Joe's positive influence on me.

On our first trip to Mexico Sheryl and I found ourselves living aboard *Casablanca* in the bay in front of Perry's resort as he had offered us both jobs to help feed the cruising kitty. And I don't mean Jack. Later, when I departed for the South Pacific, I lost contact with Joe, although Mom remained in regular communication with him.

Sheryl informed me that we could see the place as we sailed by, but we wouldn't be stopping there until we left La Paz. I viewed that as very odd behavior from my wife as she'd loved our time there as much as I had.

Twenty-five miles from the finish line the wind began to blow, and we had no choice but to pound into the building waves.

"Guess it started early," I said through gritted teeth.

I just hate crashing into that kind of junk. The boat speed slowed and hovered between two and three knots. Unfortunately, the closest safe anchorage was La Paz and to get there we would have to continue the bash for another ten miles. But, on the plus side, we would round a point of land and the last ten miles would be a downwind ride straight to the dock.

Realizing it would be very dark by the time we reached the dock we formed a Plan B. So, at 10 pm I dropped the anchor in a small, semi-protected cove a few miles north of town. We had to use the radar to get in. So much for never entering an unknown harbor after dark.

Those final twelve hours had been brutal. With the drone of the engine finally quieted, I laid down in the cockpit still in my foul weather gear and crusty with salt. My head throbbed in the sudden silence.

"Thankfully we won't need to do that again. Remember just a short motor tomorrow and you can see your mom and dad," Sheryl said jokingly.

"Stepdad... no, no... Mom's new husband," I corrected her.

"He thinks of you as his son."

"Will you stop!" I intoned, then added, "She sure seemed strange when we last talked."

"Rick, just relax, let's get some sleep and we'll get into the marina early tomorrow for some decent showers."

The next day we contacted the marina for a slip assignment and we were instructed to take slip #31, Dock 3.

Chapter 7
Ash Wednesday

"I'm not sure if I attract crazy, or if I make them that way."
~ Anonymous

"Rick let's get going we need to meet your parents around 11 at the restaurant," Sheryl reminded me.

"I told you... never mind," I muttered, bothered by her continued use of 'your parents'.

"Come on grumpy let's go," she said smiling at being able to yank my chain regarding my 'new' dad.

Earlier that morning we did the marina office check-in and paperwork routine. With that business settled, Sheryl and I set off to meet my mom and her newly wedded husband, Walter.

"My mother absolutely hates to travel. I cannot, for the life of me, figure out why she decided to fly to La Paz," I pointed out.

And Sheryl replied, "Here they come now.... why don't you ask them?"

There were hugs all around. I had to admit that Walter must have been taking good care of my mom as she looked good and seemed in fine spirits.

"Your hair's not as blue as I remembered," I teased poking fun at Mom, and I received a punch in the arm for my effort.

We got a table at an open-air restaurant and after reliving the highlights of our trip down the coast and giving the Jack update to Walter and Mom, I subtly changed course.

I was finally going to get to the bottom of this total mystery... that I had conjured up.

"What the heck are you guys doing here? You hate to travel," I asked point blank.

There was a pause as Sheryl and my mom suspiciously exchanged glances and Walter tried to make himself invisible.

"Ricky, did you see *Perry's Landing* when you sailed in?" Mom asked.

"No, it was dark, and the wind and waves were blowing," continuing on I reported, "I thought I would see some lights or something, I must have missed seeing the bay."

"No, you didn't miss it, most of the resort is gone. The last hurricane and the flooding washed almost everything away," she sadly informed me.

"Hell, I didn't know that. Where was Joe? He wasn't there was he?"

"No, he was in the States when it hit," Mom replied.

The dread I had been feeling had started to dissipate until Mom reached over and took my hand in hers.

"Ricky, Joseph passed away 2 months ago," she said softly as tears welled up in her blue eyes.

"But how? Was he sick or...?" I was in shock and completely dumb founded.

"It was all very sudden; he hadn't been feeling well, so he went in for an exam. After they found the tumor he was sent to several doctors, but by then it was just a matter of time."

Straining to keep myself together I asked, "How long.... I mean.... why didn't you tell me? We could have come back. Maybe we could have helped or something."

"Ricky, he made me promise not to tell you, the last thing he wanted was for you to turn back from your trip because of him."

My wife held my hand as tears traced my face and I asked, "You told Sheryl, didn't you?"

Sheryl spoke up, "Just as Joe didn't want to burden you, neither did your mom. She was worried that this would affect your ability to handle any problems that might happen as we sailed down."

Mom spoke up, "Joseph went to great length to explain how he felt it would be best for you if you weren't dwelling on what was happening with him."

Wiping my eyes with the back of my hand I choked out, "I wish I could have gotten to see him one last time."

A sad smile came over my mom's face as she informed me, "You are going to be able to be with him one more time. That's the reason Walter and I are in La Paz. You see, the other promise I made to Joseph, was that we would spread his ashes in front of the resort. We were hoping you and Sheryl would give us a lift out there on *Casablanca*."

"Well sure... of course, anything," I managed to get out.

Walking out of the restaurant into the bright sunlight, I was remembering what Joe would say after a couple of beers, "I worked in the rain all my life and that's the reason I am down here: no rain."

My mother and I hugged and in a low voice she said, "He loved you like a son."

"That's what makes this so hard," I replied solemnly.

With a need to find out more details about Joe, the resort and about a hundred other questions, the four of us headed back to *Casablanca* for further commiserating.

"Just a minute Rick, I need to go to the rental car," Walt said as he headed to the parking lot.

Turning to Mom I pried, "How're things with you and Walter?"

"Your new dad is a wonderful dancer," was her reply.

I stopped dead in my tracks, "Wait... What?"

Before Mom could respond, Sheryl gave away their little game with a snort through her nose and saying to my mom, "I told you he is sensitive about that. Did you see the look on his face... priceless!"

"Not funny," was my stern reply.

Trying to cheer me up, Mom said, "Ricky, laughter is the best medicine."

Walter caught up to us as we waited by the gate leading to dock three and said to me, "Gonna have a visitor tonight," as he handed me a shoe box that read *NIKE* on its side. The tattered box was adorned with a blue ribbon. It took only a second for me to figure out that it would be Joe who would be spending the night aboard *Casablanca*.

As I stared at the shoebox, my mom read my thoughts and said, "He didn't like fancy."

The sea sparkled like an emerald on the day we motored away from the dock and thankfully it was flat for the one hour run to the resort. My parents.... Damn it! Now I'm doing it! The 'folks', understandably didn't have sea-legs, so no wind and flat water were perfect for that outing.

Rounding the corner of the cove in front of the resort, I could tell right away things had changed. I scanned the shore for the familiar buildings that I had used as landmarks for setting up the sailboat race course when I had been the sailing instructor, but none were there.

Sheryl's job back in those days was that of a full-time landscaper for the resort. She enjoyed the work, and that was evident in the beautifully maintained grounds. During that period, she and Joe became good friends. In her spare time, she would try to explain to Joe, over a couple beers, why she had married me in the first place.

After we dropped anchor in twenty feet of water about two hundred feet from shore, I stood on the bow just staring at the land that had once been *Perry's Landing*.

It was heartbreaking and sobering to see the nearly total destruction of the buildings. Cement blocks that had been foundations for the cabins were the only traces left of what was once one of the most popular resorts near La Paz.

"Did Joe see this place after the storm?" I asked Mom, still in a bit of shock.

"No, but he got word from the neighbor. It was the same week he went to the doctor, so he never got back down here. In fact, the neighbor even sent Joseph pictures of what was left, but he refused to look at them, saying he knew that wasn't the picture he wanted in his mind."

"Well, I guess we should do this," I said somewhat reluctantly.

"I'll go get Joe," Sheryl volunteered since she was closest to the stairs.

Five seconds later we heard her yell, "Jack! Get away from that box! Go on.... get away from there!"

"Oh, God, no," I prayed. "Please don't let that lid be off."

"Everything's okay! Don't worry, no harm, Joe's fine," Sheryl called out as she handed the old shoebox up the companionway.

Then I noticed a light dribbling of very fine ash and yelled, "STOP, STOP! There's a small hole in the bottom corner and Jack's slobber is all over it." I quickly covered the hole with my thumb as Jack cried at my feet.

The four of us, plus the cat, crowded on the starboard rail facing the shore and after a few words, Joe was finally back home.

Later, after everything had settled down, Sheryl and I rowed to shore. We struggled to make sense of what we had been seeing.... or not seeing.

The first, most obvious change was that the beach had been completely stripped of sand by the hurricane's tremendous surge, exposing an ancient coral bed.

Further ashore, the large open-air bar that had once hosted entertainment by performers who wanted a small intimate venue and a nice vacation for themselves, no longer existed. Now all that stood in its place were a couple of poles that had supported the enormous palm thatched roof. Beyond that we could see the foundations that the small bungalows had been built upon. That was all that was left of those structures. It was evident that the surge had reached far inland.

"Look, over here, it's the truck I would use to run into town," I pointed out. It was on its side and had been stripped of all useful parts. Fast growing vines were doing their best to bury it. In addition to being the sailing instructor I had been the resorts gopher.... as in 'Go for this and Go for that'.

"I just cannot get over how there is nothing left," I lamented.

"Rick, here's a palm that I planted! It survived and seems to be doing okay," she said as a smile came over her face. It was a sad smile all the same.

Sheryl's deep passion was all things plant related, so when the landscaping job at the resort was offered, she had jumped in with both feet and a trowel.

"Sure glad Joe didn't have to see this, this would have.... uh..." I let my thought trail off.

Sheryl said softly, "You can say it Rick. It would have killed him." That was followed by an uncomfortable silence.

"Yeah, it would have," I sighed.

"I wonder how much was looted after the storm?" Sheryl pondered, talking to herself.

"Joe always closed up tight for hurricane season and I think he told me that the workers would move all the valuable stuff to storage in town. Fishing gear, the small generators and anything else that wasn't nailed down would have gone there."

We wandered around for a while, turning over boards and kicking through debris and I commented, "I don't see this place ever being rebuilt. In fact, look at the road leading out of here, it looks unusable."

The small service road that lead to civilization had huge gouges made by the torrential rains that fell during the storm. When the resort was in operation, they would pick visitors up in La Paz by panga and the trip would take about twenty-minutes in decent weather. If the conditions were not good for the boat ride, I would drive the passenger van and pick up the waiting guests. After leaving the highway we would bump along over 2 miles of very rough road back to the resort.

"Come on, we should get back to the boat. Walter and your mom are being chaperoned by Jack and after all they are still newlyweds and you know anything could happen..." Sheryl teased with a wink.

"I will not even dignify that with an answer," was my blunt reply.

When we got back to *Casablanca*, my mom had put together a light lunch (instead of playing grab ass with her husband as Sheryl had implied). While the others talked in the cockpit, I sat up on the bow and tried to make sense of it all. Joe was a great guy, he had adopted our little family, gave me my first job and then my fourth job here at the resort. He watched over Muriel and watched me grow up and all he asked for in return was for me to tell him about my adventures.

"Joe," I said, "Sheryl and I are about to go on the most interesting adventure yet, and I promise I will come back and tell you all about it over a beer," I raised my can of Tecate, then added, "Sorry about Jack getting into your ash."

From the cockpit I heard mom asking, "Is Ricky talking to himself up there?"

"Probably," was Sheryl's one-word reply.

The following day the four of us did the customary sightseeing in La Paz. I was pleased that the solemn mood of the last couple of days had given way to some smiles. The margaritas surely helped with that. We toasted Joseph (no middle name) Perry numerous times that day. We vowed that we would all meet up again in a year for more toasting.

Sheryl and I put the folks on an airport shuttle the next afternoon for their trip back to Seattle. Walking back to *Casablanca,* we passed a small group of cruisers that had set-up a table and a few chairs on the dock, not far from our slip. As we navigated through the gathering, they invited us to stay, have a beer or a glass of wine and some finger food. We introduced ourselves and in turn met about eight different people but politely declined the offer of refreshments explaining that we needed to get back to the boat.

Stepping aboard and climbing down into the cabin Sheryl started to laugh. Still outside, I was puzzled at what could be so funny.

"Rick, you gotta see this."

It took a minute for my eyes to adjust in the dim interior light but I soon saw what she was laughing about; Jack had decided to take a nap in the shoe box that had carried Joe's ashes. Apparently after knocking the empty box to the floor, he jumped in and his tremendous bulk had blown out the sides as he tried to squeeze in to the small enclosure.

Without ceremony I kicked Jack out of the box, grabbed the lid and told Sheryl I would be right back, stating, "I'm taking this box up to the garbage."

"Really?" She sounded surprised.

"Yeah it's just a shoebox now. And a broken one at that."

Once again passing through the small gathering on the dock, a tall, very thin older guy stopped me. He had thick hair that was as white as snow and blue eyes that had the look of pure mischief.

Looking at the box in my hand he asked with a smile, "Did you get those shoes here in town?"

"No, actually my friend's ashes came in this box."

Without missing a beat, he came up with, "Huh, which store did you have to go to for that?"

That was my introduction to Joey or Mayor Joey as he was known to the live-a-boards on Dock 3. Why *Mayor* Joey, you ask? Well, according to Dock 3 lore, Joey arrived in Mexico just after Cortez himself. The Mayor, it's rumored, had the very first sailboat in this marina, about a hundred years ago. Joey had become the Dock 3 go-to guy for information about La Paz. Whether it's a restaurant report or a new movie in town, or the price of bananas at the market, if you asked, he would know the answer or have it in an hour. You might ask yourself how could Joey have all this information at hand?

I quickly learned that Mayor Joey actually knew very little, but his wife, the First Lady of Dock 3 did have all the answers. Nearly as tall as Joey, Sharon is slender and always smiling, resulting in fine little wrinkles near her blue eyes. Her petite face was framed by a short hair style, her once blond hair moving to gray. The First Lady is a gatherer of information. In short, she knows what is happening in the area. But her passion was dining out. When a new restaurant, be it big or small, would open in the city she would make it her life's work to track down the location.

The Mayor was in possession of an eight passenger Ford van so for those wanting to indulge there was always room to go along restaurant hopping. Sheryl and I took part in several of those gastronomic adventures and we were rarely disappointed.

Another popular cruiser activity on Dock 3 was the *Stitch and Bitch*.......

"Rick I am going to be gone for a couple of hours," my wife announced one morning with her head buried in one of the many hidey-holes that are prevalent on a 35-foot boat.

"What's up?" I asked.

"Dianne and Jane invited me to what they call a *Stitch and Bitch*."

"Who's a bitch?" I asked somewhat confused.

Pulling her head out of the small space she replied, "No, no one's a bitch, unless you have heard something I don't know about."

"What are you talking about?"

"What are *you* talking about?"

She went on to explain, "Harmless fun.... you know, knitting, sewing, quilting that kind of thing.... there you are," she said holding up a ball of yarn, like it was a first-place trophy.

"Let me get this straight, while you sew or darn or something you girl's man-bash?"

"Hopefully," she said with a grin.

Several hours later, Jack and I were sitting in the cockpit awaiting Sheryl's return. Jack spotted her first, still down the dock a couple of slips from ours. As usual she had stopped to chat with someone from another boat.

Once she finally made it down the dock, Sheryl hoisted herself up into the cockpit, Jack made a half-hearted attempt to greet his owner by first standing and then immediately laying back down.

"Al stopped me.... he may need some help with his outboard motor," she informed me.

"I will go down and see what's up," then to the most important question, "How was your sewing circle?"

Without a word she reached into her bag and pulled out a small square made of multi-colored yarn.

"A couple of years ago your mom showed me how to knit these things," she said admiring it. I could see she was quite proud of her work.

"What is it?"

"It's your new dishcloth."

"Great, thanks for the thoughtful gift," was my reply heavy with sarcasm, then I asked, "What did you girls talk about?"

"How all men are alike and very predictable."

"Did you explain that I was the exception?"

"Oh, please.... are you kidding? You are the leader of the pack!" she said laughing.

"Well I guess we...."

"Hold it right there, you're gonna say that nonsense about, 'We will have to agree to disagree', am I right?"

After a pause I weakly retorted, "No, not even close." She wasn't close.... she'd hit the bullseye.

I eventually made my way down to Al's boat, *Solana*, to see what was up. He was sitting in his inflatable dinghy hunched over the small 5 hp outboard that was minus its engine cover.

Al was a character. Stocky with white thinning hair that often had a whacky professor look, he sported a white goatee against rose colored skin. Al was a retired geologist in his late sixties, but he had the knees of a 90-year-old. It was most painful to see Al moving around his boat or on the docks. He always wore knee pads, they were just part of his attire, he said it gave him support. Apparently, his knees were mush, but that didn't stop him from having a great disposition or making the best sundowner drinks.... he was a great guy.

"What's up Al?" I queried.

"Hey, Rick," he replied. When he looked up, I was shocked to see most of his eyebrow on the left side of his face was missing.

"Al, what the hell happened to your brows?"

"Is it bad? I haven't looked. The engine caught fire... twice."

A boat owners' worst nightmare: fire.

"How did that happen?"

"The float was stuck, and apparently a little gas dripped out. When I pulled the starter cord, a spark jumped and the fumes just kinda went poof. I got it put out in a hurry. The second time I guess there was still residual fuel down around the engine."

"How can I help?" I asked.

He answered by handing me a bucket half full of water and explained, "I think I have the problem fixed but just in case..."

"Al, I'm not sure this is in our best interest," I cautioned.

So, as I stood there, a myriad of scenarios ran through my head not the least of which involved burning down the entire marina.

We both knew he was lucky to have put the first two fires out, but luck could change. So, when he grabbed the starter cord and prepared to pull, I was ready.... maybe a little too ready. When Al yanked on the starter cord the engine sputtered, then coughed and before you could say 'don't throw the water', I threw the water. That immediately killed the engine.

Al looked up from his place in the dinghy and in a calm, but tired voice said, "I wish you hadn't done that."

Chapter 8
Discovery

"The journey, not the arrival, matters."
~ T. S. Eliot

Our 'one week at the dock' had suddenly turned into three and a half weeks, which I attributed to the elevated comfort level of life in a marina. When you have easy access to fresh food, great restaurants, hot showers and no night watches time slips by almost unnoticed. Days start to blend together and before you know it, you wake up and it's time to go.

"Wake up it's time to go." Somebody was certainly cheery that morning. "Come on Rick, time to kick the tires and light um up."

"Light the fires," I moaned my head buried under a pillow.

"I thought you had some big rule about not drinking the night before a passage," Sheryl reminded me.

Sitting up, my head told me that even though I consumed only two margaritas the night before, they must have been doubles.

"Let's go we're burning daylight," Sheryl urged me on.

"You are sure anxious to get going.... have you seen my shorts?"

"That was quite the dock party last night and no, I haven't seen your shorts."

A minute later...

"Call off the hounds, I found my shorts." It was a minor victory considering the big headache.

"Come on Rick, if we don't leave pretty soon something is going to keep us here another day. Plus, Al is back working on his outboard."

"You know we're not going that far....4 or 5 hours is all," I reminded her.

"Yes, but we will be away from the dock and just by ourselves again and I'm looking forward to that. Now that we received our cruising permits for the Galapagos it feels like we are really finally going," and she added, "even though we will be going in the wrong direction at first."

It was true. One reason for the little get together the night before was to celebrate our securing a highly sought after Autographo (cruising permit) for two months in the enchanted islands (some restrictions may apply). It would still be several months before *Casablanca* would turn her bow south and then eventually west to the Galapagos. Sheryl's enthusiasm was infectious, but it was absolutely no help to my hang over.

After another round of hugs and kisses and promises to keep in touch, we finally untied our lines with the help of our new friends from Dock 3. We made about five miles that morning before an unpredicted north wind came up and stopped our journey dead in its tracks. As luck would have it, the small anchorage that we spent the night in just a month ago when we were heading to La Paz, would provide shelter for us on our way out.

We could see the seas quickly building outside the entrance, but in the bay the water was flat with just a moderate breeze blowing. With the anchoring dance over and our post anchoring chores complete, Sheryl and I sat in the cockpit and marveled at the feeling of finally being on our own once again and off on a new adventure, even though we could still see the lights of town.

Winter was in our rear-view mirror, so to speak, and the dreaded Northers had become less frequent, so it was a good time to travel. We might still get the occasional north wind, but it wouldn't be the forceful blows for days on end that we had been experiencing.

Spring was truly the best season to be in The Sea. Along with the rise in air temperatures the water temps were increasing as well. The warmer days found us snorkeling, beach combing and exploring nearby coves by way of the dinghy. The nights were pleasant as well, so after a full day of goofing off, we would sit in the cockpit at sunset and toast the days end.

"Have you thought about where we will summer over?" Sheryl asked one evening just after dusk as we were lying on the cabin top. She was sitting with her back against the mast and I had my head in her lap as we searched the skies for satellites, shooting stars or anything out of the ordinary.

"La Paz seems logical especially if we need to do any last-minute boat stuff before heading south," I pointed out.

You see, our plan had been to stay in the Sea of Cortez through hurricane season. La Paz, Puerto Escondido or farther up The Sea was San Carlos, and all three were viable options with different pros and cons. We would then leave The Sea after hurricane season to take advantage of the Northers to push us south.

Due to a combination of unfortunate circumstances, Sheryl could not be with me in the South Pacific last time. She had missed out on one of the best parts of cruising which is relaxing on tropical beaches. My goal was to show my ship mate that cruising wasn't only long night-passages, blinding fog or being flung off the toilet in rough seas.

Traveling up The Sea we enjoyed many nice anchorages. We would snorkel from *Casablanca* ending up on shore where Sheryl could then comb the beach for all matter of treasures. At night Sheryl and Jack would pick through the bounty she had brought aboard. Jack had always been curious about the outside world so when shells, beach glass, driftwood or sand came on to the boat, he would not be denied his place at the table.

In one of the anchorages there was a sea lion colony, and we were delighted to be able to get close enough to swim with a few of the juveniles. Like all teenagers they were over flowing with energy and mischief and seemed to delight in charging at us then turning at the last moment avoiding collision by a matter of inches.

One very curious fellow even put his nose against Sheryl's dive mask just to make a point. They took turns nipping at our swim fins and performing an incredible underwater ballet. This playfulness lasted about ten minutes, until a big, really big sea lion bull figured it was time for us to leave. It only took one torpedo like charge with teeth bared from that big guy to convince us that we were no longer welcome.

My wife doesn't like sharks. Maybe the fear seeded itself when she was younger and surfed the California coast. Maybe it was watching *Jaws 3-D*? Who knows? But I can say this with confidence, my wife does NOT like sharks. Whenever we were snorkeling if Sheryl couldn't see the bottom, she would get very uncomfortable thinking about the possibility of a man eater lurking in the depths. This was despite the fact that sharks were a rare sight in the Sea of Cortez.

"Sheryl, honey, listen there are no sharks around this area, none. So don't worry," I informed her as we were getting ready to snorkel from the boat to shore. We would be swimming over some deep water so the bottom would not be visible until we got closer to the beach.

"You go in first I'll be right in," she said procrastinating.

"I will stick by you like glue, you watch my back I'll watch yours," I reassured her as I jumped off the deck into the warm, somewhat opaque water.

Several minutes later Sheryl reluctantly climbed down the boarding ladder as I was doing my customary swim around the boat to check things out. Sheryl was hesitant to leave the security of the ladder and had one last request before setting out on our swim. "Let me know if you see something and stay close."

"You do likewise." With that I started an easy kick towards shore.

True to her word, Sheryl stuck to me like a Remora on a shark. Bad analogy?

Not more than three minutes into our journey I looked to my side and suddenly no Sheryl!

Turning around I could see her doing an excellent imitation of an Olympic swimmer with legs kicking furiously and her arms stroking at a near blur. Before I knew it, she had hoisted herself out of the water and up onto the deck. I couldn't imagine what she needed at the boat, so I slowly kicked in that direction figuring she would be right back in the water.

That's when a slow-moving dark mass glided about ten feet below me. I first thought it was a sea lion...... until it opened its mouth. It was cavernous! I quickly identified what had caused Sheryl's premature departure from the pool: A Whale Shark. Not a whale and not a shark (at least in the bitey sense of the word) it's the world's biggest fish.

These huge sharks are harmless, slow swimming plankton eaters and they use their enormous mouths like a gigantic strainer. They thankfully are making a comeback in The Sea after having their numbers decimated. I was fascinated to watch the guy move through the water. He was maybe 15 feet long, with a blunt nose and eyes spaced wide apart on its head. The creature's dark skin was accented with a white polka dot pattern. The movement of its fins was nearly imperceptible but trying to keep up with him as he swam proved to be a losing effort. He then disappeared into the darkness, the entire episode lasting only about five minutes.

With the show over I climbed up the boarding ladder just as Sheryl was finishing her outdoor shower.

"We may have a trust issue," I stated trying to keep a straight face, "What happened to watching each other's back?"

"I watched your back right up to the moment when I saw that giant mouth open.... then it was every woman for themselves."

"So, when we see real sharks, what happens then?" I wanted to know.

"Well, I'll tell ya, the way I see it, I just have to be able to swim faster than you." With that Sheryl gave me a peck on my cheek then descended the stairs.

Huh?

About 100 miles north of La Paz in the Sea of Cortez, *Casablanca* dropped anchor near the small hamlet of San Telmo. The bay is protected from a north swell by virtue of a rocky spit jutting out into the sea. In calm or moderate conditions it affords an anchored boat excellent protection from waves that are generated by north winds.

A major source of revenue for most of the villagers in The Sea is the catching and selling of sea food. Clams, fish, and lobster are sold to a fish monger who then gets the catch to market in one of the bigger towns. And they supplemented that income by selling to cruisers that would stop in the bays. San Telmo was no exception and before our engine was off a panga boat was alongside of us.

The pangalero looked to be about 35 years old. His skin was a deep mahogany, he had jet black hair, brown eyes coupled with a quick toothy smile. Our command of Spanish was on par with his interpretation of English. It was clear that he was the village's sales representative.

We offered a Coke to Enrique, which he gladly accepted. Most of our conversation took place using a few words and lots of hand gestures. After a few minutes, Enrique unwrapped a blanket that had been laying on the boat's floor revealing a dozen or so tea towels with the most elaborate hand stitching we had ever seen.

Sheryl negotiated with Enrique thus adding to San Telmo's economic wellbeing with the purchase of several items. After his transaction with my wife he turned his attention to me and said a lot of things I didn't understand until he finally spoke one of the few words that I did know: langosta, the Spanish name for lobster. Sheryl had taken her purchases down below which left me alone to hammer out a deal with Enrique.

After the panga had pulled away, I excitedly revealed to Sheryl what the following night's dinner would be by announcing with a bit of a flourish, "I am going to be treating you to a little specialty of mine, *Lobster a la Rick!*"

"We don't have a pot big enough to cook lobster," was her response.

"No problem. Enrique is just going to bring us five tails, no fuss no muss, they will be here tomorrow." I was feeling pretty smug.

"So, you negotiated this deal with your excellent command of Spanish?" she queried. There was definitely sarcasm in that remark.

"I get by."

We awoke that night around 2 am (that's the time when bad things usually happen) after the wind strengthened and started gusting to 20 knots. It had also clocked around to the northeast causing the boat to rock side to side, gently at first. As the swell picked up some dishes crashed to the floor. That was the sound that alerted me to the change in weather. When the sun finally came up, it was plain to see that leaving the anchorage was a nonstarter.

As uncomfortable as we were, and make no mistake we were extremely uncomfortable, the waves outside the entrance were big with white caps. It was worse out there. We were not going anywhere; we were just going to have to tough it out.

By noon the wind speed had increased slightly. *Casablanca* was rolling side to side; we were pointed north into the wind but the swell was hitting us on our beam because it was wrapping around the land.

We were hunkered down and not feeling that great. Jack had wedged himself behind a sail bag in the V-berth, Sheryl was curled up on the settee and I was waiting for lobster tails.

Mostly to myself I stated, "Enrique will probably wait till tomorrow to come out, besides we couldn't cook them today anyway, too damn rough." With a sigh of resignation, I went back to reading a cruising guide.

Fifteen minutes later Sheryl popped up saying, "I hear an engine." Then looking out a port she added, "Rick, your buddy is here."

"I can't believe he came out in this crap!" I exclaimed as I stumbled up the stairs into the cockpit.

The boats were pitching wildly out of sync, but luckily Enrique had a helper with him to lend a hand with the transaction. His buddy held on to both of the boats keeping things as steady as possible. I passed the agreed upon pesos to Enrique and he in turn handed me a burlap bag that felt rather heavy for five tails.

When the smaller boat was safely away, I stole a glance inside the bag. True to his word Enrique had brought out the negotiated five lobster tails. Unfortunately, they were connected to five lobster bodies that sported 10 lobster claws. And they looked pissed.

"Rick how do they look?"

"Mad as hell," I muttered staring into the bag in disbelief.

"What?"

"They are alive."

"Are you trying to tell me there are live lobsters in the cockpit?"

"Guess he didn't understand," I answered sheepishly.

"You know what we have to do, right?" Sheryl said with disappointment.

"Set them free," I reluctantly replied.

"I know you were excited about our special dinner, but we just can't cook tonight in this weather and I hate to waste these poor guys for nothing." She was right.

Leaning over the side of the boat I carefully opened the bag, staying well clear of their pinchers. The boat was still pitching back and forth like a metronome, as I sadly watched our dinner sink beneath the agitated waves.

. . . . .

Sheryl thought our next stop would be Puerto Escondido where we would be able to do some provisioning. That is what we had planned, but I had a hand up my sleeve. Her birthday was just two days away, and after the langosta failure I was determined to come up with something special. I had heard that a new resort had opened on the shores of a protected bay just south of that destination.

As soon as the anchor was down and the anchoring chores complete, we jumped into the dinghy and I rowed the short distance to shore. The resort was a four story, three building complex surrounded by immaculately kept grounds. There were all matter of aqua toys on the wide, white sand beach. Paddle boards, kayaks, wind surfers you name it, they had it.

Sheryl immediately started walking the beach looking for shells.

"Hey, I am going to take a peek at the courtyard," I informed her, "I'll catch up with you in a couple of minutes."

I then hustled off to the resort office hoping that this place could help me with my birthday surprise. And sure enough, we had a bingo!

Sheryl woke the next morning, expecting her usual cup of coffee to be waiting at the table.

"No coffee today?" she said through half-open eyes.

"Nope not today."

"But it's my birthday."

"Yes, it is, so go get your bathing suit and a cover up—we're going to shore."

"What for?" she asked looking at me curiously.

"No questions, I'll meet you in the dinghy."

There was a lone figure standing on the beach as our dinghy scraped the shallow bottom approaching the shore. A handsome young man, wearing a pressed shirt and slacks, which sported the name of the resort stitched on the shirt pocket, helped me drag our small boat out of the water. He then politely offered his hand to Sheryl, helping her step out of the dinghy.

"Feliz cumpleanos senorita," He said with a smile.

That was the moment when Sheryl's jaw dropped open and she looked at me with wide eyes asking, "Rick, what's going on?"

"Just follow the gentleman," I instructed.

Lucio then escorted us to his concierge desk in the main building where he attached a yellow plastic band to each of our wrists. Then he asked my dumbfounded wife to please follow him.

"Go with Lucio, I'll catch up with you at the pool. Have fun!"

The day before, while Sheryl was scouring the beach, I had run up to the resort office and purchased a day pass for the two of us. Since it was an all-inclusive campus, this meant that we would be able to enjoy all the amenities the resort offered including all you could eat and drink for 6 hours the following day. As an added surprise I scheduled an appointment at the spa so that Sheryl could have a deep tissue massage while I brushed up on my 'day drinking' skill set.

When we met up an hour later, I was laying on a lounge chair next to one of the three swimming pools, a pool bar strategically placed within easy reach. My eyes were closed but I could tell a shadow was blocking the sun. Suddenly a big kiss was planted on my lips.

Without opening my eyes, I said, "Get lost my wife will be here soon." To which I got a punch in the stomach.

"Rick, this is so sweet you are the best. I love you," her words were slightly slurred.

"Did you have wine with your massage?"

"Yup," she beamed.

We used the pool, we ate about six meals, drank to excess and had a hellava good relaxing time. Just before our magical six hours were up and before we would turn back into low life cruisers, we were hit with an inspiration. We placed an order for a couple pizzas to go. We are soooo smart.

Chapter 9
Cat-n-About

"I wish common sense was more common."
~Anonymous

We spent a peaceful night anchored off the resort in Candeleros and early the next morning we headed for the marina at Puerto Escondido, just 7 miles north. The water was a brilliant aqua blue and flat with just an occasional ripple stirred up by the pangas that were going fishing or picking up tourists from the local hotels for their day at the beach. Wispy white clouds against a deep blue sky completed the 'Chamber of Commerce' day.

The channel leading into the marina is about a football field in length. It's narrow enough that two medium size boats could not comfortably pass each other going in opposite directions. So, when we spotted a large catamaran headed out, Sheryl slowed *Casablanca* down to allow the cat to exit before we proceeded in.

As the bright yellow 40-footer passed us, Sheryl started to kinda giggle saying, "Rick, did you see that?"

"No, what's up?"

"That guy is buck naked," she said in a hushed voice fearing the sound would travel.

"You don't have to whisper...... he knows he doesn't have clothes on."

"I hope he put sunblock on, or he's not going to be happy tonight," she pointed out.

"Wait.... what?"

"Nothing."

As the boat passed, we saw the guy was engaged in getting a fishing pole into its holder and the line reeled out. The boat was obviously on autopilot and he appeared to be single handed.

Once we were through the channel and took a slight turn to the right, a large completely enclosed bay, roughly a mile in diameter, opened up in front of us. The shape of the bay was more or less round, with several small coves sprouting mangroves near the shore. Steep rock cliffs surround the west and east side. The marina and its buildings were to the south, built on flat land that probably had been under water at one time.

The north end of the bay was quite striking. A small, rounded hill, maybe 300 feet tall, stood in the middle of what the locals refer to as the 'windows'. Story has it that several hundred years ago the bay was open to the Sea of Cortez, with the small hill poking up through the water as an island. Early day missionaries filled the shallow gaps on either side of the protruding hill by hauling boulders from the nearby cliffs. When you look north today, you see a high rock face on the east that transitions to sea level, then a 200 foot perfectly flat breakwater of rock that connects to the small hill. Heading west from the hill there is a nearly identical breakwater about the same length as the east side. Both of these flat areas are only 6 feet out of the water at high tide.

From anywhere in the bay a person can see through the 'windows' and enjoy the view of the surrounding islands. At night you can even see the bright lights of Loreto 20 miles away.

The marina developed a mooring field by placing 50 securely anchored mooring balls for boats to tie to in lieu of anchoring in the deep bay. These buoys were spaced about 100 feet apart, in no apparent pattern. When we entered, about half of the moorings had boats on them. We found an empty ball in the middle of the bay about a quarter of a mile out from the marina docks.

The dinghy was already in the water as we had been towing it since we left La Paz. Sheryl and I just needed to put the outboard motor on so that we could go to shore and check in at the marina office.

As we wove our way through the mooring field, it became apparent that about a third of the boats did not have, and had not had, anyone on them for quite some time. The birds had 'decorated' the decks and sails of the unoccupied boats and that would pose a real chore to clean when the owners finally returned.

When we reached the dinghy dock, there were several small tenders tied up, indicating that there were, indeed, a few other cruisers around.

We easily found the marina office on the second floor of a three-story building. It had windows wrapping 360 degrees, giving a bird's-eye view of the channel, the mooring field and even the town of Loreto in the distance. That's where we met the harbormaster, Javier, a smiling, good looking 30-something gentleman.

Javier talked glowingly about the marina and it's new and refurbished docks. The goal was to build a facility that would attract the million-dollar boats from all over the world. Great for the economy but not so much for the Sea of Cortez. When we finished the seemingly endless paperwork, we headed down stairs to check out the rest of the grounds.

"Let's look in that little tienda we passed on the way to the office," Sheryl suggested.

"Ice cream," was my simple response. I was then on a mission.

We found a few fresh veggies, milk and yes, ice cream! After finishing our transaction in the store, we sat at one of the tables out front which was shaded by an umbrella and enjoyed our frozen treat in the 90-degree heat.

From our slightly elevated vantage point we could see the moored boats bobbing on a dying breeze. We could also see a sailboat through one of the windows and it appeared to be motoring towards Loreto.

But something else caught my eye.

"Rick, whatcha see?" Sheryl asked as she saw me staring at the mooring field.

"That dinghy," I said, pointing to a fast-moving object. "That guy is flying. Usually you're supposed to keep your speed down traveling through an anchorage. In fact, that was one of the rules on that paper we just signed."

We watched as the small boat got closer to the dinghy dock, which was located just in front of where we were sitting.

"He's not going to stop in time...... I think he is going to plow right into the dock!" I said in alarm.

When he was about 20 feet from disaster, he slowed the boat dramatically, and in a near blur he stepped onto the dock with the dinghy painter in his hand even before the thing had come to a complete stop.

The guy looked frazzled. He was rushing up the ramp toward where we were sitting and all he had on was a bright pink beach towel that appeared to have bird poop on it. He then broke into a run as he passed us heading to the parking lot behind the office. The next thing we heard was the squeal of car tires on hot pavement.

"Rick, that looks like the guy that we saw on that yellow catamaran," Sheryl said excitedly.

"That hardly seems likely, we didn't see the boat come back in," I said while scanning the mooring field searching for the brightly colored catamaran. Knowing that she is seldom wrong when it comes to remembering faces, I added, "It does seem like something is up."

Indeed, something *was* up.

The next day, after I'd gone up to the office to drop off yet another required piece of paper, the *Casablanca* crew sat down at one of the shaded tables outside the tienda. Once again, we decadently indulged in some ice cream.

"Look, over there. Isn't that the yellow boat from yesterday?" Sheryl asked.

I looked up to see where she was pointing and sure enough, there it was, tied up to the dock.

"I wonder what all that fuss was about yesterday?" Sheryl pondered.

"I know what happened," I announced working feverishly to keep the melting ice cream bar under control.

"No, you don't, how could you?" Sheryl challenged me.

"Ok fine I don't...."

After a pause she added, "Okay smart guy, tell me."

I went on to explain to her that the guy we saw leaving on the catamaran was named Jackson. It seems Jackson liked to fish when he went sailing. It also seems Jackson liked to fish naked when he went out sailing.

Shortly after Jackson passed *Casablanca* in the channel as we were headed in, he had set a course that would take the boat to a small marina, near Loreto.

Jackson got lucky that day in more ways than one. First, he tied into what was described as, and I quote, "One hell of a beautiful fish" end quote. During the cleaning of that beautiful fish and still without clothes on, our hero slipped on some fish blood and went directly overboard.

In the excitement of catching the beautiful fish, Jackson had failed to disengage the autopilot. He had also neglected to put the boat engine in neutral. Consequently, the catamaran continued along, happily motoring north with no one on board, except for the beautiful fish. Karma.

Initially Jackson tried to swim for the wayward boat but gave up the chase after a few minutes realizing it was fruitless. After all, the vessel was moving at a jogging speed, so there would be no catching up to it by swimming.

Jackson then turned and power stroked several hundred yards to the east side 'window'. He then ran, barefoot and naked mind you, across the sharp and splintered boulders that made up that breakwater.

Jackson then threw himself into the water of the mooring field and swam 50 yards to the first boat that he knew was occupied. Luckily it was a person with whom he had shared a few beers in the past. Out of breath and without preamble Jackson had demanded the keys to Rich's car as well as the immediate use of his dinghy to get to shore.

"Wait a minute.... you're making this up," Sheryl said, looking like she was about to punch me.

"No, no. Listen, it gets better," I assured her.

I continued the story telling her how Rich couldn't help Jackson because he was in the middle of something he couldn't leave, so he tossed Jackson the car keys and untied the painter and Jackson gunned the outboard and headed for the marina.

Rich then yelled to him to get some clothes on before using his car and saw Jackson swing by a boat that had several beach towels hanging on the railing to dry. Barely slowing the small boat, he grabbed a towel sending clothes pins flying as he traveled on.

"And that's when we saw him come blasting into the dinghy dock," I reminded Sheryl.

"So how did he get his boat back?" she asked, still puzzled.

"That is where he got really, really lucky."

I went on, explaining that when Jackson set the course coordinates into the autopilot, he picked a point just outside the Loreto marina. A mile south of the marina there is a long sand bar that juts out from shore and extends far enough out into The Sea that a helmsman would have to jog around it. No big deal if someone is on board steering.

"So, you're saying the catamaran hit the sand bar?" Sheryl had figured it out.

"That's exactly what happened," I said.

I went on to tell her that while Jackson was racing toward Loreto in the car, he could see his boat about a mile out in the water happily motoring along at 6 knots, with no one on board but a beautiful dead fish.

He could also see what you had just figured out. That with any luck the boat would beach itself on the sand bar, hopefully causing little or no damage. Which is exactly what happened.

By the time he parked Rich's car and walked through the overgrowth and bramble, he got to the boat just as a few locals were trying to figure out where this mysterious craft came from and how they were going to divide it up.

Jackson eventually convinced the salvage crew it was his boat and that it hadn't been abandoned. He then climbed on board, shut down the engine, got dressed and even convinced the guys to help him get it off the sandbar. He was able to anchor nearby to inspect for damage and such.

Now Sheryl was staring at me not knowing if this crazy story was just some made up prank of mine or what.

"Nah, good try Rick, but no way that happened, no way," she protested.

"No, he told it spot on," a male voice chimed in from the next table over. As we turned in unison toward the voice, we both knew who would be sitting there.

"Hi, my name's Jackson. Or as you refer to me, and I quote, 'our hero' end quote. And you are?"

"Embarrassed," I said under my breath.

After Jackson left, Sheryl quizzed me on how I happened to know the complete story. Glancing up toward Javier's office I replied, "I have friends in high places."

Chapter 10
Misfits

"We are all born crazy, some of us remain that way."
~ Samuel Beckett

A few days after our encounter with the infamous Jackson, Sheryl and I were sitting in the cabin of *Casablanca*. It was 7:30 but the sun's rays hadn't yet spilled over the nearby mountains, so Jack was outside enjoying the cool pre-sunrise temperature.

Sheryl broke the comfortable silence reminding me, "We need to decide pretty soon where we want to head next."

This discussion was taking place because we were already several weeks into the Eastern Pacific hurricane season and *Casablanca* and crew needed a safe place to hang out for about 12 more weeks. We realized that since we had taken our time coming down the coast, it would be necessary to spend the stormy season in Mexico and we had chosen the Baja because there seemed to be more natural protection in The Sea. Baja offered several choices for refuge, so we needed to work on that decision.

"San Carlos is probably the safest, but it will be hottest," I had read this in a cruising guide. Continuing on I told her, "If we choose La Paz, I'd want to be at the dock because sailing and anchoring around there can be an unwanted challenge that time of year and it seems that would make for a long hot summer."

"Or we could stay here on a buoy and if a forecast was bad, we could head to the dock," Sheryl suggested. It seemed like an excellent compromise to me.

"It's almost time for the net," I announced as I was shutting off the alarm that reminds us that the local cruisers radio show was about to begin.

Often if there are more than two boats in an anchorage a network is set up to pass information on to fellow cruisers. These 'nets' take place on the lower power VHF radios and depending on the terrain can be heard 10 to 20 miles away.

All the nets that I have listened to are pretty much the same: First there is a call out for priority or emergency traffic, then in the smaller congregations there is the check-in with boat names. After check-ins, the person running the net will go to different scripted categories such as news of friends, arrivals and departures, restaurant report, peso report and so on and so on.

Sheryl and I try to listen to the nets whenever possible and that morning was no exception. Sheryl had settled in with her tea and I was halfheartedly listening while still perusing the cruising guides. Because we were into the start of summer and most of the part-time boaters had already headed home, the net was moving along fairly quickly with few voices to be heard or questions to be asked.

"...... and the peso closed yesterday at 19.34," the net controller droned on sounding bored. "Up next food and fishing report, news of friends or any past categories," he said, clearly pushing for an early end to that day's rather quiet net.

"Contact." Somebody was actually going to add something to the program.

"Go contact," the net controller responded, sounding like he'd been caught off guard.

"Thank you, my name is Ruby and for you that don't know me I live on the boat *Stone*." My ears perked up as I tried to discern if that was a southern accent or leaning more toward Appalachian?

Ruby continued on, "My younger daughter came home yesterday and asked me what an affair was."

By then she really had my attention and apparently Sheryl's too as I heard her do a little giggle snort thing involving her nose and her tea. I was then staring at the radio full focus.

"She said she heard that her momma was having an affair," Ruby declared.

You could almost hear a collective holding of breath coming from the entire anchorage.

"Most people here have been pretty nice, but some ain't so much," she drawled on.

"Sheryl are you hearing this?" I asked in disbelief.

"Shhhhhhhh," she silenced me.

Ruby continued her story, "It shouldn't need saying, but I am not having an affair and I know who started that nasty rumor."

There, she said it. A long, static filled pause followed her statement.

Right about then my heart went out to the net controller. Just how do you follow up something like that?

But follow it he did, saying, "Well I am sure your day will get better. With that we are closing the net for this Thursday. Have a nice day everyone. Click."

And then he was gone, replaced by a static hiss.

"What was that all about?" I pondered, trying to replay it back in my head.

"I know," was Sheryl's quick reply.

"No, you don't," I countered.

"Ok, fine, I don't."

It didn't take long to break me down, so I asked, "Ok there Nancy Drew, let's have it."

First and foremost, one must remember that all cruisers are extremely proficient in the art of gossip. The so-called 'coconut telegraph' was alive and well in Puerto Escondido.

She explained to me that the laundry room of the marina was gossip central, and the new acquaintances she had met there let it be known that there was, indeed, extracurricular activity going on involving Ruby.

To make it worse, this liaison was going on while Ruby's husband was up in the States earning money for the cruising kitty!

"Well that seals it," I said.

"What are you talking about, seals what?" Sheryl distractedly questioned me.

"Our staying here is a done deal now. How can we leave and not know how Ruby's misadventure turns out?"

"No, we don't need to get involved with any crazy drama like that," Sheryl cautioned.

"We won't, I promise," I assured her.

"You lie," was my wife's final word on that subject.

However, Ruby wasn't the only colorful character we encountered in Puerto Escondido. There was also Ken.......

After living on a mooring ball for several weeks we decided to treat ourselves to a few days at the dock. It's very convenient to be able to just step off the boat for a shower or peruse the market. The unlimited water for washing all the salt off of sails, decks, dodger and windows ranks number one on my list. But, like all things in life, staying at the dock has its drawbacks.

One morning while tied to the dock Sheryl was the first one out of bed and she kinda grog-shuffled into the galley. But instead of hearing the water running for coffee, I heard a muted yelp, followed by a loud thunk. Like a sack of potatoes hitting the floor.

"You okay out there?" I yelled from the berth.

Instead of answering me right away, Sheryl walked back and stood at the edge of the bed and in a low voice said, "I slipped off the stairs. I always look out the windows first thing after getting up," she explained.

"Did you lose your balance?" I queried.

"NO, there is a guy sitting on our dock box.... with a cup of something in one hand wearing a white terry-cloth robe! And smoking a cigarette. When I climbed the stairs to do my usual morning look around there he was. Right there near the window. In just a robe! It startled me and I slipped and fell." By this time Sheryl was not approving of my semi contained laughter.

"Is he wearing UGG'S?" I asked after getting slugged in the arm.

Walking back to the main salon she mumbled, "Who would be wearing fur booties in 88-degree weather?" Looking out the window again she said, "Huh," and then, "Good guess... seriously? Who's your new friend?"

"That would be Ken. He lives on a boat near the end of this dock," I informed her.

"You know him.... how?"

"Shhhhhhhh.... keep your voice down.... he is kinda different," I cautioned.

Ken really was different. Six feet tall, skinny as a rail except for a basketball size belly that protruded outward. He might have been 50 years old or 75 depending on the angle of the sun at the time. I went on to explain to Sheryl what I knew about Ken.

"Ken is a bit of an odd ball."

Sheryl was quick to respond, "Have you looked around lately? That seems to be the norm in this marina."

"Regardless," I said. Then going on with my story, "It seems that several months ago while living in La Paz, Ken rode his bike from the marina into town. He had just left the central market and as he peddled by one of the more popular taco stands, he noticed more than the usual amount of people gathered around it. He said suddenly all eyes were on him as he wheeled by. A couple of streets later he came to an intersection in the road that was blocked by two police cars. He was told to stop and immediately placed under arrest. He was searched and the contents of his backpack were unceremoniously dumped onto the pavement. They gave Ken a free ride downtown, to the local police station. Ken could not get an answer as to why he was headed for lock-up, but after three hours of interrogation and a threat of a body cavity search, it was determined that Ken *did not* rob the taco vender. However, the real taco bandit did use a bicycle that matched the description of Ken's. After further lengthy discussions Ken found out that really the only thing that his bike and the getaway bike had in common were that they both had two wheels. To add insult to injury, his bike was stolen while he was in custody. Worried that he would now be 'one of the usual suspects' in La Paz, Ken caught a taxi back to the marina, promptly untied his dock lines and fled the city," I paused then whispered to Sheryl, "He's quite paranoid now."

"So, where did you hear *this* story?" Sheryl asked a bit skeptically.

"Hey," I replied, "I do laundry too." Referring to the local meeting place for gossip.

Seemingly unimpressed Sheryl walked back to the aft cabin where I heard her mumbling, "Doesn't anyone wear clothes around here?"

Chapter 11
It's Summertime and the Livin' is Breezy

"A great wind is blowing, and that gives you either imagination or a headache."
~ Catherine the First

The days had grown hot ranging somewhere between the high 80s at night and what seemed like 200 degrees during the day. But as they say, "It's the humidity not the heat that is the worst part."

With the heat and moisture came the thunderstorms, locally called *Chubascos*. These gems of nature would usually develop on the Mexican mainland, which was roughly 80 miles east. As the land heats up, moisture rises forming heavy unstable clouds, resulting in the creation of thunder and lightning cells. Night fall sees these agitated cells start to cross the Sea of Cortez where they pick up more moisture thus becoming even more unstable. They travel just fast enough to reach the Baja Peninsula and hit the poor souls at anchor somewhere between one and four-dark-thirty.

Distant lightning flashes appear first, hours before the actual fun starts. The wind direction will start to change, sometimes this happens slowly other times it's a snap of the fingers. The wild card in this whole deal is the strength of the wind which can be just a gentle breeze, or it can roar over 50 knots. As the thunder cell passes over, the change in wind direction can make a once safe anchorage a very dangerous lee shore. Brief, but heavy, rain showers are often thrown into the mix as well.

Predicting the path of these Chubascos is far from an exact science as they travel along the coast making for a middle of the night nerve wracking guessing game. These thunderstorms usually start at the beginning of July and fade out sometime in September, give or take. Luckily, a cruiser whose name is Jake, from the sailboat *Jake* (along with his lovely wife Sharon and their sailcat Izzy) takes to the radio air waves every night during Chubasco season and gives his best guess as to what will happen later in the evening.

The heat, the humidity and the Chubascos are just the opening act of nasty weather during the summer months. There are also tropical storms and tropical depressions, but a hurricane is the main event.

Those monsters generally form off of the southern reaches of mainland Mexico, usually several hundred miles offshore. The hurricane season in the Eastern Pacific officially starts on May 15 and concludes, hopefully, at the end of November. Storms that form early in the season will usually follow a path that takes them west towards the Central Pacific, occasionally nearing Hawaii. The storms that form later in the season tend to track closer to the Mexican coast, eventually curving west, out to the open ocean. However, when September and October roll around all eyes and ears on Baja are tuned to every source of weather information that one can get their hands on.

"We have been awfully lucky so far, and I predict that we will continue to have that same luck this last month of storm season," I proclaim from my position lying on a settee, down in the darkened bowels of *Casablanca*. All the port lights have shades on them, fighting to keep the sunlight, thus the heat, out. I have two small fans aimed at my head and I am still rapidly losing body fluids.

"Thanks Rick. I do believe you just jinxed the whole of Baja," Sheryl reprimanded me from the aft cabin where she was duplicating my efforts to stay cool and comfortable.

My optimism was well placed, as we had had a couple of close calls with storms to that point but had managed to dodge several bullets. By that time the population of the marina at Puerto Escondido had dwindled considerably. There were a few hardy souls left, but it was generally very quiet. Ruby had moved on, still denying any adulteress activity and Ken had driven over to the cool Pacific side of Baja, while Jackson continued to fish and work on his all-over tan.

For the few of us who had remained in Puerto Escondido things started to get interesting a week later, probably due to my thoughtless prediction.

One day during the local morning radio net, the controller informed those listening, that a low had formed overnight 200 miles offshore near the central coast. The National Ocean and Atmospheric Administration, better known as NOAA, is the prime source for all thing's hurricane related. Wind speed, expected rainfall, how fast the storm is moving, what direction it's moving as well as its predicted course are all part of their report. As they had explained it to me back in Newport's NOAA station, computers gather satellite information as well as on-site observations from ships and planes. Correlating the information, the human forecasters then tweak what needs to be tweaked then they head for the dart board for the ultimate result.

The standard procedure for NOAA is to issue a daily chart showing several tracks the storm could take. When a storm is in its infancy, the tracks can vary considerably. As the hurricane matures and somewhat stabilizes the predictions start to come together as to where the beast is going to end up.

"I really don't like the early course predictions I'm seeing on this one," said George, one of the full-time occupants of the marina.

"Do ya see the wind speed is already pushing a hundred?" added George's lovely wife Barbara.

"It's all Rick's fault," offered Sheryl, who thought I had messed with the weather gods.

The four of us were sitting outside the small marina store just before sunset, eating ice cream, of course. George, or as the locals address him,

'Jorge' was looking at a computer screen that had the latest storm update displayed.

"I don't know how they can predict this thing.... it's still a week away," he said in his gravelly voice.

I spoke up, "That's the part that I can't stand ... the waiting. It makes my nerves absolutely raw."

"Oh, he is awful to live with that's for sure," Sheryl threw out.

"You mean when waiting for a hurricane?" I prompted my wife.

"That too," she said trying not to smile.

For three days following that weather prediction the marina had personnel out checking dock lines, securing dock boxes, tying down palm trees and generally rechecking everything that had been checked at the start of hurricane season. If the predictions came to pass, hurricane Serge will come up the Sea of Cortez packing in excess of 100 mph winds accompanied by heavy rains. Can I take back my thoughtless prediction now? Most of the unattended boats at the dock, as well as on the mooring buoys, already had their sails and dodgers taken down and they'd lashed their deflated dinghies to the decks. Reducing wind resistance is the key to surviving a big storm.

Having been in a hurricane before, no way was I going to be trapped out on the boat on a mooring ball with the real possibility of not being able to get to shore if things went south. Plus, unlike my single-handed days, I was responsible for my wife and our cat, so with just a couple days before Serge's predicted landfall we took *Casablanca* into the dock. The marina had filled up, thanks to the impending storm, but luckily after talking with the harbor master we were able to secure the last available slip.

After tying the mooring lines to the dock cleats and positioning the fenders, we were ready to go inside and settle in. I had noticed some unusual music wafting through the air and asked Sheryl, "Do you hear that? It sounds like one of those funeral marches they play in New Orleans."

"I think it's coming from that boat down there," Sheryl said pointing to the end of the dock. The music stopped and when it started up again, it sounded like a merry-go-round.

"Is that an accordion?" I questioned, but before my wife could answer the musician switched to playing *House of The Rising Sun*.

"I love that song and he's pretty good," Sheryl said gazing down the dock trying to identify exactly which boat the serenade was coming from.

"Let's go have a look," I offered as I took her hand and we walked toward the music. Without warning the slow mournful song that had been playing was replaced with something more upbeat.

"You recognize this song?" I asked knowing she had the answer.

"Sure do, it's *I Love This Bar*" she answered as we stopped in front of the 37-foot sailboat that was pumping out the wonderful tunes. We stood for a couple of minutes listening to his renditions.

"I sure didn't know an accordion could sound that good," I whispered to Sheryl.

Then a voice behind us said, "Amazing isn't it?" We both jumped at that, slightly startled as we hadn't seen anyone else on the dock, so it surprised us to find Barbara standing right behind us.

"Hey Barbara...... is this your boat?" I greeted her, and when she nodded, I added, "So that's George playing?"

Barbara, who George affectionately called Goldie, always had a smile on her face. She was tall with long graying hair falling to the middle of her back. Her thin frame and innocent looks hid the fact that she could probably mop up the boat with George, who she affectionately called Jorge.

"Yes, this is *DreamCatcher*," she answered with pride. Then, when there was a break in the music, she walked over to an open port hole and yelled, "Come on out here.... you have a fan club."

We could hear a little banging around then a head popped up out of the hatch.

"Heyyy Guysss," he said stretching out the hey and guys. Jorge, a stocky Vietnam vet made his way on to the dock. His curly, thinning hair was going in all directions and a big smile came to his deeply lined face when we told him we had been eavesdropping on his music.

I smiled as well when I read his t-shirt which stated: *I Hate Being Bi-Polar, it's Awesome.*

"So, we just moved in at the end of the dock which makes us neighbors," I informed him and then continued, "I guess this is where the hurricane party will be."

Barbara and Sheryl immediately started making dinner plans while George and I discussed what each of us had to do before Hurricane Serge entered our lives.

The predictions indicated that Serge would hit the Cabo area, about 250 miles south of us, in roughly 24 hours. That meant we had about 36 hours before we would start to feel the effects of the storm. After hitting Cabo, possibly packing winds of 100 mph, Serge would then start a slow slog up the Sea of Cortez, hopefully losing some of its energy as it bumped into the land along the way. Scattered clouds were already on the horizon and the Chubascos were stirred up more than usual due to Serge's presence.

Later that day, while sitting up at the newly opened roof top bar, which had quickly become our favorite meeting place, Jorge and I continued to discuss the upcoming storm.

"So according to Javier in the office there are only five occupied boats out on buoys," Jorge informed me, "but I guess a couple of those will end up being unoccupied during the storm as they plan to get a hotel until things settle down."

"Another boat came in early this morning, 35 feet or so," I reported, "and it looks like they snagged one of the closer in buoys." Then, thinking out loud I mumbled, "Should be raining pretty hard by tomorrow night."

After finishing our Margaritas, we headed back to the boats, assuring each other that Serge wouldn't be as bad as predicted. But, as always, prepare for the worst while praying for the best.

When we began to see the outer bands of unstable and moist air along with lightning in the distance, my anxiety level shot to a solid 11 out of 10. The wind had started to pick up in fits and starts, one minute a comfy 12 mph then suddenly 25 then back to 10 then up a little higher and so on through the night. To coin a phrase: *It was a dark and stormy night.*

On the plus side, at the moment, Serge looked like it would hit our area around noon. Having any storm, especially a major storm, hit during daylight hours is a huge advantage and helps to make the odds more favorable for getting out of the chaos in one piece.

Sheryl had no trouble sleeping that night, I on the other hand got up several times to look around and do a little pacing. Having lost one boat to hurricane-force winds and dodging another hurricane in my early travels, it didn't get any easier with experience, at least not for me.

And for this one we were securely tied to a dock, but I was still worrying. My heart went out to anyone at anchor or on one of the mooring balls, as it promised to be a very long day.

6am: Daybreak found the wind blowing around 35 mph, gusting to 45. The harbor had become a frothy caldron of spray, the wind making a haunting howl through the rigging of the many sailboats. Each boat seemed to be emitting a different pitch and slightly different volume, so the result was something like a cross between a wounded animal and voices in a crowded bar. It was already hard to hear Sheryl as she spoke to me from the cockpit while I was on the dock, a mere five feet away.

"Rick, you won't believe this but somebody in one of the anchorages just got on the radio and asked what was up with the weather. The office informed him there was a major storm headed this way," she shouted to be heard.

That information didn't surprise me as I had seen firsthand the same lack of awareness during Hurricane Inki in Hawaii, some years back. How could you not know?

The rain was coming in waves with big fat drops that stung the face. The marina had lost power, but the marina staff was still patrolling the docks trying to a get ahead of any potential problems. Luckily, loose halyards and overturned dumpsters were the only incidents so far. Jorge had joined me on the dock, outfitted in a bright yellow foul weather jacket.

"We just had 50 mph gust according to our wind instrument," he shouted in my ear as we struggled to walk upright. The dock itself was swaying and banging against the pilings that supported it.

Pointing to the entrance channel while attempting to be heard over a gust, I yelled, "Look, there's a boat trying to come in!"

Through the driving rain we could just make out the white hull of a sailboat that was surrounded by crashing waves, causing the boat to gyrate wildly as it struggled to reach the relative safety of the bay. We trudged to the end of the dock to watch the newcomer. In the maelstrom the buoy that the boat was headed to was barely visible. With the rain easing, just a bit, we could then see the outline of a person with a boat hook standing on the bow fully clad in bright yellow rain gear. At that exact moment a gust of wind hit the boat broadside driving the rail well under water. Then all hell broke loose.

"Oh shit!" I screamed, "That guy's in the water!"

As the gust of wind hit, the person on the bow had just snagged the mooring ball with the boat hook but when the boat righted itself that person was nowhere to be seen. We searched frantically with our eyes finally spotting a person bobbing in the water near the mooring ball. Luckily, the sailor had on a brightly colored float coat that was keeping him buoyant and easy to spot.

George yelled, "I'll call the office on the radio!"

With the wind pushing him, he struggled for control as he fought the elements to get back to his boat. George did manage to stop and fill Sheryl in on what was happening, as she attempted to make her way to where I was standing.

"He's right there!" I pointed, "Keep your eye on him."

"Got it!" Sheryl replied, a bit out of breath.

The four to five-foot waves in the harbor were pushing the person in the water towards the docks, but he was still too far out for us to lend any sort of help.

The helmsman quickly regained control of the boat and with a puff of black smoke from the exhaust, throttled up and started to circle the floating crew mate.

It was then confirmed that the man-overboard was in fact a man, as a woman's voice could just be heard shrieking over the din, "RON GET YOUR ASS BACK ON BOARD THIS BOAT!"

Without looking at each other Sheryl and I said in unison, "Did you hear that?"

As the woman tightened the circle around the one named Ron, a gust of wind slammed the boat on its beam once again, but this time when the boat came upright there was Ron, holding on to the railing! He was dangling there with his head just above deck height and his feet were still dragging in the water.

"DAMMIT RON GET IN THIS BOAT," the woman once again demanded.

I turned to Sheryl and yelled, "That must be his wife giving the encouragement." With that I got an elbow to the ribs.

Due to Ron's mass on the side of the boat there was a tendency for the wind gusts to slam that side lower into the water. So, in a matter of just a couple of minutes, Ron was dunked in over his head at least three more times.

But the fourth time's a charm, as they say. Ron had apparently tired of the water boarding and with his wife's continued encouragement he found the strength to propel himself over the railing the next time there was a dunk cycle. Ron was last seen crawling back to the helm, just as another deluge hit.

As for our fortunes, we had been pretty lucky to that point despite a gust of seventy miles per hour. The air was filled with palm fronds, branches, dust and a piece of plywood that flew like a Frisbee and imbedded itself in an office window.

Finally, there came a sense that things may have reached their peak and the storm maybe, just maybe, was even starting to calm down.

As predicted, once Serge had started to bump his way up the coast heading north, the land mass sapped a lot of its energy. By the time the storm had reached Puerto Escondido it had greatly diminished in strength from what it had been when it had ravaged Cabo San Lucas. However, the rain held on and there were reports of flooding all along the Baja Peninsula.

The following day George, Barbara, Sheryl and I sat at our favorite table in the roof top bar/restaurant surveying the harbor. One boat was aground near the 'windows' and there was a multitude of flotsam and jetsam collected along the break water.

But the big talk was the unbelievable rescue of the fellow who had fallen off his boat, only to have the boat scoop him back up minutes later. As we talked, a tall skinny guy came up the stairs followed by a petite female, both looking like they needed more sleep than they were getting. As they walked by our table George asked if they were on a boat.

"Yeah, we are on *Mystic*. We came in yesterday, during the storm," the guy replied.

Sheryl jumped right on that, saying with an air of awe, "You were the one in the water!"

With a hint of embarrassment, he replied, "That would be me."

With that we all stood up and clapped giving the couple a standing ovation. Well, to be fair, the two waiters were already standing.

"That was some show of seamanship getting that close to Ron so he could grab on when the boat sprang back up," I said.

The woman's face turned slightly red as she replied, "Just stupid luck. I was actually trying to run him down."

I didn't really know if she was kidding.

Ron went on to introduce his wife Joan Marie and explained that they had been racing the storm up the Baja when their engine quit on them about twenty miles out. He'd worked on the problem for a good while before he got it going and by that time Escondido was the only reasonable choice for safety, so they were committed.

Ron continued his story saying, "We ended up motoring around the harbor for about four hours just praying that the engine would keep going, I wasn't about to grab another ball until things settled down."

"Let us buy you and Joan Marie a drink, you need to join us for the 'after-hurricane' party," Barbara said to Ron with her welcoming smile.

"As soon as we check in with the Harbormaster, we will definitely take you up on that." Then they turned and staggered like zombies to Javier's office.

Chapter 12
Calamity!

"Trust me, you can dance."
~ signed Tequila

There is an old adage on Baja that goes something like this: 'When the yellow butterflies hatch hurricane season is over'. Well, they had a hatch and suddenly there were hundreds of yellow butterflies flying all around the marina.

Unfortunately, their appearance was in direct conflict with the National Hurricane Center which proclaimed the end was still two weeks away. Who do you trust on this one. Two hundred years of observation or the computer. The quandary for us was that late season hurricanes usually form close to the route we needed to travel, which was south along the Mexican mainland coast.

On the other hand, we had just spent more time in this marina (and bar) than anywhere outside of Gig Harbor. Both Sheryl and I agreed that we would roll the weather dice and go for it. We realized that if we didn't get going, we could end up like many cruisers with big travel plans. They would get to Mexico and never go beyond because it is such a comfortable life without the work of offshore passages. Luckily, I knew from my past travels that the rewards of a South Pacific adventure far outweigh the challenges of getting there.

The overall plan was to leave Puerto Escondido and make as few stops as possible while heading for Huatulco, which is near the Mexican/Guatemala border. Huatulco would be our jumping off point where we would then head offshore and sail to the Galapagos Archipelago.

There were many goodbyes and a few tears on leave eve.

Ken, still in his bath robe and UGGs, had returned from his summer hiatus on the coast. Jackson was still sailing his yellow catamaran, sans clothes, and catching big, beautiful fish. And Ruby? who knows?

George and Barbara had arranged for a farewell gathering up at the roof top bar, scheduled for the night before our departure. All the regulars and irregulars showed up, the drinks flowed freely along with all the tall tales. George had composed a very touching song entitled *Off the Beaten Path*, about the trials and tribulations of cruising, that had everyone verklempt when he played it for us on his accordion.

Ron and Joan Marie stopped by our table and wished us a safe voyage. Their hurricane story had been one of the most replayed tales of the night and they had taken it with good grace.

The harbormaster, Javier, and his family joined Sheryl and me at our table and he assured us that there would always be an open mooring for *Casablanca* when we returned.

The following morning, we motored out of the marina under clear skies and calm seas. We had tentatively planned our first stop to be in Zihuatanejo, some 650 miles distant.

On our previous trip down the coast we had stopped at several anchorages on the way south, getting as far as Troncones, which is where Sheryl and I had to go in different directions. She had taken a flight out of nearby Zihuatanejo as she needed to help with a family emergency in San Francisco. Meanwhile Jack and I continued on to the South Pacific. Unable to meet us in Tahiti as we'd hoped, Sheryl finally caught up to us in Hawaii a number of months later.

One of the reasons we'd decided not to stop at some really nice anchorages on our way down the coast, is that the first days of a passage are always the hardest. It takes some time on the open water to get 'sea-legs'. Our appetite, our balance and the constant motion of the boat all add up to a malaise for both Jack and me. Sheryl, on the other hand, adapts quite quickly. So rather than having to go through that 2 or 3-day process after every stop, it seemed more prudent to just keep going.

The other reason we chose to push on is that this would be the longest passage we'd had, without stopping, since leaving Washington. As the saying goes, 'If it's going to happen it's going to happen out there.' It would be a good shakedown cruise so that if something broke or quit working or any number of things, I would rather have it happen within easy distance to a safe harbor.

We were able to latch on to a mild Norther which pushed *Casablanca* out of the Sea of Cortez and towards the Pacific Ocean. It was great sailing with a reefed main and a 90% Genoa, six knots of speed and we were feeling pretty good.

It took us about 36 hours to reach the interface where The Sea meets the dark blue water and the long, deep swell of the Pacific. The short, steep waves of the Sea of Cortez did not give up without a fight which resulted in a mashed up and confused sea state causing *Casablanca* to roll, pitch and bounce wildly. Jack disappeared, retreating to who knows where, while I laid listlessly in the cockpit. Sheryl, happily humming away, was maintaining the watch.

It took nearly 6 hours for the deep Pacific swell to finally overcome the annoying short, steep waves from the north. This long regular swell was a sure sign we were indeed heading south in the Pacific Ocean.

By the fourth day, as predicted, all three of us were feeling fine. Our appetites came back, the winds remained steady, and it was some of our best sailing of all time.

Sheryl and I had decided that the watch shift would be three hours on with three hours off. During the daylight hours it wasn't as important to stick to that schedule, so if one of us needed a longer break it was usually not a problem to stretch the rest periods to four hours or even a bit more. But, at night, after three hours, a person's concentration begins to wane.

This is where we enlist help of *Otto,* the wind vane. Otto, short for Ottomatic, is the silent crew member who, whenever possible, does all the steering of *Casablanca.*

Otto's framework was made from stainless steel tubing which was attached to the stern of *Casablanca.* It consisted of a rudder in the water and another thin plywood rudder, or vane, that stuck up in the air a couple of feet off the deck. The vane on top worked on the same principle as having your arm out the window of a moving car and feeling the slip stream when you change the angle of your hand. The upper vane and the lower rudder were connected by gears and with the help of some ropes and pulleys it was attached to the steering wheel. For Otto to perform at his best, I would adjust the sails in such a manner that when I took my hands off the steering wheel, *Casablanca* would maintain course by itself for a short period of time. When this balance was achieved, we could then engage the wind vane and with just minor adjustments Otto would keep us on course, sometimes for days as long as the wind continued to come from the same direction.

A problem can occur if there is a wind shift, the vane will then dutifully follow that change, thus sending the boat in an errant direction. This happens because the upper vane is trying to stay within the slipstream. All in all, *Otto* could steer better than any other crewmate and he doesn't get tired, doesn't eat, and won't plug up the head.

We were still a couple of days out of Z-Town when a south wind came up right on our nose. Not crazy hard but enough to make for some snotty seas. We were lucky to have ample sea room so we could tack out a couple of miles and do the same on the shoreward tack. We did this because it was much more comfortable to take the wind waves at an angle as opposed to bashing straight on.

Sheryl had been below looking at an entrance chart for Zihuatanejo while I was up in the cockpit hiding behind the dodger so as not to get too wet from the spray, I called down to her, "Sheryl, could you give me a hand?"

She quickly responded by bounding up the stairs asking, "What's up?"

"Well, the AIS shows a ship coming at us from behind," I reported and we both instinctively looked behind us, but in the fading light we saw nothing.

"I see a second ship ahead, traveling toward us on the coast side, but he's not showing up on AIS." I pointed, then handed the binoculars to Sheryl so she could take a look.

"We are kinda in the middle, looks like we'll pass both ships about the same time. Sort of a ship sandwich," I said with a slight grin.

"Very funny. None the less, I am not comfortable making these long tacks until they pass us by," Sheryl offered.

That meant we were going to end up doing some much-loved bashing head on into the waves. Yuck.

Sheryl was able to contact both ships by VHF and alert them to our whereabouts. They each agreed to maintain a course that would put roughly a mile between the ships and us at closest approach.

Sheryl always acted as the communication officer onboard *Casablanca*. She would handle the radio calls to and from boats, ships or shore stations, always speaking calmly and clearly. The biggest plus having her handle the radio was that she was a female voice on the airwaves. During my single handing days my record for radio response from big freighters was a dismal 40%, but since my wife had taken over the job, she elicited a whopping 90% response. I was sure it was due to hearing a female voice, which would pique their curiosity.

"If you're good up here now I need to go down and roll up that chart and stow it away," she said climbing down the stairway.

As soon as Sheryl stepped into the main salon, I heard a familiar phrase, "Jack! Why did you do that?"

Looking down below I spotted the rolled-out chart with a good portion of the bottom chewed off and the pieces spread across the table and floor.

Jack, of course, was nowhere to be found. It seems that he will only act destructive when we are not watching. Must be a deniability thing.

"He ate the part of the chart that shows the entrance buoy location," Sheryl bemoaned.

"Don't worry, we should be fine since we're going in during the daylight anyway, we'll see it." I wasn't going to get between her and her cat.

The next day our trusty GPS informed us that at our present rate of travel we would be outside the entrance of Zihuatanejo well before sunrise the following day. The wind had backed around during the night and we were having a very pleasant, and fast, downwind sail. We never want to enter an unfamiliar anchorage in the dark since bad things are prone to happen if you do. So, we reduced sail to slow down and set our sights on a morning arrival in Z-Town.

We arrived outside the bay about an hour after sunrise. The entrance was wide, and the small boat traffic was already heading out to fish.

As we motored in, we could see the town appeared to be divided into two distinct sections. On shore, to our left, stood a long pier with a few large work boats tied alongside, as well as one big tuna seiner. A majority of the small buildings looked to be older, but well kept, with more than a few colorfully painted. We guessed that was the center of town. Gazing to our right, we saw a series of hotels or condos built on the hillside that bordered the white sand beach. Steep, winding stairways lead from the hotels down the hill to rows of lounge chairs and large umbrellas at the water's edge.

We headed to the anchorage where there were perhaps a dozen cruising sailboats. The area was off of La Ropa, the name our cruising guide had given to this stretch of beach below the hotels. I was on the bow preparing the anchor and keeping a casual lookout, while Sheryl had the wheel and she slowly motored toward the spot we had chosen to drop the hook.

Turning to face Sheryl so she could better hear me I yelled, "There's a log up ahead, go to port a little and we should miss it." She nudged the helm, and we fell off enough to miss the obstruction. Or so I thought. When I turned back the log was in our path again.

"Slow down and turn a bit more to port," I guided her and when I looked again the 'log' was gone!

I walked back to the cockpit and said, "I must be hallucinating, I swear there was something in front of us, not that far away. It looked bigger than a turtle."

"I bet you saw a crocodile!" Sheryl exclaimed.

"No way, out here?" I thought she was joking.

"The other night, on watch, I read that when the small river that flows into the bay dries up it forces the crocs out to the saltwater looking for food."

"I guess that kinda limits the water sports around here," I surmised.

"I doubt that. Just take a look," Sheryl said, pointing to the beach where a ski boat was hauling their first customer of the day up on a parasailing thrill ride. Several early morning swimmers were in the water just off the beach, as well.

"I guess we know where the croc's next meal will come from," I said sarcastically.

We anchored on the outer fringes of the group of boats not wanting to be trapped in the middle of the pack in case there was a wind shift in the night. It always pays to have an escape plan.

Our idea had been to remain there a week, replenish what we had used on our way down, then head to points south. We would stock up again in Huatulco which was about 350 miles away. And from there we would be finally heading to the Galapagos.

When the anchoring chores were complete, I grabbed the binoculars and surveyed the new neighborhood. I spied a few boat names that I recognized from the different radio nets, as well as one boat that we knew from the infamous Dock 3 in La Paz.

The boat's name was *Prairie Oyster*. Jim and Dianne had lived on the *Oyster* and sailed to the South Pacific then returned to Mexico when their cruise was over.

In La Paz, Sheryl and Dianne had hit it off from the start, both having been members of the *Stitch and Bitch*. However, it took a while before Jim and I saw eye to eye. But by the time we departed Dock 3, I had finally figured him out. I had just needed to get on what I called 'The Nut Level'. I don't know how he got to that level, whether it was drugs in his youth, PTSD or some other affliction. Maybe it was just because he was Canadian. Who knows?

Jim was short, in his sixties and about the right weight for his height. He had blue eyes and gray hair and sported a mustache with a soul patch. He admitted to being a bit of a bully growing up and he loved to pull pranks on unsuspecting dock mates, generally just 'stirring the pot', so to speak. When there was no gossip, he would make stuff up just to solicit a reaction. His wife Dianne was a sweet and quiet individual. She had long brown hair, brown eyes and must've had the thickest skin possible to put up with Jimbo the Crazy.

On our row to town we stopped by the *Oyster* to say hi and then made plans to get together for my upcoming birthday. That quick stop turned into an hour or so of gabbing and catching up on the Dock 3 goings on before we finally made it to shore.

The dinghy landing was near the working hub of Zihuatanejo. Numerous hardware stores, dive shops, tiendas and a small fueling station were located nearby. One shop, in particular, became very valuable to us. Here you could order groceries, have water delivered, as well as diesel fuel and even arrange to get the bottom of your boat cleaned for a small fee. One stop shopping with free delivery was a great service that kept us from having to schlep supplies back and forth from shore to boat and back again. You just can't beat that.

I questioned the gentleman at the counter about the bottom cleaning, what with the crocs out there swimming around. He assured me that the diver, his son-in-law, would probably be okay. It's always the son-in-law that's the first to go.

The next morning Sheryl and I were sitting in the cockpit, enjoying the first rays of sunlight peeking through the distant hill, when she informed me nonchalantly, "I've got a birthday surprise for you."

"A present for meee?" I asked with faux surprise.

"Yep! I got an email from Sparky; he and Tami are going to be here tomorrow to help us celebrate," she said beaming.

That was a genuine surprise. I was speechless.

Sparky and I have been friends for a number of years. He and I sailed from Washington to San Francisco on my first offshore adventure (we were aiming for Hawaii). It was that unplanned stop where I first met Jack and Sheryl. She was living aboard her sailboat, just one dock over from me. Her cat, Jack, thought any open boat was his for the sleeping, so when he got tired, he would curl up wherever he happened to be. So, I met Sheryl when she came looking for her wandering cat.

Sparky stayed in the Bay Area when I left for Hawaii, but he later moved down to Mexico. Sheryl and I met back up with him the first time we sailed down the Mexican coast. We had made it a point to stop in Troncones to visit Sparky and his new wife Tami, who were there running a surf and kite boarding camp.

"That's fantastic news. Seeing those two will be a blast," I replied enthusiastically.

"I was thinking that Tami, Dianne and I could have some girl time in the afternoon, you know pedis on the beach or something and then we can all meet for dinner in town," Sheryl suggested.

It didn't take me long to come up with, "So does that mean the guys will get to have guy time, like maybe on the beach, near a drinking establishment?"

"That's the plan, but you boys have to promise that we will all meet for dinner. I cannot stress this enough; you need to be in decent shape. Don't go getting all crazy, ok?" she warned me.

"Yes, mom." That remark got me a slap on the back of my head as she walked by.

The next morning when I made my way out of the aft cabin to fetch my cocoa, I found a neatly wrapped present sitting next to the steaming hot mug on the table.

"Happy Birthday, Rick!" Sheryl called from the cockpit. "Go ahead.... open it up!"

The wrapping was a Mexican newspaper with a red bow on top. I eagerly ripped opened the gift, trying to guess as to its content.

"Hey, easy, I was going to reuse that wrapping paper," she teased.

"Yeah, Har-Har."

Inside the box was a multi-colored tropical shirt that I had seen the day before at a tourist shop.

"Sheryl, did you see me looking at this shirt yesterday?" I asked with surprise.

"Yep, I saw you holding it up, and knowing that you never shop for anything other than T-shirts, I figured you were interested. So, I took a chance. I think it will look good on you."

"Good call, I liked the parrots and palm tree print, going to wear it tonight to dinner," I said as I gave her a kiss on the forehead.

Sheryl spent the rest of the morning making my favorite dessert: chocolate cake with chocolate icing. Boy, did it look delicious!

The girls' pedicures were set-up for mid-afternoon, with dinner planned for 6 o'clock. That gave me and the boys plenty of Margarita time.

When we got to the dinghy landing Jim and Dianne were already there and we exchanged greetings. Then, about five minutes later, a tall guy and a short girl walked around the corner.

"Happy Birthday Rick! Hey! Nice shirt!" Tami said, as usual all smiles. Her honey blonde hair was cut short and her blue eyes sparkled with intensity. Sparky, on the other hand, was his usual laid-back self.

"Hey," he greeted us. Truly a man of few words.

After the bear hugs, kisses and introductions were out of the way, the six of us reviewed the plan. After everyone made sure they had enough *pesos,* we went our separate ways.

"Remember: be at *Pedro's* by six," we were instructed. What did they think, we would intentionally miss dinner?

With that said the three of us guys took the first small steps to what Sheryl would later come to refer to as: *The Calamity on the Beach.*

Chapter 13
Hard Drive

*"The single biggest problem in communication is the illusion
that it has taken place."*
~George Bernard Shaw

I awoke the following morning to the sounds of cupboard doors being opened and closed. I was afraid to open my eyes, not because of what I might see, but because my head hurt so bad, I thought that the sun light might kill me, or at the very least blind me permanently.

Laying in the aft cabin of *Casablanca* I quickly deduced that Sheryl was not next to me. Then the mental fog slowly began to lift......

The high points went something like this: drank Margaritas, fell down, bashed my head, ripped my new birthday shirt and missed dinner. Well, maybe those were low points. Yup, that's the way I remembered it.

Then it was time to get out of bed to see how my wife remembered it. All the voices in my head were saying, "You are in so much trouble". No more procrastinating, it was time to face the music.

I finally pulled myself out of bed and glanced at the mirror in our room. I'd forgotten Sheryl had cleaned my head and put a *Sesame Street* character bandage on the wound. But before I saw Sheryl, I needed to brush my teeth because it felt as if Jack had slept in my mouth.

When I spit out the toothpaste into the sink, it was almost black. What the hell?

Well, so far that morning, things weren't going so well.

When I entered the galley, Sheryl was standing with her back to me and I saw on the table a cup of hot cocoa and next to it was a piece of chocolate birthday cake on a plate. I'd been afraid I might just see her packed bags instead.

Turning around, smiling, she said in a cheery voice, "Hey, sleepy head," then gave me a peck on the cheek.

I stood there trying to figure out why she was even talking to me after the fiasco the night before.

"Where's Sheryl and what have you done with her?" I asked.

"What?"

"Well, I know that I am missing some parts of last night, but I distinctly remember the words.... irresponsible, ungrateful and then I heard drunk."

"Rick, sit down and have your cocoa and the last piece of cake."

"Whatya mean *last* piece? Where'd it all go?"

"You goof, you ate a ton of it when we got home last night."

That explained the black spit. Then Sheryl came over and sat next to me and took my hand in hers.

"After I loaded your sorry ass into the dinghy, I walked back and said goodbye to the group. Spark and Jim were not in much better shape than you. But I did manage to find out that the crowd was buying you birthday shots of Tequila. By the way, those two yammered on about your dancing.... what were they talking about? There's no dance floor at *Elvira's.*"

She continued, "Anyway, maybe I was a little more upset with you than I should have been."

"You know how sorry I am about ruining my shirt and dinner and whatever else I might have done," I said sheepishly.

"Yeah, I know, just don't let it happen again. At least not before your next birthday." She stood up went to the sink and over her shoulder she added, "Get rid of your hangover, we meet the group for lunch in an hour. And a heads up: I may have ruined the computer."

"If I could just get some aspirin, that would... wait.... what?"

"We are meeting everyone for lunch, kind of a last get together before we sail away."

"No.... the computer. What did you say?"

She sat back down and confessed, "Last night after I got you cleaned up you ate your cake, then flopped into bed. I stayed up to read some e-mails. I had just poured a glass of wine and sat down. Well, my hand hit the glass, and the wine went all over the keyboard, so I shut it down immediately and dried it up, then put it away." She went on, "I tried it again this morning, but the screen was just a bunch of crazy lines."

Looking around, I didn't see the computer on the chart table, in its usual spot so I asked, "Where is it now?"

"I put it in a big tub and covered it with rice."

"Exactly what are you talking about.... rice?"

"I read a tip online that said if your smart phone ever gets wet put it in a bag of uncooked rice for 24 hours. So, I thought, what the heck, I'll give it a try. What do we have to lose?" Then she went on, "Now go get ready we need to leave soon. You don't want to miss saying goodbye to your nutty buddies."

We had a pleasant lunch at *Pedro's* on the beach that afternoon. I think the girls picked that spot to rub our noses in the fact that we, the guys, missed dinner there the night before. With an abundance of apologies for our indiscretions as well as goodbyes and promises to stay in touch, we parted ways.

When Sheryl and I got back to *Casablanca*, we found that the last of the supplies we had ordered had been delivered and were sitting on the deck. We were finally ready to leave...... except for the computer issue. When the rice didn't cure the problem, I, in my infinite wisdom, suggested that we should plug it in while still bathed in rice and see what would happen.

Extreme overheating and smoke is what had happened. If the thing hadn't been messed up before, it sure was after that.

The need for a computer on board had changed dramatically in just a few short years. On my first cruise I didn't have one. My communications to home consisted of finding the nearest telephone on shore or sometimes, of all things, a fax machine. I obtained weather forecasts from a portable radio that had its antenna hooked to the rigging. Very hit and miss. On my second trip through the South Pacific, this time on *Casablanca*, I did have a computer on board. I would hook it up to the boat's short-wave radio and with that combination I could download weather predictions, but communication through e-mail was spotty at best.

Now fast forward almost twelve years from that first cruise and the computer/shortwave radio combination is the heart of our information highway. With the computer, we can download several weather forecast sources as well as keep in touch with our families back home and other boats in transit. And it's actually very reliable. So, to have our silicone brain fried is not the best or safest way to start a passage.

We did some quick research and discovered that there was a *Costco* warehouse near Acapulco. Since we were heading in that direction anyway and we were fairly certain we could pick up a new computer there, we added that stop to our itinerary. Heck, then we could even pick up a five-gallon jug of mayonnaise if the need arose.

We left the next morning, traveled overnight and anchored around noon in a small bay to the south of Acapulco that was not too far from the *Costco*.

"Are you sure about this? It just doesn't have a good feeling, sending you out on your own," I was quizzing Sheryl for the last time as I rowed her to shore.

"Rick, I'll take one of the taxis that park near the hotel and have him wait while I shop, then he can bring me back. I've got the handheld radio so I can call you to pick me up when I return."

It had been decided that we could not both go to *Costco*, someone should stay with the boat, and sending me to buy a new computer would be sheer folly.

I put her into a cab, made some dumb joke to the driver about not losing the *senorita* and off they went in a cloud of exhaust smoke and squealing tires. I figured it would take about 3 hours max to get there, buy the thing and get back to the beach. Sheryl, bless her heart did it in an hour and a half. When I picked her up at the landing, she was holding a box that had *Dell* written on it, as well as a five-pound bag of animal cookies. Score! Glad it wasn't the mayonnaise.

The animal cookies were great, the computer not so much. When Sheryl fired up the new brain.... it only spoke Spanish! Meaning, of course, that all the programs and commands were written in Spanish without an English translation.

"I'm going to have to work on this," Sheryl said exasperated. "The keyboard is different.... I can get used to that, but I can't make it communicate in English, and my Spanish just isn't good enough."

We agreed that we didn't need the computer for the trip to Huatulco as we had the charts on board and the weather forecast was good for the following couple of days. We could wait and deal with the computer issue when we got to the dock where we would have internet access.

Anxious to be on our way, and without further ado, I pulled anchor to begin the 48-hour trip south to what would be our last port in Mexico before heading offshore.

On that brief trip, whenever Sheryl was not cooking, on watch or sleeping, she was trying to get the new computer to communicate in English. On the second day she could take it no more, saying, "I give up! When we get to port, I'll call a tech guy I know from the Bay Area. He should be able to help me get this stupid thing straightened out."

"So, what do you think the problem is?" I asked.

"It's got *Windows 7 Basic* loaded in it."

"Windows, sounds like a real pane," I responded trying to lighten the mood.

She just stared at me flatly and finally said, "You are no help."

"I am doing two shows a night for the rest of this month, right here on board," I said adding a drumroll.

"Can it, funny boy." And she meant it.

We pulled into Huatulco after having motored most of the way from Acapulco. The port is a small boat basin connected to the Pacific by way of a narrow channel. In the marina there were two main docks with numerous finger piers sticking out. The last of the provisions that we might need would be within walking distance from the harbor. This is also where we would be officially checking out of Mexico and receive clearance papers which would be necessary to check in when we reached The Galapagos. Countries aren't too welcoming unless you can prove where you are coming from.

Huatulco sits on the north end of a large gulf, Golfo de Tehuantepec, that is nearly 300 miles across. The southern end of that gulf is near the Guatemalan border.

This large gulf is separated from the Gulf of Mexico in the east by a low flat plain, or isthmus, roughly 150 miles wide. The wind can flow through this gap east to west with amazing force for days and sometimes weeks on end. With those winds come huge seas that can stretch out into the Tehuantepec some 200 miles or more. These winds are referred to as *Tehuan-a-peckers* and they must be avoided at all costs.

For *Casablanca* to get to the Galapagos we would need to cross the Tehuantepec's area of influence. Leaving from Huatulco and tracking more or less a straight line to the islands, *Casablanca* would cross the gulf nearly 200 miles out and thus experience a diminished T-Pecker effect. The only downside was it would increase our time in the Doldrums. That 'dream vacation' could include squalls, no wind, a lot of wind for a short period, heavy rain, possible thunder and lightning and blistering sun. What's not to like?

True to her word, Sheryl got in contact with her old friend Doug from the Bay Area who could help with the computer issues. The major obstacle was that the help hotline for the software program was an 800 number and that seemed to be an impossible connection through the Mexican phone service at that time. So, for one full day, telephone tag was the name of the game. And Sheryl hates phone calls.

It turned out that Windows 7 *was* a real pain.

The problem seemed to lie with the fact that the Basic version was the only version that didn't come preloaded with the option to change to any language you wanted. In the end the solution was to purchase an upgraded version of Windows 7, download and install it. Pretty simple in theory but made tedious by the need to go through a 3rd person in dealing with the company. By the end of the long day it was mission accomplished.

Chapter 14
Reefer Madness

"Life is either a daring adventure or nothing at all."
~ Anonymous

It was finally 'Leave Eve' and we were ready to go, in fact I think that was the most ready I had ever felt the night before a passage. Sheryl was more excited than I had ever seen her, as she stowed and then re-stowed supplies. And in her infinite wisdom, she had prepared several meals and put them in the freezer. If the conditions were too rough for cooking, a ready-made meal was just waiting to be warmed up.

We weren't the only ones anxious for our departure. When we checked out with the port captain the day before to get our clearance papers, he asked what time in the morning we would be leaving. I answered that I thought somewhere between 6 and 10 am. After we had some back and forth in

Spanish, mixed with some English, I was told that one of his men would be down to help untie our dock lines. I explained we didn't need help, but he made it clear it wasn't to help us, it was to make sure we left the port and the country. Was it something I said?

We cut the Port Captain some slack and let him pick the departure time. It turned out another boat had come in the night before and would also be departing in the morning. The official wanted it scheduled so he would only have to come down to the docks once in order to see both of us off and out of country.

Back on the dock Sheryl and I introduced ourselves to the crew of that other boat, *Reefer Madness*. It was a nice looking, well maintained 40-foot cruising sailboat. The owner, a 50ish something lady, explained that she loves diving on reefs so.... clever name I thought. Nicky, the owner, was tall, thin, had long gray hair and eyes that had perpetual smile lines around them. She had two crew mates onboard. We were surprised to learn she was headed for the Galapagos, as well.

The following morning, we motored out into the long Pacific swell, raised our main sail and unfurled the 130% Genoa and, as per tradition, we tossed some coins of the country were leaving over our shoulders and into the sea for good luck.

Less than an hour had passed when the first odd occurrence took place.

"Sheryl take a look at this," I called. She had her nose in a book.

"Whatya see?" she asked as I pointed to a seagull that we had just passed, about 20 feet away. "Well, I gotta tell you, it looks like he's standing on top of the water," she said with an air of wonder.

"See that's what I thought," I replied. Then the object that the gull had been standing on dove leaving the bird sitting in the water. We observed this strange interaction several more times where a turtle floating on the surface would have a seagull standing on its back, surveying its surroundings.

"Huh, that was interesting." I wasn't sure which of us actually said that out loud, but we were both thinking it. Sheryl's only disappointment was she hadn't been able to get a picture of the unusual sight.

By the third day all three of us had settled in quite comfortably as a result of the smooth seas. But, on the downside, with the winds being so light and at times nonexistent, we did have to motor about half of those first 72 hours. The constant drone of the engine was extremely wearing.

On the fourth day, *Casablanca* had traveled far enough offshore to be safe from any potential problems that could be caused by a Tehuan-a-pecker. We both relaxed a bit, having crossed that imaginary line.

As we approached the equator, another imaginary line, things began to get really interesting.

I had already transited the equator several times, so I was prepared for even lighter winds than we had experienced to that point. We had enough fuel for the engine, so that wouldn't be a problem, but as I mentioned, the constant noise of the diesel could be mind-numbing. So anytime we had even a breath of wind, we would shut the thing down, sometimes only to restart the motor half an hour later. But that half hour break was worth it.

The skies were now filling with squally, dark, heavy clouds and we seemed to be constantly altering course to avoid the larger storm cells. Some of these giants would have no wind but lots of rain and then other times they would bring what seemed like crazy multi-directional winds and very little rain. It was hard to tell their intensity in the daylight, impossible to tell at night. Thankfully, the radar aided in our effort to steer around the nasty squalls.

For safety sakes, day or night, when we saw a cell coming, we would drop the main sail and roll up the Genoa until the storm passed. They would normally last less than an hour, sometime a little longer. Lightning was a common occurrence as we approached the equator, so there was that in the mix as well.

On day seven Sheryl spotted a helicopter during her morning watch; we surmised that it was off a large commercial fishing boat. The pilots would locate the schools of tuna, then radio the mother-ship and direct them to the fish. Seems like an unfair advantage to me, but hey who doesn't like a tuna fish sandwich?

Not to be out done by my wife's helicopter sighting, on my watch I spotted something I had only seen in pictures. While reading a book, I would glance up every 10 minutes to look for incoming squalls or anything else that might be out on the water. Spotting a particularly ugly tempest about 5 miles off our starboard side, I stared in disbelief as a long, snake like funnel came out of the base of the cloud and skipped along the surface, whipping up sheets of water.

"Holy Shit! Sheryl! Sheryl! Wake up!" I called. Coming out of a deep sleep she could tell there was trouble by the tone of my voice.

"What? Oh my God! Is that a waterspout?" She gasped when she saw the terrifying cloud.

"The radar makes it look like it's running parallel to our course," I stumbled out, trying to sound nonchalant, but my voice had jumped two octaves.

We decided rather quickly to alter course and steer the boat in the opposite direction and away from the frightening squall. We stayed on that heading for three full hours before our heart rates went back to normal and were out of sight of the beast.

Before resuming her nap, Sheryl pointed out, "Well we know there was wind in *that* cell."

"Yep, probably in the neighborhood of 100 miles per hour," then I added in a teasing tone, "Sleep well."

"Yeah, right," was her response, as she rolled her eyes.

After that incident there was little semblance of scheduled watches. The weather conditions had become such that we were constantly raising or lowering the sails, which, as a matter of safety, required both of us on deck. So, instead of a three hour break we were both taking short catnaps whenever we could.

With the squally weather and lack of good sleep we were anxious to get to port. So far *Casablanca* had been making about 100 miles a day. When we plan a trip, 4 knots is the number I use as a moving average. 'We plan for 4 but hope for more' is my motto. So, we were pretty much on schedule, though we wished we were going faster. Typically, towards the end of a passage we joke about how slow it seems saying, "I could get there faster by walking."

Day nine marked *Casablanca's* third time crossing the Equator, my fourth time, but it was a first for Sheryl. The champagne had been opened and toasts were made to almost everyone we knew, past and present. We shoved handwritten notes and boat cards, that cruisers had given us, into the empty bottle, corked it back up and tossed it to King Neptune or Davy Jones, not sure which.

That night we got a radio call from *Reefer Madness*. Sheryl answered the radio immediately aware something was wrong, after all nobody calls at two am just to chat.

We were in the midst of changing watch, so I was in the cockpit and Sheryl had just gotten up. It was the middle of the night and we both looked, and felt, like hell.

"*Casablanca, Casablanca*, this is *Reefer Madness*, over."

"This is *Casablanca*.... go ahead Nicky," Sheryl replied, stifling a yawn.

I was all ears. We'd been keeping in touch by talking on the radio every other day. It was always nice to hear another voice, one that wasn't coming from my head. Last time I'd checked they were about 15 miles ahead of us.

"We ran out of fuel," Nicky stated with a combination of frustration and worry in her voice. She was not happy to say the least.

"Say again. You were breaking up." Sheryl turned to me and said quietly with a trace of disbelief, "Rick, I think she said they ran out of fuel."

My adrenaline suddenly bumped up a notch because we all knew that if you had to rely solely on the wind around the equator, a boat and crew could easily be out bobbing around for another week or more. The GPS reported that we had less than 100 miles to go. That would be torture.

"Get her position, find out how far away they are, we can get fuel to them. I checked our tanks this morning and we have way more than we need," I instructed Sheryl.

Turned out that *Madness* was ahead of us by only 12 miles. So, while the fuel-less boat languished on the flat seas, I started to fill two empty 5-gallon fuel containers.

Sheryl informed Nicky that we would catch up and at sunrise would pass them 10 gallons of diesel. The plan was for *Casablanca* to pull ahead of *Madness* where I would then drop the two fuel jugs, with floats tied to them, into the water.

The drifting boat was very easy to spot in the predawn, as they appeared to have every light on board burning. Thankfully, the seas remained flat with just the slightest undulation. However, as always, there was a squall on the horizon.

Casablanca came to a complete stop about three boat lengths in front of *Madness*. Sheryl had double wrapped the openings on the jugs with small plastic bags and duct tape so that absolutely no water would intrude, and likewise, no diesel could get out.

I carefully lowered the first jug down into the water not really sure if everything would actually float. With the aid of a gentle wind and a lot of verbal coaxing, the jug drifted to where Nicky's crew could fish it out of the water. The first one went directly into their fuel tank, but the next container would be kept on deck as insurance that they would have plenty of fuel to get into port.

The two boats floated nearly motionless about 30 feet apart. When a diesel engine runs out of fuel, they can be very temperamental in starting back up, so we stood by to make sure Nicky didn't have any problems. Turning the engine over without the thing starting tends to drain the boat's batteries very quickly, so she could end up with fuel, but not enough power to get the engine running.

After just the slightest hesitation, a puff of gray smoke blew out of the exhaust to the cheers of all concerned. They thanked us profusely for saving the day. Nicky was in tears; she was so grateful and relieved.

"We will get the jugs back when we see you in port," I yelled to them as we pulled away and continued motoring towards San Cristóbal.

After a bit, my wife poked her head up from down below and inquired, "What are you smiling so big about?"

"As long as that boat is around, we will never have to pay for another drink. That rescue will keep the Margaritas flowing," I stated, still grinning.

"Hey dream boy! Hold that thought. The big fuel transfer cost us time, so now we won't be getting in until tomorrow, so there you go." She retreated down below just as the first of many raindrops started falling on my head.

Chapter 15
Nature Calls

"Get lost in nature and you will find yourself."
~ Anonymous

Sunrise found us motoring into San Cristóbal, the port our agent had told us would be our required first stop so we could officially check in to the Galapagos. The harbor was crowded with a few cruising sailboats, many tour boats, some work boats as well as a couple of barges.

Reefer Madness was about a mile behind *Casablanca*, but since they were so close to the harbor, I could finally quit worrying about whether they would make it to port. From there they could get local assistance if they needed it

The anchored boats were uncomfortably close together, and the harbor had the makings of a disaster should a change of wind come up. We didn't plan to stay more than a couple of days. We found a small space in 40 feet of water with enough room to swing. I dropped the anchor and hoped the weather would be kind.

"Here, you do the honors," I said handing the yellow quarantine flag to Sheryl to hoist up the mast. This would signal the officials on shore our desire to check in.

"Oh, Rick I can't believe we are finally here," Sheryl whispered. I was on the receiving end of a big kiss and an even bigger hug. We were both misty eyed.

"Well it took a while, but here we are!" I proclaimed.

The trip from Huatulco covered 1,114 nautical miles and had stretched out to 11 days, 20 hours. We ran the engine for 183 of those hours, a little over 7 ½ days, and our moving average was about 4 knots. Not a lot of sailing, but heck we made it and that's all that really mattered.

The day before our arrival, Sheryl had sent a message via email to the gentleman we had hired to be our agent. Over the 6 months leading up to our departure Sheryl and Roberto had exchanged information and finally money to secure our cruising permits for the Galapagos. We had gotten a heads up from friends that had cruised here previously, and they let us know that in order to stay the longest possible time in the islands, we needed to hire an agent to facilitate the paper work. Turned out to be the best move ever.

Within an hour of dropping our anchor, a 30-foot aluminum government boat had tied up alongside *Casablanca*. The three officials, two young men in their early 20s and an equally young lady, came aboard. All three spoke excellent English and after introductions, they proceeded to check us in. The rules for staying in these protected islands seemed to change almost monthly, so when I came to the line on the check-in application that asked, *"Do you have any animals on board?"* I paused, I had worried that this question would come up.

When we had checked six months previous, we were told that as long as we had the proper Health Certificates for Jack, he would be welcome. But could that have changed? As I pondered a couple of what-if's about how to answer the question at hand, Jack made the point moot when he wandered up from below and with him came the smell of flying fish and kibble mix just out of the oven, so to speak. I thought if he doesn't get us kicked out for that stink, we're set.

It seemed that Jack's little indiscretion was witnessed by the female official who had been doing an inspection down below. One reason Jack and I get along so well is he uses the toilet for his cat business. Impressive. And when the officer saw Jack squatting on the toilet seat, the cat became an instant hit.

Anna, the young official, excitedly replayed, in detail, to her colleagues the story of Jack doing his business on the toilet. Of course, this brought up the whole question of a holding tank and thanks to Jack, all on board participated in a round table discussion concerning pump outs and such. Because of the San Diego macerator pump fiasco, I had been throwing Jack's holding tank contributions discretely over the side. I'd have to quit that practice while anchored in the islands.

After the government people departed, we secured *Casablanca* and hailed a water taxi for our meeting on shore with Roberto.

When we reached the public boat dock a tall, deeply tanned gentleman approached us and asked if we would like to book a cruise around the islands. I explained that we had just come off a sailboat.

"*Casablanca*?" He asked in heavily accented English.

"Yes! Are you Roberto?"

"At my service to you," he announced with a huge smile.

Having discerned that we still had more officials to meet, we piled into his nearby club cab pickup. We made three more stops and Roberto did all the talking, in Spanish. All Sheryl and I had to do was just sign a few papers and hand over some money for an entry fee, park fee, park pass, viewing permit (just kidding) and a couple of other passes or permits. It was very convenient that the U.S. dollar was the currency used in the islands, making the transactions much simpler for us.

Four hours later Roberto dropped us off back at the public pier.

"Now we are officially here!" I said hugging my wife.

"Let's walk through town before we go back to the boat," Sheryl suggested.

There was a definite air of prosperity in San Cristóbal, thanks to tourism. All the waterfront businesses were brightly painted and nicely kept. Not a speck of litter on the ground. Park benches lined the waterfront boardwalk. The entire scene with its colorful buildings, manicured flower gardens and the old-fashioned looking benches, made it look like a movie set.

"Rick, look up ahead, what's that?"

"Looks like something sleeping on the bench." I needed to squint because of the sun. "A seal?"

We were about 10 feet away and I told Sheryl that the 'sleeping seal' on the park bench must be a prop. Placed there as a photo op for tourists. "You know like the statue of Ronald McDonald at playland."

Getting ready to sit next to the prone figure, I was shocked at how real he looked...... and smelled. That should have been my clue right then and there. As I turned to plop down on the seat, Sheryl gasped just as the aforementioned 'prop' raised its head and let out a bark that propelled me across the boardwalk.

"That's crazy! Can you believe how tame he is?" Sheryl stated laughing at the scene.

"I don't know about tame, but he sure is relaxed." I kept a wary eye on him as we started walking toward a waterfront slide about 50 feet away.

As we got closer, we saw it was a simple children's slide positioned with the top a foot off the boardwalk and ended in a natural pool about 5 feet down. The water was about 4 ft deep and the wave action of the bay kept the water flowing in and out of the pool.

Six local youngsters where slipping down the slide into the pool where they were greeted by three young seals that would swim next to them as they hit the water. The youngsters would climb up the ladder and repeat the process. The kids were laughing and carrying on, the seals were having an equally good time. It was an unforgettable sight.

"It's just amazing, seeing those seals playing with the kids. This is magical and we have only been in the Galapagos for eight hours," I said, thinking how cool it was we would actually be spending two full months in these fascinating islands. It had certainly gotten off to a wonderful start.

We sat and watched that interaction for nearly an hour before the seals grew tired or hungry and vacated the pool.

We stayed on San Cristóbal for two more days. The Darwin Research Center was one of several tortoise rearing facilities in the Galápagos Islands, and Sheryl and I spent several hours watching tortoise of all ages being fed and cared for. There was a section of the building that housed an interpretive area, displaying some of Darwin's personal writings on the subject of evolution. As we saw and read about the unique nature of the islands, the more excited we were to leave the 'big city' and head to the less populated areas. Next stop would be Isla Isabela, the largest of the 13 main islands in the group.

Fun fact: Isabela is the only island in the chain where the equator runs right through it. So, it's possible to go from the Northern Hemisphere to the Southern Hemisphere just by crossing the street. Back and forth, back and forth, until your wife tells you to stop.

After we received our clearance papers from the port captain in San Cristóbal, we motored several hours to a small bay on Isabela.

Port Villamil is situated in a very well protected lagoon which was a much more comfortable anchorage than San Cristóbal. The port captain's office was a short walk from the sandy beach where we left the dinghy when we rowed to shore. There we once again did a check-in, complete with nearly the same forms as the previous office visit. The only exception was this time the port captain asked if our gato was still on board. "Of course," was my response. It turns out more than one boat pet has jumped ship and with the eco system so fragile, they prefer not to take chances and so try to keep track of the foreign animals.

With all our paperwork in order, we set off to explore the small town. One piece of advice we'd gleaned from our friends that had been to Isabela the previous year, was to find a tourist agency and make friends with them. The reasoning was they would be a significant source of local knowledge and information, as well as offering good tourist deals when they came up.

We found a travel office conveniently located near the waterfront. Inside we saw a young woman sitting at one of the two desks in the small room with a ukulele occupying the seat next to her.

The walls were covered with posters of different native animal species found on the islands. We introduced ourselves and explained that we would be here for around two months. The young woman who turned out to be an American from Seattle, was doing intern work at the breeding facility while working part time at the tourist office. Her name was Monica. She was in her mid-twenties, of average height and had light blond hair, cut short and she had an infectious smile. She jumped up to shake our hands seeming to overflow with energy. Monica also never stopped talking, like she hadn't seen people in a week. Which actually turned out to be true.

"I just finished a ten-day work cycle at the Breeding Station. When I'm on duty, I stay at the facility day and night just to make sure everything runs smoothly. Let's schedule a time when you can come by and tour the place," she offered.

"What kind of breeding problems do you run into, that you need to be there day and night?" I quizzed her, and for that inquiry I got an elbow to the ribs from my wife.

Monica said, "You would be surprised how many times we have to turn over a male tortoise that ended up on his back while mating." She kinda let out a little laugh at that. An uncomfortable silence followed as we digested the mental image.

We spent an hour talking with Monica and after catching up with news from Seattle, she took us on a brief walking tour of the small town.

"There are about 1800 people that live on Isabela, the number of tourists will start picking up in the next few weeks after the rainy season stops."

It was obvious that they had been getting the same rain as we had on the passage, the street was awash in a foot of water. We could tell by the height of the curbs that the water often reached three or four feet in depth along the low street.

"That will all be gone by the end of the week," She said as we waded across the street, hoping there weren't any hidden pot holes.

We saw the post office, a small grocery store and two quaint restaurants and that pretty much wrapped up Main Street.

Monica then informed us that she needed to go back and open up the tourist shop adding, "I will be working in the office for the next 3 days so please stop by anytime, especially if you need anything."

We said our goodbyes and wandered back down to the shore of the lagoon for the row back to *Casablanca*.

On the quarter mile trip back to the boat, we were delighted to see three small penguins racing under our dinghy in hot pursuit of a school of sardines.

"Now that is so cool, I never thought I would ever see penguins outside of a zoo," I said with awe. I stopped rowing, and we drifted for a bit as the flightless birds darted around us with amazing agility. Not to be out done, a small seal raced by and appeared to be trying to play with the smaller birds. He'd make sweeping passes by the school of fish not even trying to eat, but simply playing chicken with the penguins.

•   •   •   •   •

It took about a week before we were completely rested up and finished with our post-transit chores such as laundry, washing the boat during the frequent downpours of rain, as well as working through the list of things I needed to fix, which thankfully, was minor.

The following week, Monica, true to her word, invited us to the Tortoise Breeding Station, or as I like to call it 'Fornication Central'. When I told that joke to Monica all I got was a pity laugh.

We began the 2-mile hike to the breeding center from a well-marked trail head at the edge of town. There was a sign with an arrow that pointed into the nearby jungle. We walked about a mile on a wide dirt trail, shaded from the hot sun by an overhanging tropical canopy. It was weirdly quiet except for the big buzzing insects that had an alien look about them. Eventually the jungle opened up to swamp land and the dirt trail ended. Our path continued on to a boardwalk that was elevated above murky red waters. The walkway looked very new with handrails on both sides and it was wide enough for two people to walk next to each other.

After a short while, we stopped and just leaned against the railing surveying the surroundings.

"The red must come from some sort of plankton bloom," I said breaking the silence. Looking at Sheryl I asked, "What are you staring at?"

"Look right over there, that thing that looks like a stick," Sheryl said pointing toward the murky water.

Just then the 'stick' started to swim through the red ooze that covered the water, leaving an obvious trail in its wake.

"That must be a marine iguana," I stated. It was a cool discovery, and we watched his progress through the swamp until he dove underneath the surface sludge.

We continued on the boardwalk until it transitioned back to a dirt trail.

"Did you hear that?" Sheryl paused to listen.

I responded that I hadn't heard anything. We walked a little farther down the path when suddenly a loud grunt had us both stopped in our tracks.

After hearing a few more grunts, Sheryl said, "Well, we must be close."

"What do you mean?" I asked.

"That has to be a tortoise.... you know doing its thing," she said snickering.

"Sounds like a wounded animal if you ask me."

We walked on and for the next several minutes we were treated to sounds of reptilian love making, grunts and all.

Less than a mile later the trail ended in a gravel parking lot that was adjacent to a wooden structure that looked about 30 feet wide by 60 feet long. A large sign, in the shape of a circle, was painted on the front of the building. The sign was brown to contrast with the white of the wall. At the top of the sign were the words *CENTRO de VISITANTES* and at the bottom, the English translation, *VISITOR CENTER*.

In the middle of the sign there was a life like painting of one tortoise mounted on another, both with painted smiles on their beak-like mouths.

"You don't have to guess what goes on here," I said as we studied the painting.

Then the grunting began again. In earnest.

There was a gift shop located at the front of the building where a person could find postcards, tee-shirts, and of course mating turtles carved from wood, made of glass or if you prefer full-color pictures. I don't know how the cashier could stand that noise day in and day out.

As Sheryl was looking at postcards, I found a little treasure to show her.

"Can I buy this?" I held up a long sleeve blue hoodie with a picture of two of the resident reptiles making babies. Underneath the caricature were the words: FOR A GOOD TIME CALL 1-800-GALAPAGOS.

"Sure, you can buy that... that is if you never want to be seen with me in public again."

I feigned disappointment as I put the garment back on the rack.

"Hey, you two!" Monica called out from another doorway, "Come this way and I'll show you what's going on here."

"I have a pretty good idea," I said under my breath.

"Will you please stop acting like a 14-year-old?" Sheryl pleaded. Sure, now you tell me.

Monica led us through the door she had popped out of and into an area where tools were hung on pegs and rakes and shovels were in abundance. Next was the tortoise feed storage area filled with bales of vegetables, fruit, and an unidentifiable bark like substance. From there we went outside to a corral made of wood posts and railing, about 4 feet high and reinforced with chain link fencing. Inside the corral were three tortoises, varying in size from an automobile tire to a 55-gallon drum. All were moving in a painfully slow and strenuous crawl.

"These are the males we are trying to get hooked up with females over in another holding pen," Monica informed us and then went on to point out that not all tortoise are alike, "If you look closely you can see there is a distinct difference in shell shape between these males."

Meanwhile the grunting had started again.

Sheryl looked at me and her expression was clear: no stupid comments.

"This tortoise," Monica said pointing, "comes from the more tropical islands here in the Galapagos. His neck is shorter and there is no saddle on the shell." Walking to the next holding pen she pointed out, "However look at these females, their necks are longer and they have a saddle or cut-out, if you will, that allows them to extend their necks almost 90 degrees to their shell to get eatables that are higher off the ground. They are typically found on the dryer side of the islands. That is what got Darwin thinking about environmental evolution."

We were then shown to a small room where fertilized eggs were being incubated in large plastic tubs.

"Obviously, this room is climate controlled so we have the best chance of successful hatching," Monica told us, then before I could ask, she added, "We can collect anywhere from 9 to 12 eggs from one female."

Each container of eggs had a dated sign on it to help keep track of the expected due date.

"I will get some feed and then we can go see the yearlings," she said with an air of mother's pride.

The entire time she was showing us around the grunting continued and was increasing in volume.

When Monica returned, I just had to ask, "How often do the males get turned on their backs?"

"Oh, it happens from time to time, but I have to tell you the funniest sight is to see an aggressive male stalking a female who isn't in the mood. She will lead him around the corral for hours, at a blazing speed of 5 feet a minute," she answered with a chuckle.

She then walked us to another enclosure, this one was constructed of all chain link fencing. Opening the gate, Monica said to Sheryl, "Come on in and you can do the honors."

I waited outside the fence and watched as Monica handed a bag to Sheryl and said, "Throw some of this out, and don't be surprised by the stampede."

My wife reached into the bag and pulled out a handful of lettuce throwing the leaves on the ground. Right away, coming out from under every bush, from behind rocks and even out of a shallow pool, 30 small tortoise babies, maybe 6 inches in diameter, were all charging for the feed. They were climbing and crawling over one another each wanting to be the first one to the dinner table.

"They get very excited since we only feed them every three days. That's so they don't become overly dependent on humans for food."

"How long are they kept here before letting them go out in the wild?" I asked.

"We will hold on to them for 4 to 5 years, then they are distributed to the islands that match their genealogical environment. There are more pens around the back of this building that hold the older tortoises," she informed us.

We walked over to a square pen that was around 25 feet on each side. There we were greeted with a grunting, wheezing tortoise that was the size of a dining room table. He was planted on top of a smaller female. Her head was sucked back into her shell, his neck was fully extended, and he was making lots of noise.

"Like I said before, he will carry on for hours, until the female has had enough and just crawls away," Monica continued and then stated, "Well that's about it for the tour, whatcha think?"

"That was amazing, we can't thank you enough for showing us around," said Sheryl, then offered to buy Monica dinner the next time she was free.

Monica then gave us a little piece of advice, "Keep an eye out as you hike around Isabela.... there is a good chance you could run into a tortoise wandering around in the wild."

She walked us to the start of the trail that would take us back to town. We said our goodbyes and as she turned to walk away, I watched her take ear plugs out of her pocket and work them into her ears.

So that's how she deals with all that noise, I thought to myself.

●　　●　　●　　●　　●

The next morning, when I got up, I poked my head out of the hatch and was surprised to see a small seal pup resting on the floor of our dinghy.

"Sheryl you gotta see this, come here," I called.

We took pictures of the little guy sleeping peacefully, and before long he let out a soft cooing noise and mom appeared. She encouraged him back into the water, where they disappeared from view. The bad part was the baby had pooped a great deal while he slept, so I had my work cut out for me that morning. Cleaning poop in paradise.

Whenever Monica had a week off from the baby factory and was back manning the tourist office, we would stop by and chat. She was getting busier by the day arranging boat trips and guided tours for the rapidly increasing tourist population. More than once she contacted us when she needed to fill a couple seats, in order for the trip to take place. The tour boat operators were reluctant to go out with a half empty boat, the price of fuel being a big reason for this sentiment.

One such adventure for us was a 4-hour excursion to an area called *The Tuneles*. It was billed as a relaxing trip to the east side of the island where we would swim with sea turtles, maybe see manta rays along with an abundance of tropical fish. Monica had also mentioned sharks, but I didn't pass that little nugget on to Sheryl. All of this would take place in old lava tubes.

When we expressed our concerns about snorkeling in tunnels, Monica reassured us that it was more like a maze than a tunnel, adding, "It's open to the sky, I've been on this tour before and it's great. No worries." That phrase almost always makes me worry.

The next morning, we woke up to cold steady rain. "I'm sure they'll cancel our trip today," I said looking at the downpour going on.

"But we better go in just to make sure. We're supposed to meet the boat at the ramp in an hour," Sheryl said as she continued to get ready.

Thinking in the back of our minds that nothing was going to happen that day, we were quite surprised when a *panga* showed up at the ramp. A minute later a van drove up and 6 people of various ages, reluctantly disembarked the warm confines of the vehicle. As the van sped off, its passengers just stood at the top of the boat ramp and stared at their future.

The boat was made of fiberglass and it was about 25 feet long. It was 9 feet wide with bench seats on both sides running the length of the craft. Under the seats were bright orange life jackets, cheap looking, the kind you have on board just to keep you legal. A newer looking 80 hp engine was bolted to the stern. Thankfully, there was a canvas roof supported by 4 aluminum poles and a tube structure for rigidity. There were no side curtains, so the inside was nearly as wet as the outside by this stage. Overhead, in nets, was snorkeling gear for everyone, but Sheryl and I had brought our own.

The hull was painted a bright yellow, with a caricature of blue dolphins surfing through waves, adorning the bow.

The operator was a 40 something guy with a pot belly. Black hair and blood-shot eyes, he kinda went with the mood of the day. One of the tourists asked if the trip was still on, what with the rain and all, and he replied, "We will be in the water so it not so bad getting wet."

Once everyone was in the boat, Rego went through the safety instructions. Basically, we were told to just hold on and that the life vests were under the seats. Several people took life vests out and immediately put them on. I, on the other hand, had seen enough of open water sailing to believe that this short jog along the coastline would be a nonevent.

When the small boat, packed with 8 people including Rego, poked its nose out of the pass and into the Pacific Ocean, things got interesting. The steady rain obscured visibility down to less than a mile. I reassured myself that Rego must have done this trip numerous times before, in equally foul weather.

The loud engine moaned as we got into the deep ocean swell, and so did two of the tourists as their breakfasts went over the side. The *panga* ran south, about a mile offshore, parallel to the coast. Isabela was shrouded in mist generated by the heavy rain and spray was flying from the boat.

Although the land was hard to see, huge breaking waves hitting the reef were clearly visible.

"Rick, this is nasty. He's not going to go through those breakers, is he?" She said with a bit of panic creeping into her voice. Unconsciously, my foot made contact with a life vest that was tucked under my seat.

"Oh, hell no. There must be a pass that we go through, to get back close to shore," I reassured her, with a bit of panic creeping into *my* voice.

Several minutes later, and without warning, Rego turned the bow towards shore. I strained my eyes searching for flat water that would indicate a safe passage that we could transit. The rain seemed to have picked up and there was a definite chill in the air, even though we were at the equator. Our trusty, toothless driver stopped the boat just outside the surf line and I knew what his next move was going to be.

"Honey, put on a life jacket, quickly, now hurry," I ordered while fumbling trying to retrieve one from under the bench seat. The so-called life vest I grabbed weighed enough that I was pretty sure there was no buoyancy left in it.

I took Sheryl's hand and cautioned her that Rego was going to try to surf through the waves to get to the calm waters near shore. And sure enough, he gunned the engine, and the boat lurched toward the surf. As we approached the 8-foot breakers, the wave's influence took over, and we were soon surfing down the face. Below the water, the jagged coral reef was clearly and terrifyingly, visible.

When the boat started to go sideways, Rego throttled up the power and regained control of the runaway panga.

Close calls like that always make me ponder how my hometown newspaper would address the tragedy. Something like: '*Local residents drown in exotic Galápagos Islands*'. And it would probably appear on a back page, near the bottom.

Once inside the protected waters of the reef, everything became quiet, except of course, the drumming of the rain that continued to beat down on the boat's canvas roof. I was sure several of the other guests were trying to figure an alternative way home. I know the thought had certainly crossed my mind, knowing we had to go out the same way we came in. But we were there, and I figured we might as well enjoy ourselves in the meantime.

Snorkeling in the *Tuneles* was truly amazing, just as advertised. At one time these lava tunnels were fully enclosed, but thousands of years of ocean pounding had collapsed the roof leaving a maze that went from 5 feet deep to over 20 feet. Most of the corridors were just wide enough to go single file, often ending in an open expanse that would be large enough for a dozen snorkelers at a time. Sea turtles and tropical fish of various sizes and colors were a common sight, and we saw several spotted rays gliding by. I did see a small shark, but I *did not* report that to my wife.

After only about an hour in the water everyone was cold and ready to get out of the pool. Neither Sheryl nor I had packed any outer wear for after swimming, thinking that we wouldn't even be going on the excursion in the first place. We were chilled to the bone on the ride home.

The thought of the return trip heightened my anxiety level, and I really wished I had explored an alternative way home. Before Rego fired up the engine, I searched through the life vests and found two I was sure would keep us afloat if the worst happened.

Climbing the waves out of the calm waters and back into the Pacific, proved challenging for the outboard motor. The heavy-laden boat was at its power limits as it struggled to get through the surf.

Just as I began thinking again about the wording of our obit in the Gig Harbor newspaper, we broke through an incoming wave to the relative calm of the open ocean. It finally made sense, the dolphins painted on the bow of the boat, crashing through waves.

There was more shivering than talking amongst the weary passengers on the ride back to the lagoon.

•　　•　　•　　•　　•

Several days after the trip to the *Tuneles* we wandered into the tourist office. Monica was at her desk finishing up a phone conversation. She ended it with "Ok, I will see what I can do, but you only need two more individuals, is that right?" Monica was looking at us and smiling. "Alright Susan, talk to you soon, good-by."

Putting down the phone, she turned her full attention to us asking,

"So how was the *Tuneles*? Pretty awesome, huh?"

Sheryl and I had already decided to downplay the near-death experience of that trip to our lovely event planner. "Oh, it was great! A little cloudy but the snorkeling was some of the most interesting I've ever done." I was doing a good job, keeping my sarcasm under control.

"What did you think of Frank? He is one of the best guides around," Monica inquired.

"We had a guy named Rego, no teeth, kinda round belly," Sheryl answered.

"Oh heavens! Sorry about that. Rego is Frank's brother," and then in a conspiratorial whisper she looked around and added, "He likes to drink more than he likes to take tourists out."

That certainly explained our suicide ride across the breakers.

Then Monica changed course, asking, "Hey would you two be interested in going to the second largest caldera in the world?"

My first question was, "By boat?"

"No, it's an easy hike up the dormant volcano Sierra Negra, which has an enormous caldera, you can walk right to the rim. It's really something to see," She said with great enthusiasm.

Sheryl and I glanced at each other, hesitating at first, then Sheryl said, "Sure, let's have a look."

Monica called Susan back and made the arrangements for us to be picked up at the tourist office, at 6 a.m. the following morning.

The next day, as promised, a transport van met us in front of the office right around sunrise. The trip to the volcano was interesting to say the least.

A well-maintained gravel road wound through dense jungle that eventually gave way to a treeless boulder plain filled with red rocks of all sizes. The dormant volcano rose majestically out of the rocky field. At one point the driver suddenly stopped and pointed out a good size tortoise near the side of the road and a few of the passengers got out to take pictures.

In another 10 miles we were again in jungle like conditions, obviously on the 'wet' side of the volcano. The road ended in a large parking lot capable of handling 20 or so vehicles. When we arrived two other vans from different travel companies were unloading their occupants. Each of the groups had their own guide for the hike to the top and ours was a young girl from Ecuador, whose name was Rea. Rea was tall and slender with an athletic build. Her shiny black hair was tied up in a bun and she had a no-nonsense smile, a little hard looking.

After she introduced herself, she talked a bit about her background and what we would be seeing that day. During her intro I happened to notice that her legs were big knots of muscle. She must have been doing that hike awhile.

When the dissertation was concluded, our group formed up and proceeded to a small outbuilding where we signed a register showing that we were heading out on the trail. We would sign out when we got back, making it easier for the guides to find any lost souls that may have been left behind.

There were half a dozen horses at the staging area, complete with saddles, looking ready to go. "Sheryl, we get to ride horses, this will be a great hike!" I declared.

Rea turned, sizing me up and down and without an ounce of humor said, "Those are for the less capable of walking. Do you need?"

Sheryl stepped in at that point to lend me support, "He is just being a nuisance. Don't listen to him." Thanks for the kind words.

Everyone in our group looked to be in good physical shape, everybody had hiking boots except for Sheryl and me, we had tennis shoes. Several people even had fancy walking sticks, so suddenly what I had thought would be a casual stroll up the mountain was taking on a more competitive tone. But I was in no mood to let a young kid from Ecuador run me into the ground. I thought, "Bring it on!"

"I can keep up with her," I said confidently.

"Good luck," was Sheryl's only response.

After we left Puerto Escondido, we had done a fair amount of swimming but not a lot of walking......so I was beginning to worry. But we should be okay, swimming is good, right? Yeah right.

Rea hoisted her backpack up on her shoulders and this signaled the start of our march to the top.

The other hikers in our group consisted of six adults and a teenager. As we started to move, Sheryl and I fell in at the end of the line. When we got to the start of the trail, a mist began to fall. Luckily, we'd thought ahead and brought lightweight jackets having learned a lesson about preparedness on the *Tuneles* trip. Unfortunately, with the temperature around 75 and the humidity at 100%, wearing them became intolerable in short order.

The trail was wide enough for two people to walk side by side. The path became increasingly slippery as the red dirt turned to red mud in the light rain. Once the trail got steeper, the going got tougher and everyone started to spread out. Every so often when Rea would stop to point out something of interest, Sheryl and I would take that opportunity to catch back up to the group. I thought we were keeping a pretty good pace, but it appeared wonder woman had an appointment at the top and when she was moving, *she was moving*. We knew that it would be 5 miles to the top, Monica had informed us of that, and I really thought we should pace ourselves.

"Hey, Sheryl," I managed to get out even though I was breathing a little hard, "Once we get to the top, we will still have 5 miles to go."

"Yeh, we're not going to live up there, how did you think we were getting down?" she quizzed.

"It's just that if the number 10, as in miles, had come up, I might have given this jaunt a little more thought," I explained.

"Sometimes you really are an idiot," she responded, as she started walking faster.

As we climbed higher the mud finally gave way to a crushed rock path, making the going a little easier. I figured we had about a mile to go from that point. The group, and this included my wife, were out of sight just around a bend, so not wanting to get further behind I picked up my pace.

The trail took a turn around a boulder the size of a small house and then the path lead to the edge of a cliff that dropped straight down about 100 feet. This was the rim of the caldera, the business end of a volcano.

The trail continued to wrap around the rim of the dormant volcano for another quarter mile or so. I could see our contingent, they were spread out taking pictures and sitting on large volcanic rocks that were scattered about.

Rea had told us that the massive caldera was nearly 6 miles across. It was impressive. Looking down from the rim the caldera looked like a sea of black rock with steam vents near the middle of the expanse. The faint smell of sulfur filled the air. I had hoped we would see some lava, but alas, no lava.

I sat down next to my wife exclaiming, "This is incredible, looking down into the cone of a volcano like this. Unbelievable!"

"It is soooo vast, I can barely see the other side," she said, with awe in her voice.

Rea came over to where Sheryl and I were sitting, offering us each a bottle of water. Come to find out she had carried enough water in her backpack for everyone in our group. Amazing.

"We will rest here for 20 more minutes, then proceed back down the trail to the parking lot," Rae informed us, "but you may leave now if you need."

Wow, she sure knew how to kill a guy's ego. And then she moved on to talk with another couple.

"Come on, get up, let's go," I told Sheryl jumping to my feet.

"You just got here," Sheryl said as she finished her water, "Don't you want to rest a bit?"

"If you think I am going to let little miss Wonder Woman beat me to the parking lot...." With that we headed down the trail like we had just broken out of prison. Two miles further we finally stopped for a rest on a wooden bench.

"You know something? I don't remember seeing this bench on the way up," I wondered out loud.

"Did we take the wrong fork in the trail back there?" Sheryl questioned, asking the obvious.

"Nah, were okay."

"You lie." Then we started walking again.

Turned out we did get on the wrong trail, but with my expert survival instincts, and a wooden sign pointing the way to the ranger station, we arrived unharmed. We were the last ones down the mountain.

Everyone in our group was already in the van, just waiting for us so they could get back to town. As we boarded the van, the driver looked at our mud laden shoes and seemed unimpressed with the mess we were making.

Heading to our seats, we passed an older lady who asked, "Did you kids have fun?" Then she gave us a conspiratorial wink and a smile.

I gave her my best *'oh you caught us'* look.

After we got to town and were let out of the van, I limped the short distance to our dinghy. My legs hurt and my manhood was crushed, but Sheryl, bless her heart knew the right thing to say to boost my mood. "Boy, you sure showed her."

My legs, and my ego, ached for two solid days afterwards.

The remainder of our first month in the Galapagos was spent close to *Casablanca*. The penguins had become regular visitors, as well as the blue-footed boobies. Both species would rest on nearby rocks, after spending all morning feeding.

We did start pulling the dinghy out of the water at night, this to discourage the seals from using it for sleep overs and their personal toilet facilities. It had been cute the first time, but after a while, not so much.

The anchorage was beginning to get crowded and busy as the rainy season came to an end, ushering in the tourist season.

Tour boats, some 100 feet in length, others only 30 feet long, jammed into the small anchorage. The smaller boats would take tourists out on day trips, while the larger vessels, having made the overnight trip from Ecuador, provided guests with their own state rooms for the 7 to 10-day tour. These premium tours would include a licensed naturalist and access to more of the islands than private individuals were allowed.

With all the boating activity in the anchorage we needed to find a new place to view the underwater magic of the Galapagos.

Chapter 16
Taking it all in

"Good decisions come from experience.
Experience comes from making bad decisions."
~ Mark Twain

We had been enjoying Port Villamil for six weeks when *Reefer Madness* sailed into the lagoon. The last time we had seen each other was briefly in San Cristobal, when Nicky returned the diesel jugs that we had loaned her while out at sea. I rowed over to welcome *Madness* to the neighborhood. After chatting a while, plans were made to have dinner together at a small restaurant in town that evening. Nicky informed me that her two crew members had flown back to Canada, citing their unpleasant crossing from Mexico. I wasn't going to pry, at least until dinner.

That night on our walk to the restaurant, my wife requested that I not dig into what might have happened to make Nicky's crew abandon her. For the record, in my mind, a request is not a promise.

When we met outside the restaurant, I was surprised to see how tired Nicky looked, but she still had a big smile on her face.

"I owe you two dinner for coming to the rescue that night at sea," she said looking at the both of us.

"You really don't have to buy us dinner, you would have done the same for us," Sheryl said as we headed for a table.

"Rick said your crew flew home, are you single handing now?" I was surprised to hear Sheryl ask.

"Sheryl don't pry. I'm sure Nicky would rather not get into it."

"Will you please stop being so obnoxious," Sheryl said, giving me a sideways glance. She was a little irritated with me, but curious all the same.

"That's okay," Nicky replied. "Originally the three of us were going to continue on to the Marquesas from here. This was the first off shore trip for Sandy, but Bob had done some ocean sailing before, or so he said. Anyway, the chemistry just wasn't there, so they bailed. I've got new crew coming in tomorrow. We will leave in a couple of days if the weather holds."

"Now, aren't you sorry you asked?" I taunted Sheryl. Then I got *the look*.

Quickly changing the course of the conversation, Nicky asked, "So what are your guy's plans?"

There was an awkward silence as Sheryl and I just looked at each other. We had not really talked about what came next, we were simply enjoying being in this magical environment. We were in full procrastination mode.

"Well, to tell you the truth, we are still up in the air on which direction to go," I said while indicating to the server the need for another round of refreshments.

Sheryl added, "We have charts for the Panama region as well as cruising guides for the Caribbean. Just to cover all of our bases, we have special papers to get our cat, Jack, into Hawaii without quarantine, if we choose to go that way."

"Then there are the Gambiers. They're kinda off the beaten path, but actually mileage wise, just a little closer than the Marquesas," I said, realizing that we should give a little more thought to our upcoming travels.

As we rowed back to *Casablanca* that evening, we vowed to get serious with our plans... maybe in another week. Meanwhile, we had three weeks left on our visa and about six weeks' worth of things we wanted to see.

The next time we saw Monica at the travel office she was plucking away on her ukulele. It was obvious that she was new to the instrument.

"Hey, guys have I got a deal for you," Monica said, as she finished strumming.

"Before you say anything, just answer me this; will there be long hikes or dangerous surf landings involved?" I inquired.

"Rick you are such a big baby." Normally this is something that I could count on Sheryl to say. But as our friendship with Monica had grown, so did the barbs she sent my way.

"What's up?" Sheryl was all ears.

"I have a friend who just got back to town. He takes people on driving tours to unique sights here on Isabella. Having grown up here, he really knows the land and is very knowledgeable and speaks great English. I'm sure you would find his excursions rewarding."

"So, you're saying we would get to just ride in a car and sight see?" I asked hopefully.

"It's an SUV, but yeah, that's what I am saying."

"We're in, just let us know when and where to meet him," Sheryl replied.

Two days later we were bumping down a dirt road in the middle of a lush tropical jungle. Our driver, whose name was Luis, had us riding in his 5-year-old Japanese SUV. The car was immaculate, inside and out.

Luis had the look of a 40-year-old time share salesman. Walnut brown skin, the man had *the* whitest teeth which were framed by his constant open mouth smile. His dark hair was slicked back, and he sported a black pencil-thin mustache. Luis spoke excellent English with what Sheryl called a 'charming' Spanish accent.

He was short at five foot eight and probably weighed about one fifty. Luis compensated for his stature by dressing very sharp and he was, what I call, a *smoother*.

Luis seemed very fond of the peck on the cheek. He was quick to kiss Monica and equally fast when he met Sheryl. A very smooth mover. He was dressed in Khakis and wore a tropical shirt adorned with lizards. Very appropriate, I thought.

We were on our way to what he referred to as *The Wall of Tears*. While avoiding pot holes in the road, Luis filled us in on the wall's history.

He began the story by telling us, "When World War II ended, this island became a penal colony. Very few buildings. All prisoners slept outside. The conditions very bad. The prisoners were restless, so the camp boss thought up a way to keep the prisoners working."

We parked and when we opened the doors, the humidity was like a slap in the face with a wet washcloth. There was a sign at the start of the short trail indicating the *Wall's* location as well as several longer hikes to different observation points.

When we reached a clearing, the structure in front of us was so out of place it was ridiculous. It looked about 400 feet long and in some places 60 feet tall.

Luis said that the rocks were chiseled out at a quarry some distance away and then hand carried to the site.

"The wall would sometimes fall on the prisoners and crush them," Luis said solemnly.

There was a large sign laying out the history of this project. Simply put, it was the ultimate in 'busy work' simply created to prevent idle hands.

The prisoners were sent here from mainland Ecuador. The island provided a cheap way to house criminals, it was a natural prison. Because of the equatorial climate the prisoners could be kept out in the open without barracks, they were surrounded by the ocean giving them nowhere to run. The camp commander's goal was to keep the men busy and in a constant state of fatigue, so he came up with building a wall. Not to keep anything in or out, just a straight wall in the middle of the steaming, humid jungle.

Walking alongside the monolith, we could see that the stones had been painstakingly piled on one another. The base of the wall was around 12 feet wide tapering to 3 feet at the top.

"Many men died here because of that wall," Luis said in a hushed tone.

If there was ever a time when the phrase *man's inhumanity to man* would apply, this was it.

When we returned to the *'Guide-mobile'* Sheryl and I were soaked with sweat, but not so Luis. There wasn't a drop of perspiration visible on his entire body.

"Here it is very sad, but now let's go for fun," Luis stated as he started the car and turned the air conditioning on full blast for our benefit.

We ended up driving about 45 minutes. The narrow road terminated in the parking lot of a quaint little restaurant, situated on a black sand beach. There were large volcanic boulders of all sizes and shapes along the water's edge. Sheryl and I were somewhat perplexed as to why someone would build an eatery in this isolated local.

"This is kinda out of the way, do they do much business?" Sheryl inquired.

"Let us set on the deck and I will show you how they are popular," Luis said with his ever-present smile and slightly stilted English.

The restaurant was a thatched roof affair with a large deck attached to the building. Weathered wooden tables with bright orange plastic chairs were situated under large colorful umbrellas. The smell of greasy burgers made me forget about the staggering humidity.

Always acting the gentleman, Luis pulled a chair out for Sheryl. He placed a hand on her shoulder to position her in such a way that she had an unobstructed view of the beach. He then sat down with a smug look on his face.

We knew he had something to show us but damn if we knew what. After several minutes my wife, having more patience than me, finally saw the attraction.

"Wow! Rick, look over there at that big black rock!" She was pointing to a large rock about 20 feet away and near the water. The bright sunlight took a lot of definition away, but I finally saw them: marine iguanas.

As our eyes became more focused, we could see at least a dozen of the black creatures covering the rock, with many of them laying on top of one another. Their black skin against the black lava rock, made for perfect concealment, right out in the open.

As we ate our lunch, the iguanas put on a great show of surfing on the waist high waves then crawling up the beach and climbing on to a rock to warm up.

When lunch was over the three of us walked down the beach and we were amazed at the number of iguanas congregating in such a small area. Each of about a dozen large boulders were completely covered with the resting reptiles. Luis explained that after these prehistoric creatures feed in the cool ocean waters, they revive by sunning themselves on the warm rocks. Seeing the marine iguanas in the wild had been number one on my 'must-see' list and it wasn't a disappointment.

On the trip back to town, I mentioned to Luis that I would love to swim with the iguanas.

"This can be arranged; I will pick up you in the morning at Monica's office."

When he dropped us off near the boat launch, Luis hustled around to open the front passenger door for Sheryl. He took her arm and helped her out of the vehicle. I, on the other hand, had to open the back-seat door for myself. Earlier he had insisted that Sheryl ride up front with him, so she wouldn't miss a thing.

Jack met us in the cockpit when we returned to *Casablanca* and he was clearly not happy at being left alone for most of the day.

"So, I think Luis is flirting with you," I told Sheryl.

"Sure, he is, Monica warned me about him. He's harmless, besides I think it's kind of cute," Sheryl said with a smirk.

"At least he could be a little more subtle," I joked, adding, "But if he can show us where we can swim with the iguanas, he can have you." I sidestepped away just in time to miss a slap on the head.

The next morning, we lugged our snorkeling gear to the still closed travel office. Before you could say 'peck on the cheek', our trusty driver had parked and was opening the car door for Sheryl, of course not leaving out the peck.

The drive was short and in only a few miles we stopped at a wide spot on the road that had a trail that lead to the water's edge. We were looking at a small bay that had a reef separating it from the Pacific Ocean. The tide was out, and the reef was exposed several feet out of the water. Luis explained that when the tide is high, all matter of sea life can swim into the bay. Conversely, when the tide goes back out the fish or turtles or rays are trapped until the next high tide. He went on to say that some sea-life never leaves the protection of the basin. With the tides rising and falling several times a day, the bay gets a good flush on a regular basis.

When we realized that the snorkeling spot was actually just a short walk back to where our dinghy was tied to the dock, Luis decided there was no need for him to stick around while we swam. So, after giving my wife a long goodbye hug, he drove away.

We got our gear on and began swimming out toward the exposed reef, about 50 yards distant. When we drew closer to the reef, the sandy bottom gave way to thick vegetation on the sea floor. The water was 20 feet deep and somewhat opaque, but the swimming lizards were easy to spot. They would dive down whipping their tails back and forth for propulsion and then they would sit on the bottom eating the algae that had formed on the rocks.

We actually timed some of them and found that they were often underwater nearly 30 minutes. Amazing. Most of these guys had bodies about a foot long with tails adding another 8 to 10 inches to their overall length. When we got closer to the rocky reef, we saw several more lizards sunning themselves on the dark rocks. We watched in fascination as the black creatures blew a liquid out of their nose, apparently clearing out sea water, resulting in a white salt crust forming around their heads.

After snorkeling for several hours around the reef, a wave washed over the rocks sending the iguana colony scattering and signaling that the tide was on its way up, so we turned and slowly made our way back toward the beach.

As we swam, we encountered a ray that was at least 5 feet across and equipped with a tail as thick as a tree branch that hosted three long barbs. He was very nasty looking, indeed. We did not turn our back on the giant ray until we were well away from the water's edge.

That night, in bed, Sheryl informed me that she wanted to see Flamingos.

"I know just the man to get a hold of," I assured her, surmising that Luis could hook us up.

Sure enough, two days later, right around sunset, we found ourselves overlooking a pond that was the size and shape of a football field. We stood on a slight rise at one end of the large swamp where we observed about twenty of the yard ornament want-to-be's perched on one foot, dipping their long necks into the brackish water.

The setting sun reflected off of their bodies, enhancing the pink color of their feathers. Sheryl was truly enjoying herself, snapping pictures like a mad woman. All the while, Luis ran commentary on the bird's diet and of course, their mating habits. We were treated to quite a show when the flock spooked and took flight, but they soon returned, taking up their one-legged yard pose once again.

That night while lying in bed, with Jack in his customary spot on Sheryl's stomach, padding away, the last thing I heard Sheryl say before I drifted off to sleep, was one word: *Gambiers*.

The next morning during breakfast I asked my wife if that meant she was voting for going to the *other* South Pacific.

"I know I haven't been to the South Pacific before, but I have heard you, as well as many other people describe its beauty, the people and the culture. I've seen the pictures, heard the stories and it sounds wonderful and well-traveled. But after what we have seen here in the Galapagos, I think we should see more of the less visited islands. So, to answer your question, yes, my vote is to sail to the Gambiers, and Jack concurs."

With the decision to go to the Gambiers, we now at least knew the direction we would be sailing. We would be going south. Further planning would have to be put on hold so we could enjoy more of this magical island in the precious little time we had remaining.

We were able to go back and swim with the iguanas. That time we were treated to a small group of juvenile seals that came to play with us. We also had Luis take us back to view the flamingos and on the road trip back from seeing the birds we spotted a large tortoise slowly crawling near the side of the road. Of course, we stopped and watched the prehistoric reptile eating a small cactus. We were very excited to see one in the wild and would have stayed even longer, but the high humidity drove us back to the car.

When we had under ten days to go before our visa expired, we had to come to grips with the priorities of the looming long ocean passage. Although we continued doing some sightseeing, an equal amount of time was being spent getting ready to go. The relaxed pace of the island we had been enjoying, slowly gave way to full days of bottom cleaning, checking the rig and sails and other preparations. Going up the mast was not my fav because it involved wearing a harness that plays no favorites with "*the boys*". It is torture.

When we made the decision to go to the Gambiers, we also decided to leave from Isabela, even though the supply chain for provisioning was rather weak on that remote island. Monica was a big help when she made us aware of something called the '*Fast Ferry*'.

Three times a week the ferry would depart Port Villamil at 7 am and make a two-hour run to Santa Cruz Island, the most populated and most developed island in the chain. The trip ends at Puerto Ayora, a small town of around 12,000. Sheryl and I would be able to buy all the food we would need for a month at sea, as well as some small boat parts I wanted to have onboard.

"It's funny, I don't ever remember seeing a fast ferry come into the port, and we have an excellent view of the dock from our boat," I pondered, talking to Monica.

"You're picturing Seattle's fast ferry," she said smiling, "This is a little less than that."

"You're not saying that old cabin cruiser that goes in and out is the Fast Ferry? The one that always has a trail of smoke following it?" I didn't like where this was headed.

"That's the one." As I turned to leave, Monica added, "Pray for smooth seas."

I yelled back, "Always do!"

Apparently I didn't pray hard enough.

During breakfast, early the next morning, we heard the ferry come in and a little later a whiff of diesel fumes confirmed its arrival.

We got to the dock just as a line of people started to shuffle up the short set of stairs to board. A deck mate took our tickets, and we entered the cabin, lucky to find the last two seats that were together.

The 'ferry' was an older cabin cruiser that had been stripped down inside. The space had been filled with three benches that ran port to starboard with additional bench seating running along the sides. They looked much like park benches, complete with wrought iron ends and no cushions. In addition to the seats, there were six hand holds mounted on the ceiling for those that would like to stand for two hours on a rolling boat. Life jackets were located in the overhead bins that ran the length of the cabin.

"The *Minnow*" I said to myself.

"What? What are you mumbling about?" Sheryl asked as she studied the other riders.

I answered her explaining, "It took a minute, but I just figured out were I've seen this boat before. It's the boat that crashed on Gilligan's Island!"

Sheryl sighed, "It's not going to be one of those outings with you is it?"

Before I could think of something witty to say, the engine that was located under our feet roared to life. That large diesel was obnoxiously loud, so before we reached the open water nearly everyone had something covering their ears, to dull the noise.

The *Minnow* exited the lagoon and headed in a northeasterly direction, into seas that had a long smooth roll, but with an occasional side swell to mix things up. There was a small door that lead into the cabin that was kept open while we were underway, but the inside temperature was nearing *super nova* conditions. To top it off, the following wind put a little exhaust smoke back into the cabin to help people sleep.

"You have to stay awake, don't fall asleep," I whispered to Sheryl, "The fumes will kill you."

"Will you stop, I am trying to rest, it's going to be a long ride," Sheryl said with a note of exasperation.

"Okay, suit yourself," I said drifting off.

Two hours later we pulled into Puerto Ayora. The ride hadn't been too bad, though I did have one hell of a headache. On the upside, only one person had lost their breakfast to the seals.

The growing town was on the verge of becoming a city. Several low-rise buildings dotted the skyline as well as a plethora of store fronts and restaurants. Tourist season was in full swing, most of the sidewalk cafes were packed with people. There were more cars than we had seen in two months and the general atmosphere was busy, busy, busy.

We had six hours to shop before we would re-board the *Minnow* for the next '*Three-Hour Tour*' which would return us to the relative quiet of Villamil.

The markets were well stocked and there seemed to be goods from all over the world. Sheryl prefers to shop without my help, although I can't understand why. So, as usual, I would wait outside and people watch or wander close by looking in shops, awaiting her signal that my skill as a Sherpa was required.

My wanderings had led me to one of the more bizarre sights of the day. It was at an open-air fish market located on the waterfront. As Sheryl placed an order with the fish monger, I walked around the counter to an outside wooden deck. There I saw a seal, lying on the deck in the sun sound asleep. Sitting next to him was a large pelican, with its beak tucked under its wing, also apparently sleeping. As if that wasn't interesting enough, there was a crusty marine iguana lying right by the duo.

At first, I thought they must be elaborate fakes and the entire scene was staged, until I saw the iguana move out of a shadow into the sun.

"You won't believe what's out here," I called, excited to show Sheryl. I took her hand and drug her outside while her order was being completed.

"That is wild, what an odd group," she said surprised and out came the camera. After several minutes, the fish monger stuck his head out and indicated my wife's order was ready.

"Tres Amigos," he said with a smile and told us that those three gather nearly every day outside his market eagerly awaiting the scraps he would throw out. At least that explained the bird and the seal, but no one could quite figure why the lizard showed up, being a vegetarian and all.

The day flew by. We returned to the ferry dock for the 3 o'clock departure to Isabela, and I noticed a slight wind chop had developed in the harbor. Boy, I hope it's smooth on the trip back, I thought to myself.

Some of the passengers were milling around, while others guarded their newly acquired purchases with half-opened eyes. I glanced at the young lady who had lost her breakfast on the way over and she had the anxious look of someone who didn't want to get on that boat. To tell the truth, I was not looking forward to being sequestered in that stuffy, hot and humid box either. I knew that if the *Minnow* started wallowing in the sea, it would be a long ride home for me and my stomach.

"You're sure being uncharacteristically quiet. Not looking forward to the ride home, are you?" Sheryl inquired. "Think you'll get sick?"

"I'm fine, don't worry about me," I lied.

The return trip was rougher than the morning excursion had been and on top of that I ended up having to stand for the two-hour ordeal as I had given my seat up to an older lady, which probably saved me from getting sick. The bright side was that I could position myself under a fresh air vent, holding on to a leather strap that was attached to the ceiling. I stood and watched everyone else sleep, the heavy sleep of exhaust fumes.

There is an old saying: 'Life is like a roll of toilet paper, the closer it gets to the end, the faster it goes'. This adage really applied to what happens when we are getting ready to go offshore.

Five days before our planned departure from the comforts of the lagoon, which by then felt like home, we were deep into preparations. Stowing food and supplies, making sure our charts were in order, cleaning the boat bottom and worrying about the weather. By the time *leave eve-eve* had rolled around we were exhausted and getting a little snippy with each other. But, with help from Monica, I had planned a little surprise to help lighten the load.

Two days before D-Day, we met Monica for a send-off dinner in town. After a delightful meal, she drove us to a small condo complex, where she had made reservations for Sheryl and me, without my wife's knowledge.

When the car stopped in front of the building, I thanked Monica and opened the passenger side door and took Sheryl's hand.

"Why are we here? I thought we were going for ice cream?" She asked while exiting the car.

"Rick, here's the key," Monica said as she came over and gave Sheryl a big hug.

"What *is* going on?" Sheryl was starting to lose her patience.

"Come on, I'll show you," I said and led her up a flight of stairs.

As Monica drove away, I unlocked the small studio, found a switch and flipped on the lights. A sliding glass door opened to a small deck overlooking the beach and, by chance, the nearly full moon was just rising.

"Now do you mind telling me what's going on?" Sheryl said with a grin. I think she had it figured out.

Looking around I said nothing, then I spotted what I was seeking. On the table was a bottle of wine in a plastic bucket surrounded by melting ice. I used the provided corkscrew to open the bottle and poured two healthy glasses of wine. I made a mental note to thank Monica again for this impressive set-up.

Handing one of the glasses to Sheryl, I explained, "This is our last chance to sleep on land for a long time and we needed a break from *Casablanca* for at least one night. Cheers," I said as we clinked glasses.

"But I don't have anything for staying overnight."

With that I pulled our toothbrushes out of my jacket pocket.

"I think this is all you really need," I said smiling.

"You really are one of a kind," she said as she wrapped her arms around my neck, kissing me. Then she broke the embrace and asked, "What about Jack?"

"Oh, he thinks I am one of a kind as well."

"You are a goof and yes, I would like some more wine."

Chapter 17
... in a land far, far away

"A ship in harbor is safe, but that's not what ships are built for."
~ J.A. Shedd

We had only been at sea a week, but that double bed back at the condo in the Galapagos seemed like a long, long time ago in a land far, far away.

At that point, *Casablanca* had traveled about a third of the nearly 3000 miles needed to reach our destination: the Gambiers. The 'start of the voyage blahs' were over and the seas and the winds had been kind. We were comfortably riding the Southeast Trades.

I had chosen to implement our storm trysail, not because of any strong winds, but for convenience and the health and comfort of the crew. We had the main sail flaked onto the boom, and the boom was secured in place. The trysail runs on its own track, located next to the main sail track. Its sail area is equivalent to having a third reef in the main. Since the trysail doesn't attach to the boom, it can swing freely from side to side without the boom coming over to take your head off. That's the health reason. Also, when a squall or a dramatic change in wind direction happens, the trysail is self-tending, meaning the crew does not have to mess with any lines or winches. That's the convenient part.

However, there is one drawback to my setup, and that is *Casablanca* doesn't reach the speeds she would with the full main. But we always choose comfort over speed, especially on a long passage.

The sun had set, and I was on watch. Sheryl was down below just finishing checking-in with the *Seafarers Net* on the ham radio. That network is a group of amateur radio operators from around the world, that keep track of voyagers and offer assistance when they can. A fantastic organization. There is nothing like hearing a calm human voice when it's pitch-dark outside and the wind is howling, and the seas are crazy.

"Sheryl, can you come up here for a minute before you lie down?"

She came up handing me a hot cup of cocoa asking, "What's up? Oh, feels like the wind's picked up a little." She sounded tired.

"Yeah, it did. Hey, listen do you hear that?" I said turning my head adding, "It sounds like voices talking."

Sheryl listened then replied a little too quickly, "Nope, I am going to bed."

"No, no stop and listen, I swear it sounds just like people talking."

She headed down the stairs and called back, "Good night, and by the way you always hear voices in your head. Why is this time different?"

Dismayed that she didn't want to spend her off hours sitting in the cockpit, when she could be sleeping, I told her, "Maybe the voices are telling me to throw you overboard."

"If that's the case, can it wait until after I rest?" She said adding, "Have a nice conversation with your new friends." Then she disappeared below.

A week later we entered what Sheryl referred to as the '*Valley of the Squalls*'. It seemed that every night we encountered at least two of these cells and just like everywhere in the world there was no telling what kind of wind and rain they were packing. On the bright side there was no lightning. Due to the squally weather we had begun to wear our heavy rain coats at night.

Additionally, as we traveled south, the air temperature was dropping noticeably.

Reaching the halfway point in any voyage was a big deal aboard *Casablanca*. So, when we achieved that goal, Sheryl prepared a special dinner with dessert to celebrate. The next milestone would be when we were down to triple digits on the 'miles to go' read out on the GPS.

Winter had come to the Southern Hemisphere, and the trades were getting stronger and they shifted to the Northeast. This had an impact for several reasons. First the heel *Casablanca* had been on for over two thousand miles suddenly changed. Now we were on the opposite slant if you will. This made some things easier, for example, when I used the toilet, I no longer needed to hold myself on to the seat, I could just lean back and stay in place. Nice. On the other hand, on the new heel, when Sheryl would open the front-loading refrigerator, items would throw themselves out onto the cabin sole. Not so nice.

With the increase in wind strength the seas began to build, and it had become more difficult to maintain a comfortable course. So much for a leisurely cruise.

When we were just three days from landfall, Sheryl downloaded a weather prediction that looked rather nasty. There was a cold front moving in from the north and with it came even bigger seas and winds in the mid-twenties. Most unfortunate was that the weather would shift and be right on our nose. We would then have to bash the last fifty or sixty miles if we continued at the same pace. We needed to get to the islands before that front arrived.

Knowing this prediction was looking ahead 72 hours, I took it with a grain of salt. Weather prognostication isn't an exact science and being in the South Pacific makes it that much tougher due to the vastness of the area. There was a chance it could develop late, but of course on the other hand....... So, to be on the safe side, we came up with a plan to get us ahead of the incoming system.

"We should shorten our tacks and run the engine at a low rpm to try to pick up some speed," I said looking at the forecast.

Sheryl agreed and added, "After motoring for two days, I might start hearing voices myself. Then maybe you'll be the one going over the side." She had the look of someone who has been at sea for a month.

It was midnight on our last night at sea and the GPS showed the distance to go was only 35 miles. We were both holding our breath knowing we might start feeling the weather change at any moment. Our speed was okay, and our estimated time of arrival was 8 a.m.

"We're so close I think we're going to beat it," I announced and after I said that Sheryl just stared at me burning a hole into my skull with her eyes.

"What? What's wrong?" I asked.

"Do you never learn? Every time you say stuff like that it ends biting us in the butt."

"Don't be so superstitious, we'll be there in the morning, no problem." I chuckled.

4 a.m. the wind was on our nose and we are bashing into 6-foot seas. Spray was flying over the dodger and the deck got a good wash down every few minutes.

"So, funny boy, maybe now you will learn not to tease the weather gods," Sheryl admonished me as she ducked, in reflex, when heavy spray hit the dodger window.

Casablanca would come nearly to a stop when the bigger waves hit, but we were still making slow progress. Our arrival time was pushed back to around noon. I had the engine throttled up high and we were making short tacks trying to keep the wind off of our nose, allowing us to take the waves at an angle instead of head on.

"I may have misspoken earlier," I conceded.

When we were within 5 miles of the entrance, the waves had subsided substantially, however the wind was still in the 20-knot range. We were relieved to see the channel was well marked as we slid into the relative calm of the surrounding reef.

I managed to get the trysail down and the Genoa rolled up, just as we passed the entrance buoy. We safely transited the wide pass that had been gouged out of the coral reef that surrounded the small group of islands. A jungle-covered mountain rose out of the water, giving the appearance of an island in the Marquesas, however the surrounding reef is a feature that's normally seen in the Tuamotus. Barrier reefs make for a very comfortable anchorage.

Our cruising guide for the Gambiers warned cruisers to be very vigilant on the way to the anchorage that is located off the town of Rikitea. Coral patches were plentiful as *Casablanca* wound through the maze, but thankfully the passage was well marked. We quickly spotted the town several miles away, as the gull flies, however it took nearly two hours of motoring, sometimes seemingly in circles, before we dropped anchor in 35 feet of crystal-clear water.

Finally, the engine was silent for the first time in two days. We sat in the cockpit, still in our heavy coats, each of us taking in the beautiful scenery that surrounded us.

And then the rain came.

"Told you we would beat the rain," I said jokingly.

"I don't think that's what you said." Sheryl had a light dusting of dried sea salt on her face but still managed a smile.

The rain lasted for two days, which is about how long we slept. Finally relaxing, we were relieved that there were no longer any night watches. During our 'rain days' I studied a travel guide so that I would be familiar with the town and the surrounding islands. Just to be clear, Sheryl had done this exercise about two days out of the Galapagos. Very studious. It takes me awhile.

My studies revealed that the lagoon formed by the barrier reef, was about 5 miles across and that the island group is about 900 miles southeast of Tahiti, making it the southernmost point of the Tuamotu Archipelago.

The area had been closed to cruising boats from the 1970s to the 1990s so that France could stage their nuclear bomb tests at a nearby island, that doesn't even exist anymore. It's a wonder the French didn't create their own Godzilla with all the nuclear activity.

When the sun finally emerged on day three, the first thing I did was throw myself into *the* clearest water I had ever seen. Unfortunately, 'the boys' and I were not prepared for the very 'refreshing' water temperature. There was no doubt Winter had arrived; it was some of *the* coldest swimming I had ever done. Our snorkeling adventures would be short in duration, but long on scenery.

When Sheryl and I finally rowed to shore after our three-day rest, we checked in with the local Gendarme and received our 90-day clearance papers into French Polynesia.

The French official who was doing our paperwork, mentioned that not many Americans visit these islands. This gentleman seemed particularly put out that our language skills were not up to his standards. He reminded us that our 90-day tourist visa started today and *not* when we checked in again in Tahiti. After getting our passports stamped, we were dismissed and sent on our way. Nothing like the French to make you feel welcome.

The town of *Rikitea* was built along the waterfront, where the terrain was level. No more than 100 feet from shore the mountain rose, covered by dense tropical forests. Looking up, towards the top, it was evident that some terrace farming was going on, despite the steep slope.

We walked past several small warehouses that were associated with the pearl farm industry as black pearls were the number one export of the *Gambiers*. Sheryl had been hoping for the opportunity to trade for pearls, a time-honored tradition among cruisers. I believe that the days of trading pearls for a boom box or VHS tapes are a thing of the past. Now money talks, but I am sure there is still a bargain to be found.

On one of our outings we paid a visit to *Cathedral St. Michaels* the largest church in the South Pacific. Constructed in 1834 the magnificent structure was built with blocks that had been cut from coral. Honore Laval, a Jesuit priest, had come to the *Gambiers* to convert the heathens to Christianity, showing up when a civil war among the islanders was just ending. The locals that didn't die in the war were soon subjected to Laval's dictatorship. I was not sure which was worse. Building temples, churches and convents was his thing, and he put every abled bodied person to hard labor doing "God's work".

We hiked to several church ruins on the island that day and each time we were moved, thinking of the suffering this man brought to these people.

With the absence of a central market in town the locals set up food purchases rather uniquely. Their little grocery stores looked like fireworks stands back home. The merchants had small one-room buildings with rows of shelves stacked with merchandise. Customers didn't enter the store, instead they stood outside and conducted their transactions through a large window-like opening, telling the clerk what they'd like to purchase. In our case we would simply point.

We found the selections disappointing, but we were told that the inter-island cargo ship would arrive in two days and more products would be available then. I inquired and found that we might even be able to purchase diesel fuel for *Casablanca*, although there was some confusion over the quantity we could buy. The fuel for the locals came in 55 gal drums, which was way more than we could put in our boat's small tank.

I caught up to Sheryl as she came out of a small cinder block building. She was clutching two brown paper bags that were narrow and about a foot long.

"Score!" She shouted as she raised the bags high over her head like a trophy.

"What a find, outstanding work," I praised.

Sheryl had just found the 'holy grail' of the South Pacific: fresh baked baguettes. Baguettes made in these small island locations are like none other.

"Rick, what did you find out about diesel?"

"Well, the guy that works the docks says the ship may have diesel to sell, I'm just not sure if it will be a 55-gallon drum. My Gambiers language skills are not quite there yet. But forget that, let's go have bread."

It had been four weeks since the supply ship made its last appearance in Rikitea and so when it docked nearly everyone in town showed up for the event. The ship had the look of a *tramp steamer* from an old movie. It was about 200 feet long with crane booms near the center. The two-story bridge deck was placed at the stern. The hull was painted bright blue, and the bridge painted off white. Rust stains traced their way down the sides, near the anchor.

One benefit from France's nuke testing had been improvements in infrastructure. That's when the coral pass had been widened and dredged to facilitate large supply boats from Tahiti and France. They'd also built the concrete dock that the big ships could tie to.

People were milling around the dock waiting for the ship's crane to lower the first of many deliveries via cargo net. Once the net hit the ground laborers would remove the contents, then it would swing up and away, back to the cargo hold for reloading.

In addition to cargo, we were told there were eight people aboard with deck passage, meaning they slept outside until they got to where they were going. There were also six cabins available for high rollers that didn't want to be sleeping on deck. Everyone, including the crew, ate together in the mess hall. I can't even imagine the dinner conversations at the table with such a diverse group.

One highlight, for many of the locals, was a small store that would be set up in the bowels of the boat. It held quite an assortment of nonperishable items, everything from dishtowels and cosmetics to canned foods and flour.

I spoke with one of the crew who looked like he was in charge of landing the crane loads on the dock, asking him about purchasing diesel. In broken English he told me to tie alongside the ship and they would drop a fuel hose down. For the next five minutes I tried to explain I was in a small boat and needed only 20 gallons. He took a handheld radio out of his pocket and started talking quickly, in what I guessed, was Tahitian.

The dock-boss then turned to me and pointed at his watch indicating I should come back in an hour.

When I returned an hour later, I had four diesel jugs in my hands. The burly crew guy hustled me over to a three-sided storage shed that sat a short distance from the ship. Inside the shed was a 55-gallon drum with *Gazol* stenciled on the side. He had me operate the transfer pump to fill the jugs, all the while he appeared to be trying to keep himself concealed. When I finished filling the containers, he rattled off a number telling me that was the cost in French Francs. It seemed high, but I needed the fuel. After I put the jugs in the dinghy, I took a look around trying to find Sheryl.

The man who, earlier in the week, had informed me of the possibility of obtaining diesel, approached me, and apologized, saying there was no fuel for sale that day.

I didn't tell him that someone *had* sold me diesel. Out of curiosity I nonchalantly walked past the little storage shed, the one with the large *No Trespassing* sign nailed to the wall. Clearly, I hadn't seen that earlier. Oops.

I spotted Sheryl as she came down the ship's ramp, grabbing her arm and saying in a hushed tone, "Come on, time to go."

"What's wrong?" She asked.

"Well, I may have inadvertently bought fuel that wasn't for sale. I'll explain it to you on the way back to *Casablanca.*"

After my explanation, Sheryl shook her head and asked, "How do you manage to get yourself into trouble *all* the time?"

"My good looks, my big heart, my love for my fellow...."

"Please stop!" And she meant it.

On *Leave Eve* Sheryl and I were trying to look at a chart we had spread out on the table in the main salon. But Jack, ever helpful, had other ideas and was sprawled out, lying on his back covering the area we needed to study.

"Before the incredible blob laid on the chart, it looked like a straight shot from here to Moorea, maybe 900 miles. Short compared to getting here," I said lifting up Jack's tail to show Sheryl the proposed route.

We would be leaving the Gambiers after spending only 10 days there, which broke my little rule about staying in a place for at least as long as it took to get there. But we needed to move on to the rest of Polynesia before our ninety-day visa expired. Plus, the water at this latitude of the Southern Ocean was getting colder by the day.

Weather is always the final determining factor on when to pull anchor and leave a spot. In preparation we studied and analyzed forecasts from several original sources. We also listened to the *Seafarers Net* to hear what type of conditions other cruisers were experiencing on their crossings. But, when it comes right down to it, the only weather you can count on is what you have on the day you leave. Beyond that the forecasts often change, especially the further one tries to look ahead.

We sat in the cockpit that night and toasted with a couple glasses of wine, "Here's to good weather and following seas," I said clinking glasses with Sheryl and adding, "It should be a short easy trip."

Sheryl just sighed.

Chapter 18
Wake me when it's over

"Waves are not measured in feet or inches;
they are measured in increments of fear."
~ Buzzy Trent

"HOLD ON!" I yelled needlessly. We had both been 'holding on' in terror for at least five hours. My hands were frozen to the steering wheel and Sheryl had a death grip on the dodger. We were trying to keep ourselves steady as well as stay on the boat.

I heard the roar of the wave before it hit *Casablanca*. Her stern rose, and we began to surf down the enormous wave. Our boat speed was no match for the approaching giant, so when the unstable wave top collapsed, it did so right into the cockpit....

One week earlier we had departed Rikitea under cloudy skies with a light wind at our backs. The *Casablanca* Crew was looking forward to an easy, no drama, short passage to Moorea. That hope lasted for about twelve hours.

During that first night the wind had unpredictably veered from the usual Southeast trades and began coming at us from the north. This put the weather on our nose and our nice downwind sail became an upwind bash.

"Rick, here's what we should do," Sheryl said as she came up to the cockpit after downloading a new weather forecast. She informed me, "These north winds are going to continue for the next couple of days, we need to go west to avoid the Fangatau group of islands."

Originally the plan was to weave through that small cluster of atolls; with fair weather and the normal trade winds it would not have been a problem. But with these winds I agreed with Sheryl, we needed to go around and not through. Contrary winds along with the strong currents wouldn't make for a very safe passage.

It ended up taking us three days of close-hauled bashing in 15 to 20 knot winds, to clear the outer most atoll. Bashing to weather is obviously the hardest point of sail on the boat, the rigging, and the crew, hence the phrase bashing. Because of the pounding I increased my daily 'walk around the deck inspection' to three times a day, just to make sure there was no chafe or other irregularities. My worst fear was to find a stray nut or bolt on deck and not know where it came from. The decks, as well as the crew, were constantly wet, as wave after wave sluiced the length of the boat.

Sheryl and I wore our 'foulies' whenever we were on watch because more than once an errant wave would come out of nowhere throwing spray into the cockpit. My personal favorite was getting up for a night shift and putting on *wet* foul weather gear. Since salt retains water, nothing on a passage ever seems to dry out completely.

Once *Casablanca* safely cleared the last atoll in the group, we tacked east to intersect our original course. The wind continued to blow from the north, and then squally weather and frequent downpours entered the picture, as well.

It would be another long 48 hours before the weather started to shift around to the southeast, which would put the wind once again at our backs and end the relentless bashing.

With 450 miles to go we had reached the halfway point of the passage, but neither of us felt like celebrating. We were tired.

As the trade winds started to settle back in, *Casablanca* found the 15 to 20 knots on her aft quarter to her liking. We then romped along under cloudy skies and moonless nights for another couple of days.

"Less than 200 miles to go, just 48 hours if things hold like this," Sheryl informed me, doing her best to lighten the mood. We were on day 9 of a 9-day trip with 2 more days to go. That short crossing had proven, in many ways, to be tougher than the 3-week trip to the *Gambiers*.

We'd been so happy starting out knowing we only had to travel 900 miles to our next port. But the bashing and being wet most of the time was making for a very long *'short'* passage. Plus, we had run out of cookies. Oh, the humanity!

"Rick, wake up," Sheryl said using her *overly calm* voice.

"What time is it? What's wrong?" I mumbled coming out of a deep sleep and not altogether together.

"It's midnight and nothing is wrong, exactly," then she added, "I'm sorry to wake you but I think we need to reduce sail, the wind vane is kinda slewing around, I think it's because the seas are building."

"Great," was all I could manage to say.

When I poked my head out of the hatch, I was awe struck when I saw the chaos that Sheryl had been putting up with for the past couple hours.

"Sheryl, you should have called me sooner.... this is crazy," I exclaimed as a large roller sped by spewing white foam and sounding like a semi-truck.

"I figured if the noise didn't wake you up, you needed the rest," she said.

I could tell that the wind vane was having trouble keeping a steady course, which normally meant the boat was out of balance. Too much sail area quickly overpowers the vane, so correcting that was job one.

I wrestled with the main and finally got it and the boom tied down. Sheryl then raised the trysail with the halyard that ran to the cockpit. I rolled in the Genoa and replaced it with a small storm sail on the inner stay. In the hour that it took us to complete the sail changes, the wind speed had jumped up to 35 knots, but thankfully it was still coming from behind us.

The vane seemed to be working better, but still something was not quite right. It was definitely wandering more than it should with winds of that strength.

"The waves are getting huge; did you notice that about every 5 minutes a cross wave hits us on the side?" Sheryl said calmly.

"Well, we're reefed down about as far as we can be, so there is nothing to do but hang on. You want to try to get some rest?" I knew what her answer would be.

"No, but I'm going to check on Jack and maybe bring up the storm door," She said as she unclipped her safety harness and made her way below.

I knew what she was thinking: if a wave happened to come aboard the storm door would prevent the majority of sea water from going below. It replaces the decorative louvered doors that are usually in place.

Several minutes later she struggled up the stairs and clipped one end of her safety harness to the attachment point in the cockpit. As a rule, when we're outside we have our safety harnesses on and hooked to the eye bolt. This applies day or night, calm seas or rough, if we're together or especially when we are alone on watch. We have read too many stories about people lost overboard while not wearing a harness or not being tethered to the boat. The odds of recovering a person that falls over the side is extremely low.

By then the wind was dancing between 40 and 45 knots. The seas rushing by *Casablanca* were enormous, with white water being blown off the wave tops by the gale force winds. Darkness enveloped our small boat, the beam from the mast light was swallowed up by the nighttime gloom.

We both felt the need to stay up top, but I'm not sure why. When the wind started to gust over 50 knots, the seas grew even angrier and caused an unworldly moan to be emitted from the rigging keeping our nerves in a state of raw fear. It was comforting to be on watch together.

We sat huddled across from each other, under the dodger. I asked Sheryl to keep her hand on the wheel and give it a nudge if we began to wander too far off course, and I would continue to do the same from my side. We needed to speak loudly to even be heard though we were only four feet apart.

I still couldn't figure out what was up with the vane. It seemed to wander more than I had ever experienced. As a rule, the stronger the wind the more precise it steers.

Suddenly, a cross wave tumbled down on *Casablanca* and pushed the stern down with its tremendous weight. The hundreds of gallons of water were quickly returned to the sea through scupper drains, but not before completely washing down the deck.

We were both totally exhausted, but regardless, we each kept a hand on the steering wheel and as one person dozed the other kept an eye on the situation, and if necessary, pulled or pushed the wheel to help *Otto* steer the boat.

When the next large wave hit, it was like a punch to the senses. My eyes were closed, but I heard the unmistakable roar of an oversized roller approaching. In the darkness I could sense, rather than see, the huge breaker. I shouted for Sheryl to hold on as the stern began to rise, then a wall of white crashed over us and buried *Casablanca's* cockpit under a ton of seawater. Both of us were violently tossed against the cabin and a boat cushion was washed over the side. Thank God the storm door was in place.

"Sheryl are you ok!?" I asked. I could tell she was mentally running a checklist on herself.

"Yeah, I'm okay! Is the boat okay? How about you?"

We were sitting in knee deep water as the drains worked at full capacity. *Casablanca* had become sluggish with the added weight and I was terrified that another wave like the last one could sink us.

Thankfully, the next wave to board, about ten minutes later, was smaller and the cockpit only filled to our ankles.

"Sheryl, as soon as the sun comes up we need to put the sea anchor out," I informed her, then added, "We don't know how long this is going to last, and we're exhausted and need to rest."

"Rick, the waves seem to be crashing on board more," she said weakly.

"That's why we need to put out the sea anchor, it will disrupt the waves."

The sea anchor was our last ditch, last resort, survival card and it was time to play it.

Our sea anchor was basically an 18-foot diameter parachute, that had been reinforced for use on a heavy boat. The nylon material that makes up the chute is packed into a small bag. There was also 300 feet of ¾" nylon line flaked into its own bag for easy handling which was attached to a heavy-duty bridal that clipped on to the sea anchor. The combination works like this: the end of the nylon line is attached to a strong and secure point on the bow of the boat, the anchor bag goes into the water, then the line is played out and with a tug on the line the chute comes out of the bag and blossoms to its full diameter.

The para anchor breaks up the wave pattern which creates an 18-foot-wide 'slick' of relatively smoother water. Thus, basically calming the waves directly in front of the vessel as well as 'anchoring' the boat in position, minimizing the distance *Casablanca* would drift.

I had used a para anchor before, during a tropical depression that formed while I was transiting to Hawaii, so I knew firsthand the difficulty involved in its use, as well as the benefits.

Making all this happen from a pitching deck would be dangerous at best. No way we would try it in the dark, so we would just have to continue to hold on and pray things did not deteriorate any further before sunrise.

When the sky began to lighten, I could see the chaos around us, and it terrified me. Deep waves with their tops blown off by the wind marched past our small boat threatening to tumble on top of us at any time. Our wind speed indicator's last reading was 68 knots before it froze up. Actually, what had happened was the little spinning cups on the top of the mast had been blown off at that speed.

We went over the process for getting the anchor in the water as we needed to coordinate our actions very closely or the results could be disastrous. I would have to get all the gear up front and laid out, so the line could be fed out the full distance without any possibility of a tangle.

Before I could deploy the chute, we needed to turn the bow into the wind. Sheryl would need to find a lull in the wave train to turn *Casablanca* around, to bring the wind on to our nose. To aid in this maneuver, we had taken the remaining sail down and started the engine.

By heading into the wind, the boat is blown back and pulls against the sea anchor which keeps it inflated. The 180-degree turn would be one of the most critical and dangerous maneuvers we needed to make.

That turn could not take place until I had the para anchor all set up on the bow. Once I left the relative safety of the cockpit, any communication would be with hand signals.... what could go wrong?

We went over the procedure one last time.

"Please be careful, Rick, and don't fall over the side."

"Don't worry!" I shouted, "We got it, no problem." I was scared to death.

Then I clipped my tether to the jack line that runs the length of the boat. This line is attached fore and aft so when a person leaves the cockpit, clipping to it assures that if you fall over, you will still be hooked to the boat.

A person could probably still drown by being drug through the sea, but at least the boat would not sail away without you, making for an easy retrieval.

I found out very quickly that with the deck pitching wildly walking or even standing was out of the question. I had to be on my hands and knees pushing the precious bags ahead of me, battling the water that was flowing down the deck. Luckily, I'd had the foresight to hook the bags to the same jack line that I was using. We would be in deep trouble if I lost either of them overboard.

When I finally made it to the front of the boat, my extra weight caused the bow to plunge into the waves just a little more, thereby assuring that every task that needed to be performed would be done with waves washing over the foredeck, almost constantly.

Twenty minutes was all it took to get the para anchor and all the line ready to go. Once the bag with the chute was in the water, I would feed out the rope from the second bag and then stand back.

The last time I had used it, I was astonished how bar-tight 300 feet of line could get when attached to the 22,000-pound dead weight of the boat that, in turn, was being pushed back by gale force winds. If your hand was in the wrong spot, or heaven forbid, a person got tangled in the line as it was paying out.... not good.

I signaled to Sheryl that I was ready, and that it was time to do the big turnaround. We both watched the wave trains for several minutes, finally spotting an opportunity when a small lull appeared.

Sheryl turned the wheel, timing the trough perfectly, then continued thru the turn until the wind and waves were directly on our nose.

We climbed up the steep waves then down the other side. I was mesmerized at how large they were.

Sheryl's voice broke me out of my trance. I threw the bag into the tumultuous sea and when it was 100 feet away, I tugged on the line. Instantly I could tell that the chute had opened because the line started to reel out with increasing speed. I frantically triple checked to make absolutely sure the bitter end was tied to the heavily reinforced main cleat. The line was whipping out of the bag and at that point there was no stopping it. I knew it was close to reaching the end of the nylon line, so to ease the strain I had Sheryl motor forward at top speed, while she battled to keep the bow head on into the monstrous waves.

When I looked down, I was horrified to see a loop of line had gotten twisted around a nearby mooring cleat. Before I could react, the 300 feet of rope had reached its end, the 18-foot parachute fully deployed and that lightweight mooring cleat was ripped off of the bulwarks and sent flying, missing my head by mere inches.

I plopped down on the deck as Sheryl screamed to me through the wind asking if I was hurt.

I was shaking. Another couple of inches and Sheryl would've had to do the rest on her own.

On the bright side, *Casablanca* suddenly took on a completely different motion. For the first time in over 24 hours the boat wasn't being tossed around, and we didn't need to maintain a death grip to keep from being thrown overboard. The wind was still howling, but the less hectic ride was exactly what we needed.

After making sure that everything looked okay up front, I was able to crab-walk back to the cockpit.

"Rick are you okay? That thing looked like it hit you in the head and then when you sat down, I thought you were really hurt," She asked with a shaky voice. There was either a tear streaming down her face or salt water. I'm going with a tear.

"Look how much it has settled down," Sheryl said as she wiped her eyes, a weak smile coming to her face. "I kinda didn't notice at first with the noisy wind, but you're right, the sea anchor really smoothed things out," She added, with a sigh of relief.

"I'm going to stay up here for a little while, you go below, check on Jack, clean up and get some rest. We're safe now and in good shape," I reassured her and continued, "I'll be down in a bit, but you go and rest."

"Rick, I was so scared after we got flooded that last time, I thought we might end up sinking." Her tears were leaving little trails down her dried salt covered cheeks.

I took her by the shoulders, turned her around, removed the storm door and there to greet Sheryl on the top step sat Jack. He looked pissed, but with him you could never know. I realized then that I hadn't seen the big fur ball in over a day. He looked no worse for wear, so he must have found a good place to ride out the storm.

Later, satisfied that we were indeed safe, I slid the hatch open and went below. Sheryl was laying on the floor, still in her foul weather overalls, using her coat as a pillow and she was sound asleep. For his part, Jack was nuzzled up to her face, and they were each giving warmth to the other. I took off my jacket, grabbed a blanket and joined them on the floor for a couple hours of much needed rest.

Sometime later, I felt Sheryl stir and get up off the floor. After she cleaned up and changed clothes, she nudged me with her foot.

"Rick, you need to get up and wash the salt off your body," She suggested then added, "Find some fresh clothes, it makes you feel 100% better."

Picking myself up off the floor provided an unpleasant reminder that I wasn't getting any younger. I was stiff and most of my muscles ached. Thinking back, I tried to figure how much time had transpired during our ass kicking. I guessed it had been ten hours of really uncomfortable topped off by twelve hours of sheer terror. It truly was the worst sailing conditions that I had ever encountered while at sea. I never had so many breaking waves board the boat before. As always, it was the seas that made it so dangerous, in our case it seemed to be the cross swell that dumped the most water over us.

Sheryl had been right, getting the salt off of my skin had a rejuvenating effect. I was sure cleaning up helped my mental attitude as well. When I stuck my head out of the hatch things didn't look near as bad as when I had left the deck hours earlier.

Glancing at the steering wheel, a thought was pulled from my tired brain's nether regions and pushed front and center.

I made my way back to the aft cabin and pushed aside a sail bag that was being stowed on the bed, to gain access to the cabinet that held the steering quadrant.

The quadrant is an aluminum disk about two feet in diameter and an inch thick. A groove is machined around the entire edge of its circumference, and this is bolted to the rudder shaft. A small diameter stainless steel wire rope connects the steering wheel, in the cockpit, to this quadrant with the wire running around the groove. I had replaced this wire rope before setting out from Washington, over a year ago.

I was shocked at what I saw. The wire hung loosely around the quadrant, poised to fall out of the groove at any moment. It was so loose I don't know how the steering had continued to work. This answered the question as to why the wind vane had lost it sensitivity and was having difficulty steering *Casablanca.*

"Hey," I yelled to Sheryl who was in the galley, "I found the problem with the steering."

She came back to where my head was shoved in the cabinet and looking over my shoulder she asked, "What's up, whatcha find?"

"The cable that I installed last year apparently stretched out over time. I checked it before we left Mexico but missed checking it before we left the Gambiers." I continued with the sobering news, "If it had completely derailed from the quadrant, we would have lost all control and in those seas the outcome would have been disastrous."

"Can it be fixed?" She wondered.

"Sure, it will only take an hour or so. Since we're hanging on the sea anchor tightening up the cable will be a lot easier."

True to my word I had it fixed in three hours. I guess I need to hone my estimating skills.

After we'd been on the para anchor for nearly twenty-four hours, we decided that things had mellowed out enough to retrieve it and be on our way.

Getting the chute in was far easier and safer than its deployment had been. Sheryl motored slowly up the 300 feet to the anchor's location, while I brought the line in and half-assed coiled it on deck. Once we got close enough to the open canopy, I used a boat hook to 'deflate' it by pulling on its side. That is the most nerve-wracking part, keeping the nylon chute from getting tangled in the prop or rudder. Sheryl handled it like a pro and when everything was on board, we turned and set sail to Moorea, only 90 miles away.

"Nowhere did any of the forecasts say that shit was coming," exclaimed Sheryl, who normally was not prone to swearing.

"You're right. It was one of those big misses by the weather forecasters," was all I could say.

"I don't want to go through that kind of terror ever again," she informed me.

"We will figure it out, don't worry." I didn't tell Sheryl, but I had been trying to 'figure out' the weather for the last ten years... with limited success.

Chapter 19
Catching a breath

"Any damn fool can navigate the world sober.
It takes a really good sailor to do it drunk."
~ Sir Francis Chichester

We sailed by historic Point Venus around mid-morning and without further incident. The lighthouse was a welcome sight after our passage from *Hell*. Steeped in history the structure was erected where Captain Cook had set up an observatory in 1769 to watch the transit of Venus during a solar eclipse.

Casablanca would bypass Tahiti and continue on to Moorea, some 30 miles away. The reason was simple: though I had been to French Polynesia twice before I had yet to get to this island gem that I had always heard so much about. I wanted to explore it for the first time with Sheryl. It would be much more interesting than the big city of Papeete and a much better introduction to French Polynesia for her.

We dropped anchor off the famous *Hotel Bali Hai* in Cooks Bay. As the sun was dipping behind the mountains, Sheryl and I enjoyed a wonderful swim around *Casablanca*. Jack looked on, probably puzzled, trying to figure out why our heads were floating on the water.

"Think about this," I said as I swam up to my wife, "Two days ago, we were drenched and wet and cold, what's the first thing we do when we get here?"

"We get in the water," She said smiling, relaxing while floating on her back.

Remarkably, I think we were already beginning to forget the passage that had just culminated. There is an old saying that talks about cruisers having short memories or they wouldn't keep on cruising.

Several days later, when the boat was again livable, we found our cleanest dirty clothes to wear to shore. After launching the dinghy, I rowed the short distance to the dock near the hotel where we tied up the small boat.

During a walk around the area we managed to find a couple of small stores, a place that would do our laundry and best of all a pizza joint with outside seating. While waiting for the first slice to touch our lips since Mexico, I struck up a conversation with a couple seated nearby. They were an older man and his wife who were off a 40 something sized cruising boat that was anchored close to *Casablanca*.

Phil was short, with a grizzled look, brown leather-like skin, a few chin hairs, big arm muscles and the requisite hoop earring. Her husband Jerry, on the other hand, was rail thin, tall, buzz cut hairstyle and really didn't speak much.

"You kids just come in?" Her voice boomed louder than needed, since we were just sitting at the next table.

Before I could answer, Phil went on, "We got caught in that bullshit, excuse my French, a bunch of days ago."

Sheryl replied, "We were coming from......"

"And you know what? That sucker was nowhere in the weather prediction we got," She continued. Phil was a loud talker.

Jerry added rather meekly, "Nowhere."

Suddenly changing subjects, Phil asked, "You kids seen the rays at the beach?"

"No, we *just* got off the boat today," We replied nearly in unison.

"Well, go to the sand beach south of the hotel and take some meat, you know tuna, sardines something fishy, then wade out to your waist and they will come right to ya. You can pet them. It's very cool. Go early cuz the tourists over-run the place by 10."

Our pizza arrived and there was a momentary silence as we savored the circular piece of heaven. After coming up for air I asked Phil if she had run into a boat called *Reefer Madness*.

"Nicky is the captain.... she was sailing to the Marquesas," I stated.

The look I got from that woman could have melted steel. All she said was, "Yes, I know Nicky."

Wanting to avoid getting punched out, I dropped that inquiry like a hot piece of pepperoni.

Not much else was said after that. We quickly finished and grabbed a to-go box for the rest of the pie and headed for the boat.

"Rick, you sure can turn a peaceful meal into something so much more," Sheryl razzed me.

"Boy, did you see the look Phil gave me? I thought she was going to grab me by the throat," Then I added, "Guess we won't be seeing much of those two while we are here."

"Especially if Nicky is around," Sheryl assured me.

The next morning, after again tying up to the hotel dock, we talked to a nice Polynesian lady at the front desk and she filled us in on the exact location of the 'ray buffet'. The directions sounded vague. We were only told to look for a long, white sand beach, about 800 meters away. We actually had no trouble finding the beach, turns out it was the only white sand beach within miles.

I carried a small backpack that held a water bottle and two cans of tuna fish. Sheryl and I navigated the narrow path next to the road, finding ourselves at the beach a short time later.

"No one here, but this must be the place." I was eyeing the shallow water for movement.

"So, what do we do? I don't see any rays," Sheryl asked, looking a little leery.

"Well, let's grab a can of tuna and wade out a bit."

Before she could say "This is nuts", I grabbed her hand and together we shuffled out to knee deep water and then continued on till it was up to our waists.

I opened up the can of tuna and at that same moment Sheryl grabbed my arm, like she wanted to head to shore. In the aqua blue water, I spotted what she had already seen. Three discs roughly the size of garbage can lids were barreling our way from about 25 feet out. Thinking they were intent on knee capping us, I started a slow backward retreat. When the three got to within arm's reach they stopped and hovered in place, looking at us with small marble like eyes.

The five of us just stared at each other until I reached into the tuna can and pulled out a pinch. The larger of the rays moved in so close that he was rubbing against me. When I submerged my hand holding the tuna, the one I called *big boy* used his toothless mouth to start gumming my fingers.

The others were not far behind and they would literally push each other out of the way to get more tuna. Sheryl and I held bits of the meat while the velvet soft, puppy like creatures, rubbed against our legs making smacking noises as they ate.

We quickly went through the two cans of tuna. With nothing more to offer, the rays lost interest in us and made their way over to some newcomers that were just wading in.

Before reaching shore, I felt something rough brush against my lower leg. Looking over my shoulder, I spotted the long, sleek shape of a shark circling back toward us, apparently scavenging for leftovers.

"Hey, look behind you," I said softly to Sheryl.

"Damn!" She went from knee deep water to shore seemingly in one motion, and we had been out about 100 feet from the beach.

I just shuffled slowly, thinking if he bit me it would probably be more like a dog bite. Growing concerned that the empty tuna cans, that were stuffed in my short's pockets, might agitate *Sharky*, I picked up the pace to shore taking the cans out of my pants as a precaution.

Sheryl and I had a marvelous week on Moorea. We rented bikes from the hotel and peddled around the island getting our legs back in shape. We hiked several challenging trails that were nearby the anchorage, but most of our free time was spent in the water either snorkeling, cleaning the bottom of *Casablanca* or just motoring around in the dinghy.

All too quickly our time in Moorea drew to a close. There were a few minor boat problems that needed to be taken care of before the long trip to Hawaii, so we would head to Papeete for provisions and repairs. There we could find everything we would need.

That four-hour sail to Tahiti was, thankfully, uneventful. The trade winds blew in the teens with large white puffy clouds racing us across the water. We were happy to find the narrow pass through the barrier reef well marked. We dropped the sails as we motored through the deeper water of the channel. About a dozen surfers were riding the swell that formed in the shallow water adjacent to the entrance.

Jack and I had been to Tahiti several years ago. The city of Papeete had held little interest for me except that it was a great port for provisioning and boat parts. In fact, I had even been able to get a new diesel engine straight from Japan delivered to a local marine store on that trip. The old motor that had been in *Casablanca*, was tired and suddenly decided that it did not enjoy the cruising lifestyle, so it refused to function reliably.

We picked up a mooring ball outside of a new marina that had just opened less than a month before our arrival. It was the first time we hadn't had to deal with anchoring since we left Mexico. While I was out fiddling with the mooring lines, we got a surprise call on the VHF radio.

"*Casablanca, Casablanca* this is *Reefer Madness*."

"Rick, Nicky is calling on the radio. She must be close by," Sheryl called to me with surprise in her voice.

I grabbed the radio mic and replied, "Hey, great to hear you, let's switch channels to talk."

Turned out *Madness* was moored just six boats over from us. Nicky said she had been watching the surfers in the pass when she spotted us coming through. We made plans to get together and have dinner on shore that evening.

"I'm looking forward to finding out how Nicky knows Phil, the gal we met in Moorea," I pondered, adding, "Remember the cold shoulder we got after bringing up Nicky's name?"

"You don't think the wise move would be to say nothing, possibly avoiding an awkward situation?" Sheryl questioned, giving me an almost pleading look.

"Nah," I replied.

"You're hopeless," she said shaking her head.

Later that day we met Nicky at a shore-side restaurant that was run by a French ex-pat. I attempted to order a hamburger and was told by the surly middle-aged waiter, "We do not serve *hum bag errs*"

Not to be deterred I went on, "Then I will have an order of French fries, instead."

The look on the waiter's face made it clear that 'joke time' was over.

Sheryl to the rescue, "He'll have a salad."

To which I added, "With French dressing, *por fa for.*"

When the pride of France left with our meal order, Nicky said, "He will probably spit in your salad."

"Nah, he likes me. Anyway, how was your trip to the Marquesas?"

For the next 15 minutes Nicky talked about her trip to the islands after leaving the Galapagos. Generally, she had an okay passage. Her and the lone crew mate started out fast but languished the last week of the voyage. It seems that they were low on fuel and running out of food and making very slow progress the last few days. Their coffee supply ran out well before landfall, and that may have led to some difference of opinion on board.

"So, I'm single handing again until my new crew gets here for the trip to Hawaii."

I was sensing a pattern.

"Wow, that's too bad about your crew bailing," Sheryl said, then added, "When are you leaving for Hawaii?"

"Two weeks from now, give or take, that's when my new crew will be here. There's some boat work to be done and a shake down sail. We will head to the Tuamotus to get east and then turn north to Honolulu," Nicky answered with confidence.

Sheryl gave me the subtle, *'don't open your mouth'* glare that I am quite familiar with.

Due to some bad past experiences with buddy boating, we try to avoid the awkwardness of having to tell someone we don't want to sail with them, especially on a long voyage. The plan that Nicky had just laid out was our choice of routes as well, with almost the same time frame.

So, to deflect the conversation in a new direction I asked Nicky, "Do you know a woman who has the skin of an old catcher's mitt? I think her name was....?"

Nicky replied, "Phyllis or Phil for short... yeah, I know Phil." I could tell by her tone I had hit a nerve.

"She sends her greetings," I lied. About this time my wife looked down at the table and slowly shook her head.

"I find that hard to believe, the last time I saw her we had unpleasant words," Nicky informed me.

There was silence as I picked through my salad looking for any of the waiter's misdeeds. Then Nicky offered, "When I got to Nuka Hiva my crew flew out and there were a couple of projects on *Reefer Madness* that I needed advice on. Jerry and Phil had been in the harbor for a week or so before I met them, and Jerry was nice enough to come over to the boat a few times and help with a couple things. Well, the next thing I know Phil is accusing me of flirting with her husband and taking up too much of his time. She made a big stink and so here we are."

We really liked Nicky, so I offered to help out until her crew arrived.

The following two weeks I split my time between *Casablanca* and *Madness*. None of the work on either vessel was serious, just time consuming. And unlike Phil, Sheryl wasn't bothered in the least and actually enjoyed the little bit of alone time it offered her.

Eventually both boats were ready to go and the process of buying and storing food began in earnest. By that time, it was no secret that we were all headed in the same direction around the same time, so it was sort of assumed we would leave together. The one exception was that in our plan we would be hauling *Casablanca* out of the water at Apataki atoll, for a quick bottom paint job. The facility was fairly new, and I figured it would be easier and cheaper to do the painting there, rather than Hawaii.

"Sheryl, Rick, I would like to introduce you to Marvin, he's going to crew with me to Hawaii," Nicky announced one evening as she approached our table with a guy in tow. They then joined us at the outdoor beach bar that was just a block from the marina.

Marvin explained that he was a captain and a helicopter pilot and had been involved with the search and rescue branch of the Coast Guard. Nearly six-feet-tall with piercing blue eyes and a buzz cut, he talked with the swagger of someone who was important, or at least he thought he was.

After the usual 'feeling out' process that guys do, I got right down to it and asked, "Have you done much offshore sailing?"

"No, but I have picked a few sailors out of the water during some pretty hairy storms," He replied rather smugly. "Plus, I have done a lot of day sailing," he added.

Of course, it took every bit of restraint I could muster not to say something, something like, *"this won't be like any day sail you've ever been on"*.

After more small talk, Marvin excused himself and went looking for the latrine.

"So, you guys, what do you think of Marvin so far?" Nicky asked tentatively.

Sheryl was quick to reply, "Oh he's cute and those eyes!"

"I know!" said Nicky. "Big arms, too."

"You both sound like you're back in junior high," then I added, "Let's see how captain blue eyes fares after a month on the open ocean," I followed that with, "So where did you find *Captain Morgan*?"

It took a minute for Nicky to figure out who I meant and then she said, "I placed an ad in the crew wanted section of a west coast sailing magazine and we exchanged e-mails. He had a month of leave coming and he says this is his dream, to sail the open ocean."

Sheryl looked at me and smiled asking, "Rick, are you a little intimidated, maybe?"

"Hardly but I bet......"

"What did I miss?" Questioned Marvin sauntering back and flashing his wide, ultra-white smile.

"Not a thing," Nicky responded, almost dreamily.

When we got back aboard *Casablanca* after meeting *Captain Courageous* Sheryl asked what I thought of the arrangement.

"Well, let's see how far his looks get him when things go to hell," I answered.

"Oh, still just a little sensitive having a macho guy around, are you?" She teased smiling coyly.

"I just think he doesn't know what he is getting into and most of all with whom," Then I added, "And I am far from the jealous type."

At that Sheryl replied with a stream of laughter that lasted an uncomfortably long time.

During our last week of preparation, before leaving for the Tuamotus, our primary goal was to stuff as much, in the way of provisions, into every spare bit of space that we had left on *Casablanca*. Not only food, but paper towels, toilet paper, anything that we might need in the next six weeks. We would be spending a week or more in the Tuamotus without the luxury of any stores for shopping. And the trip to Hawaii could take as long as a month.

Provisioning in French Polynesia was crazy expensive. While many food items were subsidized by the government, making the prices more reasonable, liquor was not one of them. Hard alcohol seemed to start around 50 dollars a bottle at the markets and skyrocketed from there. However, there was a catch.

A few days before leaving Papeete, we stopped by the immigration office to make sure our paperwork was in order. Everything was perfect until the lovely Polynesian girl we had been dealing with, asked about our *Liquor Voucher*. Explaining that we had no idea what she was asking for, she held up an official looking paper, that was written in French. Between the three of us we figured out that because we had checked into the country in the Gambiers, it had not been included in our paper work.

The young lady gave us directions to the liquor warehouse along with a slip of paper that was basically *'keys to the kingdom'*. Due to an antiquated rule from a hundred and fifty years ago, sailors were allowed enough liquor to have one bottle of alcohol a day until his next port. For Sheryl and me that meant, in theory, we could buy up to 60 bottles of whatever. The best part was there would be no duty or taxes on the purchase. They figure a sailor is due his daily ration of rum on a voyage.

Once in the liquor store we were like kids in a… liquor store. Every American brand, many that I hadn't seen in over a year, stocked the shelves. A variety of wines held Sheryl's interest. We spent an hour filling up two shopping carts before we were done. The prices were very reasonable, and they would deliver everything to the dock at the marina the next day. The one restriction that was made very clear, both at the immigration office and the liquor barn, was that we could not open any of our newfound gains, until we were out of French territorial waters. Like that's gonna happen.

The plan was in place, such as it was; *Casablanca* and *Reefer Madness* would make the two-day sail to the Tuamotus, where we would go to Apataki for a quick haul out, and Nicky would go to nearby Rangiroa, before we both headed to Hawaii.

Like most cruising plans this one started on a pleasant note with a fine forecast. Both boats left the mooring field at sunrise, under clear skies accented with a few puffy clouds. The wind was light on our nose.

".... and the forecast called for 48 hours of light winds and smooth seas! So, don't ask me what the hell is happening," I bemoaned exasperated. It seemed that the weather forecasts were getting further from reality with every passage.

The sun had just begun to set as we pounded into 4 to 5-foot seas and 12 to 18 knots of wind, still dead on our nose. The day had started out as predicted with light conditions and a happy crew, but by noon the wind had come up and the seas started building about two hours later. It was definitely not the worst conditions we'd ever been in, but none the less, it was uncomfortable and not fun. At least Sheryl and I were able to maintain a decent watch schedule, although neither of us slept very well that first night.

Reefer Madness was sailing close by and we could see their mast light in the night but lost visual track of them after the sun came up. We were still in radio contact with Nicky and commiserated about the terrible weather.

"How's everything on board?" Sheryl asked at the midnight check-in.

"Fine," Came Nicky's terse reply.

Sheryl, as was her custom, brought out a hot cup of cocoa and said good night.

Just as she was preparing to lie down, she asked, "How do you think Marvin's doing?"

"If the wind lets up and doesn't get any worse, he should be fine, besides, he is, after all, in the Coast Guard so he must go out on ships sometime," was my answer.

The night drug on and the conditions did not improve, in fact, we seemed to be pounding more than ever. Since the boat was fully loaded with provisions, not to mention a year's worth of booze, we sat lower in the water and hobby horsed more than usual.

The following day the conditions were unfortunately about the same. The wind was forward of the beam, blowing 15 to 18 knots and the seas were steep, but spread out, with wind chop producing white caps.

Our random check-ins with *Madness* did not give us any indication of how it was going over there. They were around 5 miles behind us and, for once, I chose not to pry into their state of affairs.

Sheryl downloaded a new weather forecast, and it was troubling.

The winds were now supposed to strengthen to 20 knots. That in itself is not the end of the world, especially if you're anchored safely in a lagoon somewhere, but it's getting *into* the lagoon that might be the problem.

Many of the atolls in the Tuamotus are ringed with a barrier reef that surrounds the island and gives great protection from the ocean waves. In order for ships, cruising boats or even small craft to get to the villages or towns that are within a reef they must transit a pass that can be either natural or manmade. Often these reefs are not exposed or only rise up a few feet above sea level. When the wind blows hard for a long period of time, the resulting wave action pushes a tremendous amount of water over the barrier into the lagoon. The extra sea water inside the reef needs a place to go, so it flows out at the point of least resistance: the pass.

To safely transit a pass in calm conditions, the rule of thumb is you wait for *slack tide*. Slack tide is theoretically the hour or so when the tide is neither coming into the pass nor going out of the pass. Big ships can be more flexible because they can just power through the currents.

The outflow can reach up to 8 knots or more, often resulting in a standing wave which makes traveling through a pass a bit hair raising, even in calm conditions.

Unfortunately, each atoll was different and there was no way to know if you could get into a lagoon until you actually saw the conditions in the pass.

We arrived outside the pass for Apataki an hour before sunset. The entrance to the lagoon was on the lee of the atoll, meaning that we were in relatively calm water with 15 knots of wind. The pass, however, was a frothy white capped river pouring out of the atoll into the surrounding sea.

We got to within a mile of the entrance and after studying the water for several minutes through the binoculars I told Sheryl, "There's no way we can get in there before sunset, the current is crazy, we wouldn't stand a chance."

I was bummed enough for both of us.

"So, I think the best plan is to hang out here tonight. We are in fairly calm water, we can just drift, letting the wind blow us away from shore. When we feel that we need to get closer we turn on the engine and motor back, then drift back again. We should be able to get some rest until sunup." That was my plan, such as it was.

Sheryl looked at me with deep skepticism and then observed, "You're delusional if you think we can get any sort of rest, hanging outside this entrance."

"I don't know what else to say, we can't go in under these conditions. I'm just hoping that things will calm down enough by daybreak to try."

Suddenly the radio came alive and Nicky was calling to tell us that she was having an overheating problem with her engine. I explained our proposed plan of hanging out until sunrise and suggested that maybe she should divert to our location instead of going to Rangiroa. Once we were anchored in the lagoon, I could take a look at her engine. She agreed and several hours later we could see the running lights from *Reefer Madness* bobbing in the swell about a mile from our position.

For the next eight hours we hung outside the entrance to Apataki, motoring back to the original position about every three hours. Nicky was farther offshore and talking to her on the radio it sounded as if they were working hard to maintain their position.

As the night drug on, Sheryl did manage to download a new weather forecast, and it did not show any change. Winds would remain fresh, 15 to 20 knots with 6 to 8-foot seas at 14 seconds.

An hour before sunrise I was still optimistic that things would change enough to allow us to proceed into the lagoon. As dawn slowly lit up the morning sky, my optimism dimmed. If anything, the pass had become even more turbulent.

A short time later Sheryl came on deck grabbing the binoculars from their holder and surveyed the pass. Without taking her eyes from the glasses she whispered, "We need to head back."

"Wait, you mean *back* to Tahiti?" I said with astonishment, though the thought had crossed my mind, too.

Handing me the binoculars she added, "That pass is not going to get any better today, we're just wasting our time hanging out here. We can go back, re-group and try it again, hopefully with a better weather forecast."

"The thing that gets me, is that once again the forecast didn't match the conditions we encountered. We would have never left Papeete if I'd had a clue it would be anything like this," I lamented, as my frustration began to boil to the surface. What worried me most, was that we still had to travel over 2500 miles to Honolulu. If you can't count on the weather predictions, it could prove to be a very long and tense voyage full of unwanted surprises.

"You're right. We do need to go back. I'll call Nicky, explain what our plans are, and she can do what she wants." A tough decision on my part, as I had never turned back in the thousands of ocean miles I had traveled. But, given the situation, it was the logical and safe move.

Almost before I finished telling Nicky of our new plan, she was turned around and heading back to Tahiti. Obviously, she was relieved to have that decision made for her.

The trip back was much like the trip out: lots of wind and waves with little sleep. My mood was not great when we finally tied up to the marina buoy whence we'd come. The prospect of traveling in nasty weather for the upcoming long passage to Hawaii had me questioning why the hell we were doing this in the first place. The thrill and the rewards of offshore voyaging were slowly being edged out by sleepless nights in a small storm-tossed boat. I knew in my heart that *Casablanca* was a great offshore cruiser and would hold up better than her crew in tough situations, but I was getting plain tired of battling Mother Nature.

"Who are you talking to?" Sheryl asked sticking her head out of the hatch.

"Just the usual guys," I said pointing to my head.

That unsettled weather lasted a week in which we spent our time cleaning and straightening out the boat.

Nicky, on the other hand, had several problems to remedy such as the overheating problem that had cropped up. The first thing she did was put her dinghy in the water then she and '*captain blue eyes*' motored to shore. She swung by *Casablanca* on her way back to *Madness* sans Marvin.

Sheryl invited Nicky onboard, but she declined, saying she needed to get back to the boat and clean it up, but she did fill us in on the details of the last couple days.

"Well Rick, you were right about macho man, he folded pretty early in the game. On that first night of rough weather, he started to make suggestions on how we should be handling the storm. By the next day, he was practically giving orders on how we should be sailing. He got sick and didn't make it out on deck then blamed me for making it an uncomfortable ride." She continued, "But the worst part came when the engine started to overheat, and I asked for a little help to figure out what was going on and he refused to come below. I am so thankful that you guys called and said you were heading back; I was at my wits end trying to figure out how to handle *Marvin the Ass*. Anyway, he is staying on shore until he can get a flight out. The ass."

I thought she seemed close to crying, so I changed the subject by asking, "What's up with your engine?"

"Don't know. I changed the water pump impellers, but that didn't help. So, I'm going to get hold of a mechanic that the marina recommended.

We talked a little longer, then Nicky dinghied back to her boat.

"Ok, Ok, let's hear it and get it over with," Sheryl said after Nicky was out of ear shot.

Smiling, I knew exactly what she was referring to. "What are you talking about?" I asked, with as much surprise as I could muster.

"You know darn well, predicting that Marvin was going to be a flop, maybe a little '*I told you so*' will lift your mood," Sheryl taunted.

"Don't be silly, I take no pleasure in being right all the time," I said smiling, "But, seriously, it's too bad that Nicky has such trouble with crew. I think the word *Reefer* should be dropped from the boats name and simply call it what it is."

"You may want to keep that idea just between us," Sheryl cautioned.

For the next several days I was moody, thinking about the trip to Hawaii. I looked online at the possibility of shipping *Casablanca* back to the west coast, though I knew that was never going to happen. We hadn't even set a new departure date.

I was in a funk. But while I wallowed in procrastination, Sheryl had been doing her homework.

Chapter 20
Apataki

"You can always tell a cruiser.... but you can't tell him much."
~ old adage

"Back so soon?" Sheryl asked as she heard me climbing aboard *Casablanca* from the dinghy.

"If the mechanic had his way, I would have been back even sooner," I replied.

"Hopefully, you didn't cause any problems for Nicky."

Reefer Madness was still having over heating issues. Nicky had contacted a local mechanic to have a look, after I had spent a day trying to figure out the problem for her, to no avail.

"No, I didn't cause any problems but the mechanic who, by the way was French, made it clear my help was not needed. Plus, Frenchie had a helper, and with four of us crammed around the engine compartment, the space was getting tight."

Sitting in the cockpit, I could see down into the cabin where Sheryl was banging away on the computer.

"What are you working on?" I inquired.

"Rick, what do you know about weather routers?"

"Well, I know big shipping companies use them to keep their cargo ships away from serious storms," I stated, then added, "And I also know that ocean racers use routers to direct them closer to stormy weather for the sake of speed. Why do you ask?"

Sheryl turned the computer toward me as I came down the stairs. On the screen was a picture of a sailboat heading into a huge black storm cloud with the caption: *Don't let the unknown spoil your day!*

"I've been in contact with a guy named Jeff Duval, he is the owner of a service called *World Wide Weather*. It's pretty interesting. For a small fee, he will study the wind and waves for our proposed route and direct us around any problems the weather might throw at us. I got the idea after looking for an alternative source for weather forecasts," She said with excitement in her voice.

"So, he sends what he thinks is going to happen in an e-mail over the ham radio?" I was intrigued.

"Yeah, here's the deal, we give him all the vital stats on *Casablanca*, sail area, hull speed, how much fuel we carry, cruiser or racer all that stuff. Then he looks at where we want to go and plans out the safest and fastest way to get there. He will contact us every other day with updates or.... and this is big.... if something pops up, he can tell us how long it will last or how to alter our course to be more comfortable."

Being able to know how long a weather system would last was a key to cruising with less anxiety. Our most recent voyages had been rough, especially not knowing if things would get better or worse, mainly because they were not predicted in the first place. So, I was warming up to the idea of having a third party looking at the BIG weather picture for us.

The next day Sheryl sent all the data to Jeff regarding the boat specs, our intended destination and emergency contact information. This last request gave me pause, wasn't he supposed to keep us from having to use that bit of info?

We told him that our first stop would be in the Tuamotus. He wrote back inviting us to use his service for free on our passage to Apataki. He would work up a sail plan and let us know the optimum time to depart.

While there was renewed excitement aboard *Casablanca,* that was not the case on *Reefer Madness.* The engine problem that Nicky was experiencing was serious enough that the engine head would need to come off and be machined. This would be no small undertaking. Her time was running out and she would need to get a visa extension from Immigration to stay and have the work performed.

We, on the other hand, needed to get going. The end of our allotted 90 days was fast approaching, and we had no reason for an extension. Plus, I still wanted to pull the boat for a quick bottom job at Apataki atoll.

Two days later, Jeff from *World Wide Weather* sent an e-mail to Sheryl letting her know that the passage to Apataki would see favorable conditions for the next week.

We were stocked up and ready to go, so there really wasn't much to do the night before leaving: *Leave Eve.* We rowed over to *Reefer Madness,* to share one last bottle of wine and a few appetizers.

Nicky looked somber, in part, I'm sure, due to our leaving. She was also facing a rather significant engine problem. Even though her spirits were at a low point, she managed a smile.

"This better not be the wine you're not supposed to open until you're out of territorial waters," She joked and then added, "I found crew for the trip up and I know he won't back out. It's my ex-husband."

Nicky laughed, "I wish you could see the look on your faces. Rick, you can close your mouth now. My ex and I are still very good friends and he offered to help me sail to Hawaii, so I took him up on his moment of weakness and said okay."

The three of us talked and drank well into the evening. Under the influence of a nice bottle of contraband wine, we made promises to stay in touch and hopefully meet up in Hawaii.

That night, getting ready for bed, Sheryl pointed out it seemed Nicky's crew mates had come full circle with her ex-husband in the mix. He had been crew on her maiden voyage.

"Full circle crazy," was all I said.

The sky was overcast when I unhooked from the buoy the following morning. Sheryl had gotten an update from Jeff, late the night before, stating the weather was still a go but he indicated that there was a chance of a morning marine layer, in other words low clouds. It was predicted to burn off by noon. As a free gift added to the already free service, Jeff plotted out the timing for slack tide at the atoll to which we were headed. I was really warming up to this guy.

The two-day passage turned out as advertised with smooth seas and light trade winds. The white puffy cotton ball clouds were a welcome sight during the day and the night was so calm and clear that we were able to participate in something we hadn't done in some time: star gazing. Jack even joined us in the cockpit, although wearing a safety harness and leash always made him a little cranky.

"That's the Southern Cross," I was pointing out the constellations that I knew, to Sheryl and the cat. "That group right there is Cetus the Whale. And if I am not mistaken that's.... Yer-anus."

"Har, Har haven't heard that one in a while, probably not since third grade," She chided me good naturedly. Then before I knew it, we were locked in a rather passionate embrace and Sheryl whispered in my ear, "You need new material."

A minor commotion brought us back to reality.

Jack, after having seen enough, chose to head down stairs. Unfortunately, his leash was tied short so when he jumped from the stairs, he came to an abrupt stop and just hung in midair, gently swinging back and forth in rhythm with the motion of the boat. He was not happy.

By late afternoon on the second day, *Casablanca* was lined up and heading into the pass at Apataki. What a difference good weather makes!

The entrance was unrecognizable from the frothy outflow we had seen two weeks earlier. It hadn't reached slack tide, but we chose to try to get into the atoll, anyway. The outgoing current was only a couple of knots, so with the engine at 3/4 speed *Casablanca* lugged through the pass and a mile later were in the calm clear waters of the atoll. The clarity of the lagoon was astounding. Our depth sounder was reading 45 feet to the bottom, but the coral and brightly colored fish looked only a few feet away.

The haul out facility was almost twelve miles from the entrance, so we needed to hurry to get there before dark. Again, as is the case in French Polynesia, the channel was well marked and meandering. I was sure we crossed over our same track at least once during our quest to the far side of the atoll.

The last remnant of sunlight disappeared as we were tying up to one of the round floats near a concrete boat ramp. We had made it.

"This must be the place; I can just make out some sailboat masts back in that clearing. We'll need to go in tomorrow first thing and see if they can haul us out," I said. While I was thinking about the upcoming haul out, my wife was thinking about what had just ended.

"Rick, can you believe how pleasant the last two days were?" Then she continued, "I know it was only a short trip, but it was nice knowing that Jeff was watching the weather. With him giving us semi-daily up-dates, we are going to have more accurate information on what's ahead of us on the way to Hawaii. I still plan on down loading the high seas forecasts as I usually do. I have a feeling that this is going to be a pleasant trip."

"Whoa there, you are making predictions. You always tell me it's bad luck, that I am responsible for all bad things that happen."

"It is bad luck to make predictions and you are responsible for all bad things," She said as she kissed my cheek.

The next morning, after putting the dinghy in the water, we rowed to shore, landing on a stretch of crushed coral next to the concrete ramp.

"My gosh, look at this!" Sheryl had walked over to the ramp.

Looking to where she was pointing, it was indeed an unusual sight. Near the top of the incline, the name 'Apataki' was spelled out in one-foot tall letters made of black pearls embedded in the cement. They weren't perfect jewelry quality pearls, but black pearls all the same.

"These are probably worth more than our boat," I joked.

Sheryl looked up and said with some hope in her voice, "Looks like I should be able to trade for some pearls here." So far, her luck at finding inexpensive pearls had hit a wall.

Sheryl chose to walk the beach while I found the office and made the haul-out arrangements. After a short hike I saw a small drift wood sign that read office nailed to a palm tree. It had an arrow pointing down a grass path.

Chickens were running around pecking at the multitude of bugs that skittered across the ground and a grunting pig caught my attention as I got closer to a small building. There was a clothes line on one side of the structure, that had colorful sheets gently waving in the tropical breeze. The door was open, so I poked my head in and immediately determined that this was someone's residence. I stood in the doorway while my eyes adjusted to the dark interior.

"Can I help?" Came a man's voice causing me to jump in surprise.

"Yes, ah, ah, we would like to haul out, is that possible?"

The short, dark-skinned fellow was clearly amused at sneaking up on me and he showed it with a huge, toothless grin.

He extended his hand and introduced himself as Rene. I followed Rene into the house where we sat down at his kitchen table. He spoke very passable English. I explained that we wanted to paint the bottom of our boat and only needed to be out of the water a few days.

"How deep the *kel*?" He asked.

It took me a minute to figure out what he needed, but I finally replied, "Oh, the keel. We draw 6 feet," when he looked at me a bit confused, I added, "two meters."

Rene grabbed a small book and thumbed through the printed numbers.

"We can haul today, good tide," Then he asked, "You have paint for the bottom?"

"Yes, we have everything we need on board. I didn't see a lift.... how do you take the boats out?"

"Chariot," was his one-word reply.

Before I could get a definition of chariot, Sheryl wandered in.

I introduced Sheryl to Rene, and she commented on the beautiful beach near his house. As we were leaving, Sheryl showed me some shells she had found. She also told me she'd seen a couple kids feeding a shark. Apparently, it would come into very shallow water and take pieces of meat from the children, the entire time their dog was running up and down the beach barking at it.

"Nurse shark," Rene said smiling, "not hurtful."

"Well, you wouldn't see me feeding that guy. He was about this big," She said stretching her arms as wide as she could.

We needed to wait for the afternoon high tide to haul-out, so I convinced Sheryl to go snorkeling with me in the meantime.

"Bommies, what the heck are bommies?" Sheryl asked.

"They are the coral heads that grow from the bottom of the lagoon to just beneath the surface," I explained, and then I added, "The sea life that lives around them...... incredible."

"Sharks."

"What?"

"Will we see sharks?" There was a look of concern on my wife's face.

"If we do, they won't be the dangerous open ocean kind, these guys will be small, no big deal," I said giving her my best sales pitch.

We mounted the out board on the dinghy and after the twentieth pull it sputtered to life, followed by an abundance of blue smoke.

We motored about a mile from shore, towards the center of the lagoon. There we dropped the small anchor on a shelf about six feet down, making sure we didn't disturb the coral itself.

"I'll get in first and check it out." With that I slipped over the edge of the inflatable, dove down, repositioned the anchor and then motioned for Sheryl to join me. The Bommie that I had chosen was nearly 20 feet in diameter. We began to circle around the pinnacle of coral. Our heads were on swivels at the beginning, keeping an eye out for any unwanted guests.

We slowly started to relax and enjoyed the explosion of color that made up the small ecosystem. My wife and I circled the coral island several times in both directions, on each pass spotting something interesting that we hadn't seen before.

We'd been in the water about twenty minutes, when I felt Sheryl's hand grip my calf with a vice-like hold. She was pointing to a patch of water, but I saw nothing. We surfaced, and she told me she saw a shark.

"Don't worry these guys won't hurt you," I said trying to sound convincing.

"Rick, I'm going to the dinghy," She stated. There would be no debate on that.

The inflatable was about twenty feet away, on the far side of the Bommie and I told Sheryl, "Okay, let's just swim slowly back to the dink. I will keep an eye out, but I am sure there won't be any problems." Before I'd gotten the last words out of my mouth, I could see Sheryl was already climbing up the ladder into the boat. So much for staying calm and not attracting attention.

Just to prove my point about the minimal danger the shark posed, I slowly swam back, even diving down to get a better look at a colorful tropical fish or two.

Reaching the small boat, I teased, "See I told you he wouldn't be a problem."

"Rick, before I climbed out, I saw two more sharks."

That got my attention, so before I got out of the water, I took one more look around and sure enough shark number one had invited his family to supper. At that point they were just meandering around and didn't look to be aggressive, but those cold dead eyes gave me the creeps, so I exited the pool. Promptly.

"See, I told you they were harmless."

"You know I don't believe your BS about those guys not biting. Besides, you got out of the water pretty fast when the others showed up, Mr. Tough Guy," she chided me.

"I just make it a point not to be out numbered."

Despite the party crashers, the snorkeling had been great. Sheryl even found a really nice *vacant* shell to add to her collection.

A few hours later I found out what a *chariot* was.

Casablanca slowly motored towards the concrete ramp that held an oversized boat trailer submerged in the clear water. The trailer was attached by a thick cable to a winch at the rear of a backhoe. Several hydraulic hoses stretched from the machine to the trailer.

The tractor sat at the top of the ramp, about twenty-five feet away, and it was chained to a palm tree.

Two of Rene's sons were in the water, with dive masks on, to guide *Casablanca* onto the trailer. When we came to a stop, the boys and their dad started a running conversation in Tahitian that culminated with the backhoe's engine revving up. I could see Rene working several levers that were connected by hoses to hydraulic lifts on the trailer. There were three lifts on each side with large pads connected to them. These lifts would raise the pads to cradle the hull, thus spreading the weight of the boat evenly on the trailer.

The boys dove down and made sure the alignment was correct. When everyone agreed that things looked right, Rene forced the winch drum into gear and slowly began to drag *Casablanca* out of the water to the top of the ramp. Then the trailer was hooked directly to the tractor, and we were pulled into the large flat field where we were positioned near several other boats.

They promptly delivered a ladder to us so Sheryl and I could climb off the boat since the deck was now about 10 feet off the ground. Rene had one of the kid's pressure wash the hull, making it ready for painting.

All the 'out of the water' chores were completed in two days. In that time, we had applied three coats of paint to the bottom, greased 6 thru hull valves, as well as lubricating the folding propeller.

One evening, we enjoyed a special treat as Rene's wife cooked us a dinner of fresh fish, which we savored at a picnic table overlooking the lagoon.

On launch day, Sheryl climbed up the ladder nearly breathless telling me, "Rick, Rene's wife will trade pearls for wine!" She went on to explain to me that wine is very hard to acquire due of the remoteness of the atoll. No supply ships.

"That's good news, lord knows we have plenty to spare, and we'll be well out of French waters before the law shows up."

Sheryl spent the next hour looking at black pearls of all shapes and sizes. Some were just malformed black blobs, while others were perfect in shape, with a deep black color, seemingly able to absorb light.

Once *Casablanca* was back in the water, we contacted Jeff the weather man and relayed to him that we were ready to go whenever the weather looked right. He e-mailed back that he would start the route planning right away, and we would hear from him within a day or two.

Sheryl and I spent the next morning exploring the atoll on foot. We hiked out to the barrier reef and watched as large South Pacific waves crashed onto the coral, sending spray eight feet into the air. We had a picnic on a small patch of sand and after eating, I laid back to listen to the rhythm of the sea, while Sheryl scoured the beach for treasures.

"Hey, wake up, look what I found!" Sheryl was holding a small oyster shell. "Help me open it up."

Using a fork from our picnic basket, I pried open the bi-valve and much to our surprise there was a very small, perfectly round, black pearl about the size of an apple seed.

"Congrats, you found your first wild pearl, very nice," I said handing the tiny ball to her.

Sheryl was ecstatic. After carefully wrapping her prize in a napkin, she proudly placed it in her pocket for safe keeping.

On the way back to the inflatable, not far from Rene's residence, we spotted a man standing ankle deep in the lagoon. He seemed to be throwing bits of bread into the water with one hand and holding a beer in the other.

With an Australian accent he was delighted to tell us, "Say mate, they have a tamed shark here that you can feed and pet." He continued to throw bread into the water and finally a gray fin cut through the surface. There was a splash in the area around the floating bread chunks, then the shark darted away. Next the man placed his hand in the water, swishing it under the surface.

"This should bring him back," The Aussie concluded.

We watched for a couple of minutes, then left when the shark didn't reappear. We walked on and met up with Rene who was hurrying down the path heading towards the guy feeding the shark.

"I see the nurse shark is back," I commented to Rene as we passed.

"Not nurse shark, bad shark," He replied as he picked up his pace running toward *Crocodile Dumb-de*.

"You know, Rick, I *thought* that looked like a different shark than the one I saw the other day."

We got into the dinghy and headed for *Casablanca*.

"Did you hear that? It sounded like a scream," Sheryl asked.

I replied, "No, didn't hear a thing."

Chapter 21
Flash Dance

"Oh, the shark, babe, has such teeth, dear, and it shows them pearly whites."
~ Mack the Knife

From: **World Wide Weather**

Casablanca crew, Good Morning

Sheryl, after studying the weather models for your area, the forecast looks excellent for at least the next ten days. Once we get to the equator, we will adjust course, if needed, to get through with minimum inclement weather.

Your first GPS waypoint will be at the equator. I will have you try to cross the equator at around 145 degrees. That will make for a more pleasant ride to Hawaii. Please keep in mind that the Equatorial currents tend not to be as established at this time of year, however there are times when the current will build unexpectedly in strength and ruin your easting. Just a heads up.

I will be in touch every other day unless you have a question or if there is a change in the forecast.
I look forward to sailing with you to Hawaii.
Sincerely, Jeff

I had been reading the e-mail from Jeff, over Sheryl's shoulder. "Well, we sit at 146 degrees now, so going east to 145 shouldn't be too bad," I said.

Hawaii is roughly 2500 miles northeast from French Polynesia. Due to the southeast trade winds, as well as the currents near the equator which move in a westerly direction, a direct or rhumb line route is ill advised. Instead the smart money is to achieve as much easting as possible before you get to the equator. In our case that would be around 145 west longitude. Once you cross into the northern hemisphere, a crew can then ease the sails and have a good run to the islands with the wind behind the beam.

A simple way to achieve the desired eastward travel is to use the Tuamotus as a stepping stone, as we had. A one or two-day sail to the outer islands helps a boat get east rather painlessly, providing the weather cooperates.

"So, how long will it take us to get ready to go?" I asked my wife.

Sheryl replied, "However long it takes you to get the anchor up. I've precooked and frozen a bunch of meals and everything is stowed and tied down. We could leave now. The weather is calm and its even close to slack tide."

We were both excited to get the show on the road.

After two gorgeous days at sea we received an e-mail from Jeff instructing us to adjust course. In the message he gave us some good news: *"...... so, as a result of the high moving east, the winds should be favorable to set a course directly to Honolulu. We will deal with the ITCZ when you get closer to the equator. Happy sails. Jeff."*

That was significant news. Even though the sailing had been outstanding, it's nice to visualize a straight line to your destination.

By our fifth day out, the three of us had fallen into the *'life at sea'* mode. Conditions were nearly ideal as the seas, for the most part, had a nice long period. Winds were from the southeast and just behind the beam making for some very nice sailing indeed.

It was our custom on long passages to spend the mornings together in the cockpit, especially when the days were pleasant and we'd both had plenty of sleep. On one of those relaxing mornings Sheryl was drinking tea and reading 'Harry Potter' out loud as I stretched out on the other side of the cockpit.

Just as I was drifting off to *Hogwarts*, there was a sharp bang that came from the area of the wind vane and *Casablanca* went immediately off course.

"Sheryl grab the wheel! We must have hit something and broken *Otto*."

When I got to the stern, I could see the paddle that steers the wind vane had disconnected from the frame work and was only attached to the boat by a small diameter safety line. The paddle skipped behind the boat threatening to disappear if I didn't act fast.

Luckily, I was able to quickly retrieve the paddle, using its safety line to haul it up on deck.

The paddle is of stainless-steel construction. It is two feet long by ten inches wide, formed into the shape of an airplane wing. The paddle is connected to the framework using a shear-pin that is designed to break if it hits an object in the water that could do serious damage. What I found was shocking.

"Sheryl look at this," I said.

In a disbelieving voice she asked, "Are those teeth marks?"

Sure enough, the part of the paddle that was deepest in the water had a series of *grooves*, four deep impressions on both sides of its surface.

A Brit that I met up with in Fiji, had lost the end of his towing generator to a shark, but this was a first for me. Though on my first ocean voyage a large shark had followed the boat for two days. Probably because I was throwing scraps over the side.

"Certainly makes you aware that we are not alone out here," Sheryl said, surveying the surrounding ocean.

I had a new shear-pin on board and the paddle was reinstalled an hour later. It normally wouldn't have taken that long, but I admit to my reluctance to bend over the side with my hands near the water. Not to mention Sheryl kept screwing with me by saying *"is that something in the water?"* about six different times.

The nine days it took *Casablanca* to reach the equator went by without further incident. The sunny days and star-filled nights provided for a very delightful trip.

Jeff's weather prognostications had been spot-on, so when he wrote and informed us that a change was coming, we took notice. However, the change that was coming was not a surprise, it's one of the first weather patterns that offshore sailors learn about.

The Inter-Tropical Convergence Zone is better known by its acronym ITCZ, which is much easier to say. This is the weather band that stretches around the globe, near the equator. It is where the northeast trade winds from the Northern Hemisphere meet the southeast trade winds from the Southern Hemisphere. As you can imagine with the two weather systems colliding, the band is in constant flux. It can move north or south of the equator up to several hundred miles, depending on the season. In addition, the width of the band can change dramatically.

Sometimes a crew can get through it in one day, sometimes it will take a week. The weather there is fluky, ranging from thunder storms, heavy rain to dead calm with no wind, but it is always hot and humid.

When one transits the equator, the wise choice is to find the skinniest part of the ITCZ and push through it at that point if possible. It's like trying to hit a moving target, an opening you see one day will suddenly close up, making the next day's travel quite a trial. In a small, slow sailboat, well, you get what you get. This is where Jeff the weather guy earns his money.

"What did Jeff say?" I asked Sheryl as she had just down loaded his most recent message.

"He says to stay on the rhumb line to Hawaii and that the ITCZ is about the same width east or west. We should start seeing a change tomorrow and to expect two, maybe three days of confused weather. He also said it might be helpful for us to start motoring when we contact the Zone to get through as quickly as possible, provided we have enough fuel. Jeff will keep us updated every day until then."

"This is where your pre-cooked meals are going to come in handy since it will most likely be crappy weather." Then I added, "After that: next stop Hawaii!"

We both saw lightning in the distance on our watches that evening, and the stars were periodically blotted out by the passing clouds.

The following morning the sun was veiled in gray clouds that stretched from horizon to horizon. The wind was nearly non-existent, and the swell was long and had taken on an oily look.

"Guess we're here, we might as well start the engine and get some miles in," I announced as Sheryl and I were switching watch. She was coming up to the cockpit, and I was heading to bed.

"So, Rick, what do you want to do this weekend?" She asked.

"Oh hell, I don't know. We could go sailing, I guess."

This was an old joke that we often used to elicit a smile from the other. Of course, being a thousand miles from anywhere on a sailboat... well you get the picture.

We were on day two of the ITCZ crossing when we got hit with a rain squall that released so much moisture, the visibility was down to about fifty feet all around. The wind was zero, the sails were stowed and the engine chugging away.

I sat in the cockpit, in my rain gear, for about an hour before I said to hell with it. I rotated the radar screen so that I could watch it from the cabin. Sitting on the top step it was easy to open the hatch, take a look around then retreat back down to the dry cabin. We both took turns doing this routine for the next eight hours, staying dry and not having to wear cumbersome rain gear.

That evening *Casablanca* crossed the equator, so we were back in the Northern Hemisphere for the first time in over six months.

On day three in the *Zone* the wind filled in and the gray clouds began to break up, exposing small bits of blue sky. Our spirits soared. We had made it through some unpleasant weather as well as passing the half way point, in miles to go!

What we didn't know at the time was that a trough of low pressure situated a thousand miles away had moved north. The result of that weather shift caused the *Casablanca* crew to have to endure more ITCZ crappy weather.

"Jeff said he is sorry for the poor weather. He explained that the Convergence Zone moved northward and caught back up to us. His best guess was that we would pass through it in approximately 24 hours," Sheryl was reading the update off the computer.

Several hours had passed since the news came in that we were going to spend more quality time in nasty weather. I was laying down on a settee and Sheryl was on 'top step' watch, my eyes were closed when I heard what sounded like aluminum foil being balled up. A millisecond later a bright flash permeated my closed eyes and a thunderous bang rattled *Casablanca* as well as my fillings.

"Oh man! Rick, that was close!" Sheryl yelled as she jumped off her perch.

"Grab the chart plotter and hand-held radio! Put them in the oven," I called as I jumped up in a flash (no pun intended). "I'll check outside, you check the bilges!" I climbed the stairs and as I opened the hatch, another lightning flash followed immediately by thunder made me re-consider the wisdom of going out on deck.

The rain was beating down and with every burst of lightning the moisture bubble we were in lit up like a flash bulb had just gone off. No way was I going on deck! This intense game of lightning roulette lasted for 30 minutes before finally tapering off.

When things calmed down several hours later, I did go on deck to have a look around. I found no damage, but I am absolutely sure the lightning hit very close to us. We were lucky that our electronic instruments were not affected. Putting the radios and such in the oven works as a *Faraday cage* and helps protect delicate circuits. That's providing you do it *before* the lightning hits and that you're not baking at the time.

Well, it took a little longer than 24 hours to exit the lunacy that was the ITCZ, but of course that wasn't Jeff's fault. To that point his predictions had been very close to reality, and we were enjoying a very good passage. *Casablanca* was now less than a week from landfall, with no regrets so far.

Three days from Honolulu tragedy struck.

"Rick," Sheryl was calling from behind a closed door that separated the galley from the head facilities. "There's something wrong with the toilet."

Being the smart ass that I am I answered, "Yeah, I noticed that the water swirls down the drain the opposite way now that we're in the Northern Hemisphere."

"That's cute," She said sarcastically, "But it seems to be plugged. It won't pump out."

Silence.

"No funny quip?" She asked.

"You're jerking my chain, right?" I said with growing dread in my voice.

"Try it yourself, I don't know what's wrong with it," She said opening the door.

I did, and it didn't. Dammit.

The throne on *Casablanca* was big, sturdy, and made of bronze. It had a vertical handle and a foot pedal. When your business was complete, a step on the pedal followed by a forward and back motion with the handle and away goes trouble down the drain. But Not This Time.

Doing work on the toilet requires taking the bathroom door off so the whole unit can be hauled out of the confined space of the head area and schlepped into the main cabin. No small feat considering it weighs around fifty pounds. But it's doable... at a dock.... in calm conditions.

I never had the occasion to work on the unit while underway and I definitely was not looking forward to this disaster in the making.

I did luck-out in one rather big respect; it was only liquid in the bowl. Thank you, Sheryl.

I gathered the necessary tools and started to undo nuts, bolts hose clamps and hoses. Before I loosened the last hose, the one that transfers the sewage, I grabbed a bucket so that the contents of said hose could be contained. I undid the last clamp and stuck the end of the hose in the bucket and was surprised when nothing came out. My deductive reasoning led me to believe that the plug was not in the toilet itself, but rather in the hose. Good, that means no dragging the bronze bastard through the boat, spilling whatever was left in the toilet all over the place.

Enter Jack.

Jack is always interested when I work in the head, and today was no exception. With my face crammed down in a tight corner he decided to jam his oversized body into the same small space.

"Sheryl, please take Jack out of here," I pleaded, spitting cat hair out of my mouth.

"I think he needs to use the toilet," She said.

"No, don't say that, I still haven't fixed the plug you so graciously left me."

"Do not go there! All three of us use that thing, so don't blame me," she said in self-defense.

With the end of the sewage hose in the bucket I used an old straightened out coat hanger and jammed it up inside the hose. With that I was able to coax a little liquid into the container.

"It's blocked with big chunks of crystals," I reported, "This should be easy to fix."

When urea mixes with saltwater, it forms a crystal-like substance that sticks to the inside of the sewage hose on a boat. Even though the toilet bowl is thoroughly flushed a certain amount will always remain in the hose. Slowly, the residue builds until the day it plugs, right when your cat needs to pee.

A monthly dose of vinegar easily takes care of the problem, by breaking down the crystals. Running vinegar through the system was my job and I couldn't remember the last time I performed that ritual. I knew my wife would be asking me that question before I was done.

The 2-inch hose that connects the toilet to the ocean is a little over 6 feet long, so by my calculations the 5-gal bucket would have no problem handling what might be left in the line.

The plug seemed to be near a 90-degree bend. I jabbed and prodded and just as a sizeable chunk broke loose *Casablanca* fell off a wave, burying the toilet thru hull under water. The resulting back pressure shot the loose plug into the bucket along with about 2 gallons of sea water and 3 gallons of some seriously stinky stuff. Jack got hit with spray from the bucket and jumped across my face with full claws, while I managed to get doused with a fair share of affluent as well.

"It's unplugged," I announced triumphantly.

Sheryl's only response was, "That is one nasty smell."

We spotted the big island of Hawaii on day 19. Honolulu was still more than 100 miles away, so we would probably not be able to make it in during day light hours the following day. Anxious as we were to get to a dock, one more night at sea would not break our hearts.

"Have you tried washing with something stronger than soap?" Sheryl inquired.

Annoyed I asked, "And what do you suggest?"

Sheryl replied, "I don't know... bleach, maybe?"

The left-over stink bomb from the toilet repair seemed to have taken up permanent residence in the head. We were still cleaning up two days later, and the smell just wouldn't go away.

"Rick, here's the latest from Jeff. I will read it to you."

"Good morning Casablanca crew. By now you should be near the big island of Hawaii. The forecast for the next two days looks very good, so your landfall on Oahu should be without any drama. This will be my last report. If you have any further questions or comments, please do not hesitate to contact me. It has been a pleasure sailing with you, and I hope to be able to assist you in the future. Sincerely Jeff."

At 8 pm Hawaiian standard time *Casablanca* bobbed two miles off of Waikiki. The entrance to the Ali Wai boat basin was a mile west of our position. As predicted, we had missed getting into the boat basin before sunset. But there was no wind and a small gentle swell, so we would just drift until the sun came up in the morning and then head in to a slip at the local yacht club. It should be a nice quiet night.

Sheryl was leaning against me and Jack was on her lap. "The lights from the city are absolutely amazing," She said as she sipped her tea.

"If you think about it, we haven't seen this many lights since we left Mexico," I observed and added, "By the way here's a little trivia for ya. According to the log book it's been exactly 7 months to the day since we left Huatulco."

"That's kinda weird," Sheryl responded.

"I don't know about weird, but I thought...."

"No, not that. Look at all the police cars going back and forth on the main road."

Sure enough, there were at least six cars with flashing blue lights racing both ways on the road that borders the beach. Before too long the blue lights were joined by the red lights of the fire department.

Our VHF radio had been turned off. So, I hit the power button and turned to channel 16 just in time to hear, "*... warning stay tuned for further up dates.*" Then the pre-recorded message started again. "*Attention: at 7:50 local time the office of tsunami preparedness has issued a tsunami warning. This warning covers beaches and property facing south to southwest. Stay tuned for further updates.*"

For the first time in a very long time, neither of us could speak. We just stared at each other, in disbelief.

"Jeez, this is a first," I said breaking the trance. "I'm pretty sure we are in deep enough water, so we shouldn't be affected if something does come in." I didn't add that if the place got wiped out by a giant wave, we would have nowhere to go.

"Look over there!" Sheryl was pointing to the basin's entrance.

What I saw was a steady stream of boat navigation lights exiting the harbor. At the same time, the radio came alive with a multitude of voices on different channels. They were all talking about strategy for getting safely offshore a couple of miles and then just drifting until the event was over.

"Let's get the radar turned on so we can see what the hell is happening. So much for no drama," I said under my breath.

For the next hour vessels of all sizes steamed through the pass seeking the relative safety of open water. Our plans for having a nice quiet last night at sea were turned upside down. In a remarkably short time *Casablanca* was surrounded by at least 30 boats, half of them showing up on radar as over 50 feet long. It seemed nobody wanted to get very far from the entrance, consequently there were a lot of boats in a small area.

For six hours we stood watch, constantly having to adjust our drift because some knuckle head was asleep and not paying attention to the surroundings.

At 2:30 A.M. the tsunami warning was rescinded. The Coast Guard asked those who left the harbor to please stay out until day light, if possible, for safety's sake. Some did, most did not.

We tied *Casablanca* to a dock at the Hawaii Yacht Club at 7am the next morning. We were back on US soil for the first time in nearly two years.

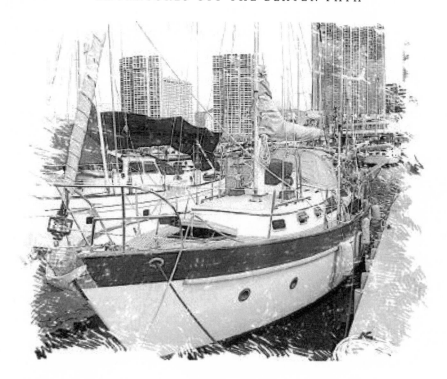

Chapter 22
Hawaii

"Bureaucracy is the art of making the possible—impossible."
~ Javier Salcedo

After checking in with the yacht club and finding our slip, my first call was to the United States Customs Office. I spoke with a bored sounding gentleman who explained to me that they had no customs official to send to *Casablanca* until Monday morning. It was only Saturday. I explained again that we had just arrived from French Polynesia and we sure would like to get off the boat and go to a grocery store.

"No problem, you can go to a store if you need to, just don't leave the city," I was told.

"Can my wife come with me?"

"That's your decision," He said, obviously thinking he was being cute.

"One more question: what about the gun smuggling, foreign speaking, nasty looking guys that traveled with us?" I really didn't ask this, but I was surprised that entry to the country seemed rather lax.

Enter Jack.

Before departing on this trip, we did some research on bringing a pet to Hawaii. On the advice of our vet we had Jack tested for rabies as well as a microchip placed in his head (which could explain a lot). We had those results sent to the Agriculture office in Hawaii, where incoming domestic pets are processed. This forethought on our part would negate Jack having to spend a month in quarantine.

So, Agriculture was the second phone call I made, and the second bored sounding official I had the pleasure of speaking with. This one a woman. Again, I explained that we had just entered the US.

Apparently a ten-year-old cat is far more dangerous than a boat load of smugglers, because she promised someone would visit *Casablanca* within the hour.

"We need to confirm that your cat is on board the vessel," she explained and then she added rather nonchalantly, "Your cat will need to come to the Agriculture Department at the airport for a chip scan."

"I'm not sure I understand. Someone will check to see if the cat is onboard, but I have to take him to the airport for a scan to make sure it's the same cat?" Bewildered, I asked, "Couldn't the person you are sending scan my cat when they confirm it's on board?"

Silence filled the phone waves.

"Sir, we are not set-up to scan pets that come by boat. The officer does not have a scanner, but he will be more than happy to transport your cat to our kennels and then you can pick him up in the morning."

That sure as hell wasn't going to work.

"He uses the toilet," I stated.

"Excuse me sir, who uses the toilet?" the lady inquired.

"My cat."

Again, silence filled the air waves.

"That may be so, but he still needs to come to our office," she informed me.

After pointing out the absurdity of having to take Jack to the airport, it was agreed that we could bring him in and take him right back with us.

Sheryl and I, along with Jack the cat, caught a cab to the airport immediately following the visit from the Agriculture guy who confirmed that yes, indeed, there was a cat on *Casablanca*. The man even took a mug shot of Jack to make sure we brought in the same feline.

I asked the pet police officer, "Why can't you scan the animal when you come to confirm?"

"We never thought of it," He said like a light had just gone on in his head.

Once we got to the Agra office it took about 30 seconds to determine the cat that had arrived on the boat was the same cat trying desperately to get out of his carrier at that time.

Apparently, gun running, no problem. Pet cats, big problem.

There was one other piece of bureaucratic nonsense that occurred when we applied for a long-term slip in the government run Ali Wai boat harbor.

We had stayed at the yacht club only temporarily until a more permanent and more affordable moorage situation could be found. Most transient boats end up at the Ali Wai, which is a large 699 slip marina adjacent to Waikiki Beach. So that is where we found ourselves a week after arriving, in the government offices that control the boat basin.

"Okay, that about does it, the boat inspection looks good, we have your insurance papers, your boat documents, you will be in slip C- 24," this from an overweight, lifetime government employee. Balding with small red veins on his bulbous nose, he had watery blue eyes and seemed to be bored with his job.... Must have been something in the air.

"Okay, after lunch you need to take your boat out to the 2-mile marker just outside the entrance, turn around and come back. After that you will be free to go to your assigned slip," He instructed and then after seeing the baffled look on my face he added, "You must prove your boat is seaworthy and can proceed under its own power."

"Wait, What? We just traveled 2200 miles from French Polynesia. I can confirm that we *are* seaworthy," I explained.

"Sorry," He said, but I could tell he didn't mean it. "The fellow that will watch you is at lunch and will be back in an hour."

"You can't watch us?" I asked.

"Nope, has to be somebody watching from the break water. So, we will call you on the radio to let you know when to proceed to the buoy," He said, stifling a yawn.

"So, we can wait here at the dock, until lunch is over?" I asked heading for the door.

"I'm sorry but there is another boat coming in for an inspection," He said, this time he did yawn.

Feeling abused, I asked him, "Really? We have to just wander around? How about we go to the slip and wait for you to call us?"

"Sorry," was his one-word response.

As I left the office, frustrated by another set of stupid, inane rules, I walked down to where *Casablanca* was docked and explained to Sheryl that we needed to go out and float for an hour at sea.

"Let me talk to him," She said jumping off the boat onto the dock.

"Good luck.... don't hold your breath," I called to her as she marched through the office door.

I am not exaggerating when I tell you it was less than a minute later when she came back out the door with a big *shit-eating* grin on her face.

"What's up?" I asked.

"We're good," She said.

"Okay, try to tell me what's going on, if you can quit smiling for one second."

"We are clear to go to our slip and we don't have to do a sea trial," she said obviously pretty full of herself.

"What the hell did you say to that guy to make him cave-in?" I asked, truly amazed.

"Charm," Was her reply.

Chapter 23
Surprise

"Something about today wants me to be hung over tomorrow."
~ Anonymous

We settled into a very pleasant routine at the boat basin, in slip C-24. Sheryl and I would take morning walks on Waikiki Beach around sunrise before it filled up with sunscreen lathered tourists. There was a large park next to the marina that we would also frequent. One highlight was watching radio-controlled sailboats skim across a one-acre pond.

We were enjoying life and had decided to stay in Honolulu for an extended length of time, so we could explore the possibility of settling down in Hawaii.

"Great news! I got the job!" I was practically yelling at Sheryl from the dock.

"Rick, that is fantastic news! So, the interview went well, I take it?"

A week before we had been in a local marine store and I saw an ad on their bulletin board concerning an open moorage space at a small marina in Keehi lagoon. Knowing that we were only allowed a few months at the Ali Wai, I was keen to check out the advertised slip.

We immediately grabbed a cab and headed for *The Maluhia Sailing Club* on Keehi lagoon.

The taxi dropped us off near a gate that had several palm trees bordering it. A cyclone fence ran a hundred feet north and south from the gate with palm fronds woven through the links. The fence ended at the water's edge. I pressed the call button at the locked gate.

"Yeah?" Came the tinny voice from the decade's old speaker.

"We're here about the slip that's for rent," I said hopefully.

"Upstairs." Then a buzz sounded at the walk-through gate.

"Was that a guy or a woman?" I whispered in Sheryl's ear.

An elbow to the ribs and a hiss, "Shut up."

We walked down a short path that appeared to be carved out of a jungle. Exotic looking plants with giant leaves lined the crushed gravel walkway. Birds cooing from the trees added to the ambiance. Giant insects buzzed our heads.

The path lead to a two-story building that looked to be vintage 1940. Rectangular in shape there was a balcony that separated the two floors. On the bottom floor there was a small bar. It was an open-air sort of thing with the front facing the water and accordion type folding doors bunched up at one end.

Looking out at the water, I could see three long docks with maybe 15 boat slips on each dock.

We climbed the stairs and when the door opened, we were greeted by a wall of cigarette smoke.

"I'm going to wait downstairs," Sheryl said turning and heading back down.

Walking into the small, rapidly clearing room I saw the occupant, a woman, was stubbing out a cigarette in an old coffee can. She was seated at a tattered desk that was covered with files and papers and in one corner sat a picture of a young couple standing in front of the marina. A battered three drawer green file cabinet sat to the right of the desk and the face of its top drawer was covered with *sticky notes,* some faded and looking a century old.

The short, squat, 60-year-old woman looked at me with blood-shot eyes and with the gravelly voice of a heavy smoker said, "Sorry about the smoke, things are screwed up right now, and I'm stressed outta my ass. Are you here about the job?"

"Ah, well, I came about the slip that's for rent," I stammered.

"Yeah, that's right," She mumbled as she started to fumble for another smoke. "If the city catches me smoking in this office, I will be up shit creek... again. Law says I can't even smoke in my own office, that's BS. Kid, open the door for me, will ya?" She said as the lighter flamed on. "What size boat and do you have a holding tank?"

Turns out, I was speaking to Madge, the recently widowed owner of the marina. Madge's husband left her with the business and obviously the business was making Madge a chain smoker.

I gave Madge the low down on the boat, our travels, the plans for staying in Hawaii for the foreseeable future and she seemed unimpressed.

"You can have the slip," She croaked. "Hey, I need someone to run this place, ya know anyone?"

And that is how I got the job interview that resulted in my becoming the *'soon to be'* manager of *The Maluhia Sailing Club*, Sand Island, Keehi lagoon, Oahu, Hawaii. 96819

"I start in two days and we get free moorage at the dock! And yes, the interview went well. But I believe Madge would have hired anyone with a pulse. We got lucky walking in when we did," I exclaimed. I was excited about my new job.

"I couldn't believe how smoky her office was. That smell hit like a punch, I thought I was going to puke," Sheryl said. She was sitting at the table eating strawberries. "Stay away from her second-hand smoke."

The next day I took the bus to Sand Island. I wanted to hang around the marina and get a better feel for the complete operation, even though Madge had walked me through the facility after the interview. It was an opportunity to have a nice quiet look around without the constant cloud of smoke following me.

The bar was closed, but a surfer looking guy, that I recognized as the bartender, was at a table doing some paper work. I introduced myself and explained that I would be running the marina starting the next week.

"That's cool. Marge needs a break in the action," He said pushing his long blonde hair back with his hand. "Welcome aboard, Dude. So, you know we have a small bar menu, but stay away from the clams. I dunno if Marge told you, but your bar tab is covered as long as you work here."

"Marge? I thought it was Madge… I've been calling her Madge," I said confused.

The bartender kinda scratched his head as if trying to retrieve something from the back of his mind, then said in a slow, spacy drawl, "Oh ya, right man, it is Madge."

As I walked away from that odd conversation, I had to pinch myself. I have always harbored a desire to run a marina, now I get to run the marina, have free food and drinks as well as free moorage. It just doesn't get any better than that. With a spring in my step and a smile on my face I boarded the bus back to the Ali Wai, anxious to fill Sheryl in on our good fortune, compliments of *The Maluhia*.

After getting off the bus, I stopped at a nearby fast-food place to grab a strawberry milkshake for Sheryl and a chocolate one for me. We were going to celebrate!

Five minutes later I arrived at slip C-24.

"Luucee I'm home!" I hollered in my best Ricky Ricardo imitation.

No answer.

I stepped over Jack, who was sunning himself in the cockpit, "Hey, anybody home? I've got treeeats."

Peering down the hatch I could see Sheryl sitting at the dining table. In front of her was a small stack of papers and a manila envelope.

When she looked up at me, she was as white as a ghost.

"Honey, what's wrong?" I couldn't tell if she was happy or sad or who the hell knows.

"Rick, when I went to get the mail from our post office box, there was a registered letter that I had to sign for." She took a breath and then added, "Here you need to read this." Sheryl handed me a very official looking three-page type-written letter.

I tried to comprehend what I was reading. It felt as if the blood was leaving my head. I had a touch of dizziness and a bit of a shake in my hands.

"Rick! Rick! Here sit down. I know this is a shock, are you okay? You don't look good," Sheryl hovered above me as I stumbled back and sat down.

"Yeah, I'm okay, fine, I just don't know what to say. I can't think of anything that could be more of a shock."

I was slowly regaining my composure. "Huh," Is all I could say.

Sheryl sat next to me and took my hand.

"Rick, there is one more piece of news.... we are going to have a baby," She whispered.

"Rick, honey just take a deep breath; I will get you some water. Do not faint on me you big baby. *Rick... Rick... Rick............*"

Chapter 24
New Crew

"You can't go back and change the beginning,
but you can start where you are and change the ending."
~ C. S. Lewis

"Rick, Hey Rick! Wake up! Your mom and Walter will be here soon. You and Cassie need to get cleaned up," Sheryl said sounding a little tense.

"I wasn't sleeping, more like day dreaming."

"Regardless, let's go." And she meant it.

I had been laying on a small patch of sand at the water's edge, while my 13-month-old daughter tried to bury my feet using her bright orange toy shovel. It had been one of the few times that I was able to get away from the insanity that had consumed Sheryl and me since that day in Hawaii. That peaceful time with Cassie gave me a chance to try to put in perspective just what the hell had taken place.

I clearly remember that fateful day when it all began. I had just been hired to run a small mom and pop (minus the pop) marina in Honolulu. That afternoon, when I arrived back to *Casablanca,* Sheryl presented me with two life changing pieces of news.

Number one on the hit parade: Sheryl was pregnant. And contrary to what she says, I *did not* pass out. I just caught my breath there for a second.

Number two: Joseph Perry, aka Joe, had left a parcel of land to Sheryl and me. It was the land that his resort had been built on in Baja California Sur, Mexico. Unfortunately, the resort had been wiped out by a hurricane a while back. His Will deeded the land to us, along with some seed money to rebuild the resort for our own. The Will stated certain criteria that had to be followed, such as we were to employ the workers who had jobs at the resort before the hurricane. Joe also recommended that Sheryl run the financial end. Citing her past experience with her own business, as well as her organizational savvy, Sheryl was the right pick. I think the Will even had a clause about me staying out of the business side. Joe was still sticking it to me even from the urn.

The news of the pregnancy had immediately put me into panic mode. Sheryl had miscarried before and I was not sure living on *Casablanca* was wise. I floated the idea of her flying to San Francisco so that she could stay with her mom while Jack and I sailed the boat back to the Bay Area.

"There is no way you get to sail back without me. You don't worry about me and the kid, we will be just fine. Besides a couple of weeks at sea will be good for the four of us. I think things are going to get hectic very soon, and the crossing might be the last semblance of peace we have for some time. No, Buster I'm going. End of discussion."

"Jeez, I just asked you to pass the salt. A little cranky, are we?" I said good naturedly. And then I got the stare.

We needed to wait until spring before sailing back. That's when the North Pacific High would move to the south giving us more favorable winds. I took the job as manager of the marina and Madge, or Marge, was less than thrilled about me leaving in a couple of months, but she let me in on a little secret.

"Kid," she rasped, "by the time you leave, hopefully this place will be sold."

"So, the marina is for sale? Will it remain a marina?" I queried as I had heard rumors about the place being torn down.

"Doubt it, the state regs suck and it would cost thousands to update this old place. Condos," Madge answered and started to cough so hard I wondered who would end up going first, the marina or her.

So, a couple of days later we moved the boat over to Keehi Lagoon and found the slip that had been assigned to *Casablanca*.

While I worked at the marina, Sheryl dove into surprise number two: Our potential Mexican resort.

Before *Perry's Landing* got blown away in a hurricane, it had been one of the top-rated destinations in the Baja part of Mexico. Small companies would book retreats at the *Landing* and famous entertainers would sneak in from time to time seeking quiet days of relaxation. From kite surfing to offshore fishing or a day of snorkeling, Joe had a knack for keeping the guests entertained.

Perry had built the resort from the ground-up. After spending years coming down to sport fish, he sold his construction business in the States and built the getaway he'd always wanted.

According to his Will, Joe wanted that legacy to continue. Of course, he knew there was a chance that we would decline the offer, so the Will stipulated that if we refused, the land would be sold, and his estate would go to charity.

But for Sheryl and me the timing seemed perfect. We were nearing the end of our offshore adventure and were wondering what to do next or where to settle down. Not to mention we were going to have an extra crew member before long. A resort was sure to be an adventure all its own. I hadn't lived on land for most of my adult life, so this would be a big change for me.

The resort and its grounds had been one of a kind. At the center of the property sat a large restaurant/bar, open on three sides and covered with an enormous, thatched roof made from palm fronds. A small stage had its place near the back, where a few well-known entertainers had treated guests to impromptu jam sessions in the past.

Eight small bungalows were built near the beach and they were rarely without guests. Joe's sport fishing holidays were legend, always good fishing with a party atmosphere to boot. It was not uncommon for guests to book a room a year in advance.

A swim-up bar had been located at one end of the large pool. At the opposite end was a waterfall feature with a slide that kept the kids entertained and away from the bar.

Private planes could land at a dirt airfield near the edge of the property. But all of that was gone, just like the rest of the resort.

Fortunately, Joe had a plan even in the afterlife. He had set up a trust fund and once Sheryl and I agreed to rebuild *Perry's Landing* plans were put into motion that he had obviously made in the months before succumbing to his illness.

Joe had a neighbor who lived next to the resort whose name was Manny. Manny was an ex-pat as well as a licensed civil engineer. Joe and Manny were close friends and Manny agreed to help supervise the rebuilding of the resort, providing Sheryl and I were on board with it. His help proved to be invaluable.

The work started at the property about the time Sheryl and I began the passage to San Francisco. Thankfully, the crossing was uneventful. With help from Jeff at *World Wide Weather* we avoided the worst of the poor weather. After 48 hours of heading north from Hawaii, we were able to turn east and set a rhumb line course to San Francisco. The voyage lasted 22 days.

We once again chose to stay at *Emery Cove Marina*. Its location was close enough for Sheryl's mom and Joni, her sister, to fuss over my wife while awaiting the big event.

With the expectant mother in expert hands, I flew down to Baja to meet with Manny, who had been supervising the work being done at the resort. When I showed up to the site, it was my first face-to-face meeting with Manny. Asking one of the Mexican workers where I might find *Senor* Manny, he pointed to a rust stained, faded yellow tractor that was repairing the old access road.

Watching, I couldn't help but notice the operator had a big grin on his face as he skillfully moved and leveled a pile of dirt. The other thing that caught my eye was the scrawny dog that sat next to him on the seat. Shutting down the noisy diesel, he jumped down off the tracks.

"You must be Rick," He said holding out his hand.

"And you must be Manny," I countered. Manny was around 5' 10 in height, deep brown eyes and tanned skin. Sweat dripped down his completely hairless shaved head. This man was blessed with a mischievous smile that went from ear to ear, which in turn made his eyes twinkle.

"I cannot thank you and your wife enough for letting me help out here. When Joe passed, I lost a good friend, a fishing pal and drinking buddy, so I started to question what I was doing down here. I was bored, and I was kinda becoming a hermit. Then I got the call from the lawyer explaining what Joe had in mind and after talking with your wife I knew this would be a good way to stay busy and help keep Joe's memory alive." Manny's eyes watered up. The dog that had been riding the bulldozer came over and sat obediently next to Manny.

Petting the medium sized Shepard type dog, I asked, "What's his name?"

"Don't know. He wandered in when we began working and he hasn't left," Manny continued, "I bring him food and I tried to get him to come to my house, but he ends up here every night. The workers call him *Bola-Tuerca*. I think it means 'nut ball' in Spanish."

We spent the next couple of days going over the plans for the reconstruction. Many of the same drawings that the original builder had used would work for our repairs. One change from the previous layout concerned the location of the new structures. We had chosen to move the bar and the bungalows back away from the water's edge by a hundred feet. Plus, it was decided to raise the buildings up several feet above the level of the beach. Both these changes would make the buildings less vulnerable to another big storm surge.

As we walked the site, I saw there were a number of laborers working at different locations. Some were working on the construction of the bungalows. One small *casita* was nearly finished and several more were in various stages of completion. At the location of the old swimming pool, two men with shovels were removing sand that had been deposited by the storm.

Manny pointed out that the pool could not be moved, and he wasn't sure how much damage was under the sand. "If the damage is extensive, you can fill the whole thing in, but I think we may get lucky and be able to save it with a little work," He said optimistically.

I realized why Manny always had a smile on his face; the work was fun. I ended up traveling to the resort several times a month, not that I really needed to, but damn it *was* fun running the equipment and playing in the dirt.

Back on *Casablanca*, Sheryl was nearing the end of 'her marathon' as she put it.

Close by the marina where *Casablanca* was moored was a condominium complex. We rented a one-bedroom unit for the short term, so that when the "new kid on the block" joined us there would be some kind of normalcy. At least for a while.

I'm not sure Jack had ever lived in anything bigger than a boat, so when we moved into the condo it took some getting used to for all of us. It seemed no matter what room we were in, Jack would come in, plop down, making himself an unmovable object and a tremendous obstacle. I don't think he cared for all the extra space because he liked to keep his humans close.

One afternoon, shortly after moving in, we couldn't find Jack. The main door had been closed but the slider that opens to the small balcony was open. Our residence was on the second floor so we figured he wouldn't have jumped that far to the ground. Our balcony connected to the unit next to us with a short wall separating them. I had briefly met the neighbors; they were a young couple, and I knew the two of them were at work, so I climbed over the wall to look for the cat.

Their slider was opened about a foot and as I stole a look into their condo, I could see Jack coming out of their bathroom.

"Dammit, Jack! Come here.... come on good kitty," I said through clenched teeth. He ambled towards the door then stopped and sat to clean himself. No way was I going to break into my new neighbors' home to grab him.

"Jack come here!" I tried to sound calm and loving but he just sat on his big butt staring at me.

"Jackie boy come here sweetie," Sheryl cooed from our balcony. With that encouragement, Jack got up and walked past me, jumped up onto the short wall and back to our side of the fence.

As I drug myself over the wall, Sheryl reminded me, "Someone left the toilet seat up and that's why he went next door." Tough to argue with that. Our neighbors were in for a surprise.

With the delivery date just days away, my mom flew down from Washington, leaving Walter to tend to the senior's garden at the retirement community. Sheryl's mom motored over from the coast and Sheryl's sister, who lived just a few blocks away, would use her time at our place as stress relief from her twins. With two moms and a sister always in attendance, our small condo really shrunk in size. I would make it a point to slip out and walk to the marina where *Casablanca* was moored, and work on a project I called *quiet time*.

It was during one of my quiet time naps on the boat, that I was awakened by a cell phone call. "You better get back here. It's time." And then the phone went dead.

When I opened the door, Mom, Bets, Joni and even Jack were sitting around Sheryl as if they were warding off something evil. Worried smiles were on the human faces, Jack had milk on his.

"Ok, what's up?" Even though I already knew.

"Sheryl's water broke, time to get on the road," This was from future grandma, Bets.

"I'm no Obstetrician, but maybe I should take a look," I said trying to sound clever.

Sheryl took this opportunity to enlighten me, saying, "Will you please stop being a smart ass and let's get going, things feel like they are moving right along."

With that we piled into two cars and made it to the hospital just in time to have Sheryl go through about six hours of quick breathing and several more hours of bone crushing hand holding.

The birth went well. Thank God there were no complications. But it was pretty easy to see where they got the inspiration for the stomach scene in the movie *Alien*.

After all the pain, the uncomfortable sleep, the bloating along with the wild cravings, we were given a veritable treasure. A baby girl with wisps of blond hair and bright blue eyes. She weighed in at nearly eight pounds. We named her Cassiopeia, Cassie for short. It was the name that we had agreed upon if it was a girl, overruling my suggestion of Zelda.

For the next month between the grandma's, Joni, Sheryl and me, Cassie was held almost constantly. Sheryl recovered quickly, and I learned a butt load about diaper rash.

While we were adjusting to our new house guest, Manny had his own challenges down at the work site. It seemed that a building inspector had questioned one of the permits and the entire project was brought to a halt.

"Congratulations on becoming a dad." I could hear the smile in Manny's voice over the phone.

"And I know it's a bad time but you may need to come down so the local building inspector can meet you. They are holding us up on a technicality. It's really nothing, just a way to exert some authority."

"Yeah, ok, I can come down in a couple of days. Is there any work you can do in the meantime?"

Manny enthusiastically replied, "Sure, Nutball and I have some water connections for the reverse osmosis shed we can work on. By the time you get down here we will be making fresh water from sea water."

Joe had started to build a water making facility for the resort, but it wasn't completed or operational before the storm wiped things out. Essentially salt water is pumped through a series of membranes and the result is fresh water and as long as you have power, there is an unlimited supply. Costly water deliveries from the nearby community well would become a thing of the past.

The little problem that Manny was dealing with brought to the forefront something that had previously gone undiscussed around the grammas. We would soon need to relocate down to Baja in order to get the resort completed and running. Sheryl and I had figured that at six months Cassie would be able to start living aboard *Casablanca* while we were having our own small *casita* built. Our residence would be the last to be constructed, knowing that living on the boat would work for the interim.

"It's not going to be fun bringing this subject up to your mom or mine," I groaned.

"Do you really think they haven't figured it out by now?" Sheryl asked while she performed diaper change #5 for the day.

"So, Jack and I will take *Casablanca* down sometime in the next six weeks," I said. It was more of a question than a statement.

"As much as Cassie and I would like to travel with you and Jack, it probably makes more sense for us to fly down," Sheryl opined, with a hint of disappointment in her voice.

"That's the other thing. We do need to buy a vehicle of some sort. Once the boat is down there, I will fly back, and we can all drive down together. We are going to need something for transportation while living down there anyway," I said sharing my plan.

Sheryl added, "In that case Jackie can stay with us and you will be a true single hander for maybe the first time in quite a while."

She was right, all of my offshore sailing has been with the cat aboard, so this would be different.

I flew down to La Paz, and with Manny in tow, we visited several local government offices which were responsible for the permitting of construction or conversely, the stoppage of said construction. Manny had been right, all they wanted was a little face time and a donation to their favorite charity and work could resume.

I hadn't been down to the site in a while since the baby had been born. I could tell Manny was anxious to show me the progress that had been made after my last visit and before the shutdown occurred.

Driving down the newly graded road in my rental car, I was shocked as I came around the last corner that lead to the resort. I stopped and retrieved my camera. Sheryl had wanted pictures of the progress and from my present vantage point on a small hill, I had a clear view of the resort and the beach front.

The restaurant/bar looked structurally complete and with the massive, thatched roof in place, it was an impressive sight.

There was a crushed coral pathway leading from the small parking lot to the restaurant's entrance, then continued through some newly planted palm trees and disappeared behind a large *Bougainvillea* bush on its way to the beach. There was a second walkway lined with bright white rocks that led from the restaurant to the row of bungalows.

Another one of the small bungalows had been completed, but the other four were still works in progress. They were being built using cement block and plaster and would have thatched roofs. They each had one bedroom and bath, but unlike the originals there would be no cooking facilities. The thought was that we would expand the kitchen's ability to make and serve meals. Guests would be able to eat at the restaurant, do takeout or even have a meal delivered to their room.

Manny and Nutball met me down at the water-making shed. With his usual smile he showed me the workings of the reverse osmosis machinery.

"We tested it to 100 gallons an hour, with no problem and we were taking it easy, so I think we're good to go," Manny said as he threw a stick for the dog. He went on, "So we need to figure out where you want your residence. I've got a couple of locations that look good building wise, but of course it's up to you."

We spent the rest of the day discussing where to put a small office for checking in and business stuff. Then we looked at a location for the home I wanted for my family. Our house would be the last thing to be built, but not until the resort was up and running. All the while we walked the property, Nutball would run along with us, a stick in his mouth, begging for a throw.

From the shed we walked on a path, past some newly planted shrubs and came out at the location of the old pool. I was shocked at what I saw.

"Damn, Manny you saved the pool!" I was excited.

"Well not quite, there was damage at the one end, so I had the guys take out the bad part. Then we formed and poured a new end. So basically, it shortened the pool by about six feet. Then to test the water maker we filled it up to make sure it still held water. We have a little more work to do but it is coming along," he informed me and then he added, "The showers will be in a small building right over there and the swim-up bar will be started in a week." Manny was grinning ear to ear.

Just then, Nutball dove into the pool for a lap before getting out and shaking like... a wet dog.

"So, Manny, I'm going to sail down soon, and the family will follow shortly after that. We can't thank you enough for all your work on our behalf. We could have never done any of this without you, we will be forever grateful."

"Well, I believe that this saved my life and gave me a purpose. Like I said I loved Joe like a brother and I still talk to him, when things get crazy."

We shook hands, I think maybe we both had tears in our eyes. As I started to walk away, Manny called to me, "You need to come up with a name for the resort, so I can get a sign made."

Chapter 25
Off the Beaten Path

"A journey is measured in friends, rather than miles."
~ Tim Cahill

I carried Cassie up to the bungalow that Sheryl and I were using for the day, so that we could clean up before the other guests arrived. We were preparing for what would be a 'soft' opening for the mostly completed resort. The restaurant/bar had been finished a month earlier, and the bungalows had been completed and furnished not long after that. We had invited some close friends to help put the newly hired staff through their paces.... sort of a test-run with friendly customers. The palapa style restaurant had the seating capacity for around 40 guests, but there would be far less than that at the evening's event.

As promised by Sheryl, Walter and my mom showed up right on time, having just flown down from Seattle. One of our staff met them at the airport and brought them out to the resort. This was their first time down since the day we had spread Joe's ashes.

"Ricky!" Mom gave me a hug and as she looked all around, she exclaimed, "I can't believe the change, it's amazing! But enough of you and Walter.... where is my beautiful granddaughter?"

"Nice to see you, too," I said feigning hurt feelings.

"She's with Sheryl and Nutball. We are staying in the last casita down the path," I informed her, pointing her in the right direction, "Sheryl's expecting you so go right in. Don't worry about the dog, he's harmless. Ever since Sheryl and Cassie moved down here, Nutball has not left Cassie's side whenever she is on shore."

I took Walter on a brief tour around the grounds before I showed him to the bungalow that he and Mom would occupy for the next couple of days.

We walked from the small parking lot located next to the office, down the path that led to the pool. We strolled past the small building that housed the men and women's rest rooms and showers.

"Rick, this is fantastic, I mean last time I was here it was a mess. There was nothing here, now look at all this," He said pointing around as we walked.

"Most of the credit has to go to Manny, he got the ball rolling and never stopped pushing," I went on, "You will meet him tonight at dinner, a really great guy."

We came to a fork in the path where there were two wooden signs on a post, one pointed in the direction of the restaurant and the other pointed to the beach.

"We can walk down to the beach and then there is another path that leads up to the cabins."

As we started to the beach, Jose, our main grounds keeper stopped us.

Senior Rick, may a word please?" He was a small deeply tanned man with a worried look on his face.

Jose explained in broken English that I was needed at the pool area. I apologized to Walter and informed him that I had to take care of a minor problem, and that he could go to his cabin or go see Sheryl and Cassie.

"Don't worry 'bout me, you tend to business," Walter said as he shuffled away.

"Thanks, Walt," I called out, but I don't think he heard me.

I followed Jose back down the path to the pool area and when I arrived, he pointed to the men's side of the shower building. Without a word I entered and in one of the two stalls was a woman sudsing herself up.

Quickly looking away I was, as they say, befuddled as to what to do.

"Um, excuse me miss." No response. So, a little louder, "Excuse me, I think this is the men's shower room."

The water shut off and a women's voice proclaimed, "No, you're wrong, this is the ladies shower."

I backed out to the entrance and double checked the signage. She was definitely in the men's shower, but what I couldn't figure out is who she was and why she was using the pool facilities. I thought I should stand guard to keep someone from going in and causing an awkward scene.

Finally, a thin older lady with short gray, wet hair and a frown on her face came out, looked at me, then looked up at the sign that read 'men's shower' and begrudgingly said, "Guess you were right."

"Excuse me, you are?" I asked.

"Jan Campbell," She said staring at me like she wanted to rip me a new one. "And who are you?"

I explained to her who I was, and she informed me that Sheryl had invited her to the resort so that she could write up a review for a travel magazine.

"So how was the men's shower?" I asked, as she walked away.

"Great till you showed up," She said over her shoulder.

I walked over to the bar to see how things were shaping up. We'd invited about a dozen people for the run through and I was nervous about how the whole thing would work out. We had no experience in the resort business, but we were happy with our staff and the set up, so we were confident that common sense would prevail.

The restaurant staff were eager to get things under way, although we still had several hours before dinner would be served.

I wandered down to the beach, purposely taking the long way back to our cabin.

"Rick, so how's the big resort mogul doing?" I turned to see Bets, Sheryl's mom, sitting on a beach chair looking at a brightly colored shell.

"God, I'm stressed. Your daughter is the pillar. She thought of all kinds of business stuff that never even occurred to me. And her eye for design and detail really added the finishing touches," I replied. Then I went on, "And she is a wonderful mother, you did a magnificent job raising her, Bets. You know you are welcome to spend as much time down here as you like. We will always have a room for you. In fact, we are planning to build two small cottages near where our house will be, for you and my mom."

"Thanks Rick, you're a good husband and father," she replied. "And that thing I said at your wedding about killing you in your sleep if you weren't good to my daughter, you can rest well." Then, after an awkward silence she asked, "Did your mom and Walt show up yet?"

"Yeah, Mom's with Sheryl and Cassie and Walt is wandering in that direction."

Bets said, "I'll go see them in a little while, let Muriel have some time to catch up with Cassie and Sheryl."

"I gotta run, so see you tonight," I said as I started to take the path towards the cabins, but I stopped when I saw a boat sailing into the bay.

A big smile spread across my face.

That must be *DreamCatcher* I thought. We had invited George and Barbara to the opening and I even asked George to play his accordion after supper. We hadn't heard back, so we assumed they would be no shows. But there they were, and they even came by boat! That is cool, I thought to myself. They anchored not far from *Casablanca;* it would be an easy row to shore for them.

When I finally reached the bungalow where we were staying, I was greeted on the porch by Nutball, who was waiting patiently for his new best friend to come out and play. Cassie and the dog had become instant companions. Whenever Cassie was around, the two were inseparable. With my daughter just learning to walk Nutball would stand next to her as she grabbed a fist full of fur for balance. As she took small tentative steps, he would move slowly making sure she had hold of him preventing her from taking a face plant.

As I opened the door, Nutball looked in expectantly.

"Naba, Naba, Naba," said my drooling daughter as she made a break for the door, outfitted in only a diaper.

"Rick don't let Cassie out I just got her cleaned up," cautioned Sheryl.

"Yeah, okay, come here you little fart," I said as I grabbed her, lifting her high into the air.

Pointing to the door she fussed, "Naba."

"No sweetie, you can't play with your nutty buddy right now."

Carrying her into the room I found Sheryl sitting on the bed painting her nails.

"I do not believe I have ever seen you paint your nails before," I said dropping Cassie on the bed from a foot up, eliciting a loud laugh as she hit the soft mattress.

"Big night... might as well gussy up," she said craning her head for a kiss. I bent down and gave her a peck on the lips, and she said, "Walt stopped by and said there was a problem at the pool?"

"Yeah, did you invite a travel reviewer for tonight's thing?"

"Manny set me up with a local ex-pat that writes travel and lodging reviews. She lives in La Paz, so I contacted her and invited her to the opening. Why do you ask?"

"She was in the men's shower, at the pool. I walked in on her and she was covered in soap suds. Not the best time or place to meet our first reviewer," I informed her.

"Huh, that's odd, you didn't offend her, did you?"

"Nah, does that sound like something I would do?" And before she could reply I asked, "How was my mom? She barely spoke to me when they got here in her rush to see you and Cassie."

"Everything is wonderful with her and Walter. They are excited that we're settled down and can visit us more often. And the way she fusses over Cassie, makes me think she really wanted a girl instead of... no offense... a boy." And then quickly changing course she said, "Spark and Tami called. They're at the airport and rented a car for the couple of days that they will be here. And he said to tell you he brought his gear. What gear?" Sheryl asked.

"If there is decent wind, he said he would teach Juan Carlos how to kite surf and that way once JC gets the hang of it, he can teach guests who want to try it out. He's donating some of his older equipment for us to test out, to see if it's even anything we would like to promote." I explained.

Switching subjects, she asked, "Rick, have you thought about what you're going to say at tonight's dinner?"

"What are you talking about? You told me to be polite and don't say anything stupid."

"Tonight is a dedication, a re-opening of the resort, so you should probably say a few words at dinner. Not everyone is up to speed on why we are suddenly running a resort here on Baja. In fact, I think it's a surprise to most people that we're even here. We did kinda keep it on the down low," She said holding up her hand and admiring her nails.

The invitations that were sent out to the guests stated that dinner would be served at 8 and that there would be an open bar before that. We really hadn't talked to our friends about what brought us back to Baja. We had been purposely vague.

At 7 pm Nutball and I walked over to the restaurant, leaving Cassie and Sheryl to finish getting ready. The invites said beach casual for dress, so I was a little surprised how long it was taking my wife to get *casually* dressed. It must be a learning moment for our daughter.

As I approached the restaurant's entrance, I was happy to see that the sign I'd had made by a woodworker in La Paz was still covered up. I didn't want anybody to see the name of the bar until it was time. Not even Sheryl knew what I'd come up with. As they say, '*with great naming, comes great responsibility*' so I had been given a talking to about things that might be offensive to some.

"Rick, sometimes your humor is funnier in your head than when it's said out loud," She had cautioned me.

Sheryl made sure that I understood that stupid names and phrases or any sort of bathroom humor would not be acceptable. I told her not to worry, which made her worry even more.

A simple chalk board at the entrance welcomed the guests. Once we fully opened, it would be used to announce the specials that would be served on a particular night or any entertainment that would be planned.

For our special opening, in addition to welcoming our honored guests, the reader board informed every one of our signature drink: *Kealakekua Bay Punch*. That was a concoction I had thrown together when I was a single-handed sailor in Hawaii and at a loss as to what to contribute to an impromptu potluck. I found a bottle of rum and a jar of Tang, squeezed a few limes and the rest is history.

When I entered the palapa, Nutball took his place near a palm outside the entrance and waited for Cassie. Soft Tropical Rock music played in the background courtesy of our good friend Dave Calhoun. When a schedule conflict prevented Dave from attending the opening, he compiled a great playlist of his music for us to play throughout the night. It was almost as if he was there.

As my eyes adjusted to the interior, I spotted Manny sitting at the bar talking with Angel, our bartender. "Manny, you are looking sober this evening, how'ya doing?" I asked sliding on to a bar stool next to him.

"Great," He said as he took another sip of his Margarita. "So, is everyone here? I noticed a sail boat anchored near *Casablanca.*"

"That belongs to George and Barbara, the boat name is *DreamCatcher.* They live up in Puerto Escondido."

Just then there was a bit of a commotion outside and looking up I spotted Jim and Dianne. We'd first met them in La Paz and then after we sailed to Zihuatanejo they happened to be there as well. Jim had been a participant in the *Calamity on the Beach* fiasco.

I went over to greet them. "Typical Canadians," I joked, "arriving early for a party." Shaking Jim's hand and a hug for Dianne, I added, "Glad you guys could make it."

Unfortunately, the rest of the Dock 3 crew weren't in La Paz at the time so that reunion would have to come at a later date.

Sheryl walked through the door carrying Cassie and Dianne left the guys and made a beeline to talk to my wife and to gush over our daughter.

Once all the guests had filtered in and were accounted for, introductions were made, and Angel started mixing drinks. People milled around enjoying the view, chatting, and catching up on what we were doing, which was certainly a surprise to most. A common question we heard was, "So are you done sailing?" And our standard reply was, "For the time being."

The "moms" showed up and both Bets and Muriel easily slipped into their comfort zone, talking about Sheryl and me. All the women took turns holding and fussing over Cassie who, by that time, needed a Nutball fix and squirmed to get free of hugs and go outside to see her four-legged pal.

After an hour of shooting the breeze and making sure everyone had been introduced to everyone else, it was time to sit down for the first meal at the *Last Resort*.

Wine was served by the wait staff and it seemed that everyone was having a good time, judging by the volume of the conversations. I was elated at the easy way they all seemed to mix.

Sheryl broke away from a discussion with Tami and stood next to me. In a hushed voice she said, "Rick, now is a good time to say something, and please don't be crazy, okay?"

"But I didn't come up with anything," I whispered.

"Then just wing it and no stupid jokes," Sheryl said forcing a smile.

After we'd all taken our seats, I stood up, cleared my throat and twelve faces looked up at me. The thirteenth was my daughter who had more important business as she tried to make a break for the door babbling, "Naba, Naba, Naba."

"I want to thank you all for coming tonight. My wonderful wife told me I needed to say a few words and not to tell any stupid jokes. And I agreed, so here goes. Two peanuts were walking down the road and one was a salted." Sheryl buried her face in her hands.

There may have been one or two groans, so I went on, "Let me tell you a story about why we are all here tonight. And I promise to make it short. A man named Joe Perry came into my life when I was a youngster back in Gig Harbor. That came about because a few friends and I would build snowmen in the winter, only to have some teenage knucklehead with a new license and driving their parent's car, run over our creations. So, the next snowman we built was around a fire hydrant located near my front yard."

Glancing at my mom she had her face in her hands. I seem to have that effect on people, so I continued, "Sure enough the teens came a calling and boy were they surprised when they tried to run over Frosty." There was a clamor of laughter from the tables. "Anyway, *Perry Construction* had been contracted by the city to repair the damage to the hydrant. One weekend several of us boys were hanging around the equipment that the workers were using to repair the water line. Since the crews didn't work on the weekends, we would sit on the bulldozer and pretend to knock down houses. To this day I don't know how it happened, but the tractor started up and lurched into gear. My friends scattered and left me on the dozer which is why *they* are not here tonight. Anyway, as I was about to run into a car, Joe Perry came out of nowhere and shut the beast off. I was inches away from smashing the neighbors brand new Buick."

By this time everyone was asking my mom if this was all true.

"Oh, heavens you can't imagine," She said shaking her head with a good-natured smile.

"After the tractor fiasco incident, Joe recognized that I needed a little direction in my life, so he gave me my first job. He became a good family friend. Looking back, Joe was like the bumpers they put in bowling alleys so young people can't roll gutter balls. He helped me stay in the lane and out of the proverbial gutter."

I could feel myself start to choke up and looking at Mom she had a sad smile on her tear-stained face.

"Now the reason all of you are here tonight is that I recognize each of you as having some of the qualities that Joe had in his heart and soul. And, like Joe, you have all made a positive impact in my life. Sheryl and I thought that there would be no better way to celebrate the opening of *Perry's Last Resort,* than with people that would be his friends if he were here today."

There was polite applause from our guests. I then signaled to Angel to have the staff pour champagne into the glasses that were placed in front of everyone.

"But before we toast Joe Perry, I want Manny to stand up. Everything you see here at the *Last Resort* is due to this man's hard work and extreme dedication to his friend. When Joe first moved down to Baja, he and Manny became good friends. They would fish together, drink together and raise hell together."

I could see Manny starting to get a little embarrassed being in the spot light.

"So, with this in mind I give you......," and with a little flourish I pulled the wrap off of the new sign that hung above the bar. It read: *Manny and Joe's Fish Tales Bar.*

I went over and hugged Manny, he was speechless.

"Let's all raise our glasses to the two men who brought us here tonight. Here's to Joe and Manny. May they be forever in our hearts, and in our bar. Cheers!"

Epilogue

It's been six months since the soft opening of the *Last Resort*.

Business has been good. After working out some of the early operational bugs things have smoothed out nicely. Plans are underway for an additional three bungalows as the originals are usually booked up well in advance and we hate to turn anyone away.

Manny is taking great pleasure at filling in as bartender for Angel at *Fish Tale's* one day a week and in his spare time he's organizing a sport fishing tournament and the interest in that venture seems to be building. It's been a godsend having such a positive individual working with us.

A month ago, Sheryl, Cassie, Jack and I finally moved into our new home which is just a short walk from the resort. Did I mention that it comes with its own rescue dog? Now that we are on shore full time, Nutball, Cassie's nutty buddy, is a permanent resident at our house. I'm not sure how much Jack likes his new foster brother, but with all the face licking Jack is getting from Nutball, well, he will eventually be won over.

But on the bitter sweet side of life, we sold *Casablanca*. The boat that protected us for thousands of sea miles and numerous storms seemed overkill in the relative calm waters of the Sea of Cortez now that she wasn't our home. She sold to a nice family from the Seattle area, whose intentions are to sail to the South Pacific, so *Casablanca* will be back in her element once again.

So, for now I'm a dirt dweller, without a boat, for the first time in a very long while. But I have always tried to look at life as an adventure. And this part of my adventure takes place near one of the most beautiful bodies of water on earth.

Cassie is teaching me about fatherhood as well as helping me re-live my childhood. And Sheryl continues to tolerate my jokes. So, I'm feeling like a pretty lucky guy and I am excited to see what happens on this new path.

What's next for us? Who knows, but I've heard it said that life's more about the *journey* than the destination. I think I need to add that it's actually more about who's on that journey with you.

AUTHOR'S NOTE

Adventures Off the Beaten Path chronicles the latest adventure my wife Heidi and Rosie the cat embarked upon aboard *Cetus,* our Fantasia 35 sailboat. This time our travels took us over 10,000 miles, first sailing down the West Coast of the United States. After spending several months in Baja Mexico, we traveled to the mainland. When we left Mexico, we took a path less traveled and ended up in the Galapagos before heading for the very remote Gambiers in the South Pacific. The route described in *Off the Beaten Path* is the same as we took in *Cetus.*

In keeping with the spirit of my first two books, *Adventures Aboard Rick's Place* and *Adventures Aboard S/V Casablanca,* I have taken our real-life travels and fictionalized them. This gives me a little more leeway with characters and events and provides for a faster pace to the stories. As before, the major events are real, but characters are often a composite, taking names and characteristics of different people I know or have met along the way. Many names have been changed simply to avoid any messiness, such as lawsuits and such. Our toilet trained cat Rosie actually got a lawyer, resulting in her character being renamed Jack.

A big thank you to Reagan Rothe and the Black Rose Writing team for once again working with me and putting my story in print.

I would be remiss if I didn't give a shout out to several people who have helped us along the way. Monica and Doug Edwards have always been our link back in Washington State. They take care of our mail, send boat parts when needed and keep us up to date on the going's on of the family as well as providing a wonderful place to stay when we get back for a visit.

As he did for the first two novels, Travis Johnston was kind enough to lend a few of his excellent drawings to grace some of these pages. His talent speaks volumes, more than I could ever put into words. Thanks Trav.

George Gray wrote the song *Off the Beaten Path* which is featured at the beginning of this book. The lyrics perfectly sum up the feelings that I tried to convey in my story. Well done Jorge!

Carly, our daughter, helped with the proof reading assuring me it was an interesting story and giving me moral support to go forward with it. Having spent her childhood and teen years as a live-aboard boat kid, her eye for detail was an immense help in keeping things readable.

None of this would be possible without my friend, my cruise planner, my wife, Heidi. I have often said that the writing was the easy part. Heidi had the tough part, she read the draft countless times, fixed hundreds of mistakes, and made sure what I was writing was coherent, (it didn't always start out that way). Without her encouragement and patience and understanding, I would be that guy at a bar telling crazy stories. She also provided the photography for the photos within the book. Thanks hon.

And finally to our many friends, who gave me the push to write *Off the Beaten Path*: I hope you're happy with what you've done.

—TJK

ABOUT THE AUTHOR

Terry and his wife Heidi began sailing in 1978 and have been liveaboards for over 30 years, half of those with their daughter, Carly.

Terry's three books are based on their travels through the South Pacific, through Mexico, Hawaii and the Galapagos Archipelago.

The first voyage was aboard *Cassiopeia*, a Golden Gate 30 sailboat which they built from a bare hull.

Currently making plans for their next adventure they, along with their boat cat Rosie, are enjoying Mexico's Sea of Cortez aboard *Cetus*, the Fantasia 35 sailboat they have called home for over 25 years.

NOTE FROM THE AUTHOR

Word-of-mouth is crucial for any author to succeed. If you enjoyed *Adventures Off the Beaten Path*, please leave a review online—anywhere you are able. Even if it's just a sentence or two. It would make all the difference and would be very much appreciated.

Thanks!
Terry J. Kotas

Thank you so much for checking out
one of **Terry J. Kotas's** novels
If you enjoy our book, please check out our recommended
title for your next great read!

Adventures Aboard: Rick's Place

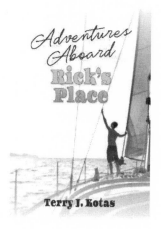

Adventures Aboard: Rick's Place is a story of a solo sailor, based on the author's true-life adventures.

Follow Rick through his carefree youth and then later in life as a series of events leave him jobless and wondering just what comes next.

Live vicariously through this charming landlubber turned sailor as he fulfills his dream of escaping the rat race and sailing off into the sunset.

Culminating with a life-changing event, this humorous tale gives a realistic look at the adventurous cruising lifestyle and will leave you longing to visit the beautiful isles Rick explores as he sails the Coconut Milk Run.

Made in the USA
Middletown, DE
10 September 2021